"I work best alone."

"I'm afraid you don't understand," Rorie said as she stood and looked at Gabriel Hawk. "I am going to San Miguel. With you—or with another protector."

Hawk grabbed her by the shoulders, and she trembled beneath his big hands. "I'm the *only* man available who knows San Miguel on a firsthand basis and who has contacts in the country who can help find your nephew."

Rorie stared him directly in the eye, calling on every ounce of her willpower not to show him any weakness. His nearness both aroused and frightened her. He was big and dark and dangerous. He was gloriously, intriguingly male. And suddenly she knew that he *was* the only man on earth capable of helping her. Gabriel Hawk was the powerful guardian angel for whom she'd prayed.

She just hadn't expected her protector also to be a fallen angel....

Dear Reader,

A new year has begun, and in its honor we bring you six new—and wonderful!—Intimate Moments novels. First up is *A Marriage-Minded Man?* Linda Turner returns to THE LONE STAR SOCIAL CLUB for this scintillating tale of a cop faced with a gorgeous witness who's offering him lots of evidence—about a crime that has yet to be committed! What's her game? Is she involved? Is she completely crazy? Or is she totally on the level—and also the perfect woman for him?

Then there's Beverly Barton's *Gabriel Hawk's Lady,* the newest of THE PROTECTORS. Rorie Dean needs help rescuing her young nephew from the jungles of San Miguel, and Gabriel is the only man with the know-how to help. But what neither of them has counted on is the attraction that simmers between them, making their already dangerous mission a threat on not just one level but two!

Welcome Suzanne Brockmann back with *Love with the Proper Stranger,* a steamy tale of deceptions, false identities and overwhelming passion. In *Ryan's Rescue,* Karen Leabo matches a socialite on the run with a reporter hot on the trail of a story that starts looking very much like a romance. *Wife on Demand* is an intensely emotional marriage-of-convenience story from the pen of Alexandra Sellers. And finally, welcome historical author Barbara Ankrum, who debuts in the line with *To Love a Cowboy.*

Enjoy them all, then come back next month for more excitement and passion—right here in Silhouette Intimate Moments.

Yours,

Leslie Wainger

Leslie J. Wainger
Senior Editor and Editorial Coordinator

Please address questions and book requests to:
Silhouette Reader Service
U.S.: 3010 Walden Ave., P.O. Box 1325, Buffalo, NY 14269
Canadian: P.O. Box 609, Fort Erie, Ont. L2A 5X3

BEVERLY BARTON

GABRIEL HAWK'S LADY

Silhouette

INTIMATE™ MOMENTS®

Published by Silhouette Books

America's Publisher of Contemporary Romance

SILHOUETTE BOOKS

ISBN: 0-373-07830-7

GABRIEL HAWK'S LADY

Copyright © 1998 by Beverly Beaver

This edition published by arrangement with Harlequin Books S.A.

® and TM are trademarks of Harlequin Books S.A., used under license. Trademarks indicated with ® are registered in the United States Patent and Trademark Office, the Canadian Trade Marks Office and in other countries.

Printed in U.S.A.

BEVERLY BARTON

has been in love with romance since her grandfather gave her an illustrated book of *Beauty and the Beast*. An avid reader since childhood, she began writing at the age of nine and wrote short stories, poetry, plays and novels throughout high school and college. After marriage to her own "hero" and the births of her daughter and son, she chose to be a full-time homemaker, a.k.a. wife, mother, friend and volunteer.

When she returned to writing, she joined Romance Writers of America and helped found the Heart of Dixie chapter in Alabama. Since the release of her first Silhouette book in 1990, she has won the GRW Maggie Award, the National Readers' Choice Award and has been a RITA finalist. Beverly considers writing romance books a real labor of love. Her stories come straight from the heart, and she hopes that all the strong and varied emotions she invests in her books will be felt by everyone who reads them.

With love and appreciation to all my wonderful readers, who have let me know how much they enjoy my books. And to my very special editor, Cathleen Treacy, who demands my best and works diligently with me to achieve that goal.

Prologue

Hawk knew he couldn't stop them. But dear God, could he live with himself if he didn't try? It wasn't as if he hadn't seen innocent people die before. Hell, there had been times when he'd seen guiltless bystanders die—men and women who just happened to be in the wrong place at the wrong time. Killing was a part of his job. A part he hated. But he did it with expert ease and skill. Perhaps too much ease. With each passing year of the twelve since the CIA had given him his first assignment, he'd grown harder, colder and more ruthless.

He had no family, few friends and no special woman. The only real passion in his life was the adrenaline rush of danger. And lately, it took larger and larger doses to achieve the desired effect.

So why the hell was it bothering him so much that Emilio and his amigos were planning to kill the young couple? He hadn't been sent to San Miguel to infiltrate this renegade rebel faction so he could play savior to the country's reigning princess and her Anglo husband. He'd been sent here to discover the whereabouts of a stolen U.S. missile.

Maybe he'd gotten too good at his job. Maybe somewhere

along the way, he'd crossed the line. It was so rare that he ever felt anything, that he ever gave a damn. Maybe, just maybe, this was a sign.

Get out now or you'll lose what little is left of your soul.

If he tried to save Cipriana and Peter Dean, he would not only blow his cover, but he would very likely get himself killed. Emilio didn't take prisoners. He eliminated anyone who interfered with his plans. In that respect Emilio was like the island dictator, King Julio Francisco, a ruthless bastard who had grown rich while his countrymen lived in abject poverty.

The only chance the young couple had was if his message got through to Murdock, and if his old buddy could inform rebel leader, General Mateo Lazaro, in time to stop the brutal execution. If anyone could get through to Lazaro, Murdock could. He was the only contract employee that the agency considered as good an operative as Hawk. But the powers that be at Langley were careful about using the big man. Aloysius Murdock had a well-earned reputation for being a mean, deadly, uncontrollable son of a bitch.

Murdock was one of the few men on earth whom Hawk trusted completely. But even Murdock couldn't perform miracles. Time was running out. If Lazaro didn't come to the rescue in the next hour, Cipriana and her blond, pretty-boy, missionary husband were going to be decapitated and their heads sent to Cipriana's father.

Lifting her three-year-old nephew from his bed, Rorie Dean cuddled him close as she stroked his back and whispered soothing, reassuring words. When the soldier grabbed her arm, she winced from the pain.

"Give the little prince to me," Captain García said, reaching for the boy.

Frankie clung to his aunt, whimpering when the captain tried to pull him out of her arms. "No. No. Tía Rorie!"

"Take your hands off this child!" Stepping backward, she lost her balance and tumbled onto the bed, but kept her hold on Frankie.

"*Señorita,* I have my orders. King Julio fears for Prince

Francisco's life, now that the rebels have taken his parents prisoner."

Righting herself into a sitting position, Rorie glared up into the dark, scarred face of the captain of King Julio's private guard. He was a large, barrel-chested ape of a man, but his keen black eyes hinted at a shrewd intelligence.

"I understand His Majesty's concern for Frankie's safety, but surely he doesn't mean for you to take the child away from me. My brother and Cipriana left Frankie in my care when they went to Puerto Angelo. If he leaves this house, I go with him."

"I'm sorry, but King Julio wishes his grandson to be brought to the palace immediately. Alone," Captain García said. "Arrangements have been made for you to take the next flight out of San Miguel."

"What's happened?" Clinging tenaciously to Frankie, Rorie lifted herself up off the bed and stood to face the intruders. Two guards waited outside her bedroom door while three marched inside. She glowered at the captain. "What are you not telling me?"

Clenching his jaw tightly, García took a deep breath. "The rebels have executed *la princesa*…and your brother," he said in a low voice, his dark eyes cutting back and forth from Rorie to the child she held.

For one brief moment, Aurora Dean's heart stopped beating. Peter dead? It wasn't possible. Not her kind, loving, wonderful brother. And not Cipriana. Beautiful, sweet Cipriana. "Are you sure? They disappeared only two days ago." Rorie held her hands over Frankie's ears. "Is there proof that they're dead?"

"*Sí, señorita.*" The captain swore in Spanish, his anger slurring the words. But Rorie understood all too well. She wasn't sure she wanted to know the details.

"What proof?" she asked.

"*Madre de Dios,* those animals sent their heads to King Julio."

Rorie gasped, but shut her mouth quickly as nasty, sour bile rose in her throat. She swallowed the hot bitterness and willed herself not to vomit.

Frightened and sleepy, Frankie wept. Huge tears trickled

down his round, full face and droplets clung to his long black eyelashes. Rorie wiped away the tears, then kissed his precious forehead. "Everything is going to be all right. You must be a brave boy for Tía Rorie. We're going to see Abuelo Julio and stay with him."

"I am sorry, Señorita Dean, but you cannot come with us to the palace," Captain García said. "Two of my men will take you to the airport as soon as you are dressed and packed. But Prince Francisco must come with me now."

"No!" She couldn't—wouldn't—allow anyone to take Frankie away from her. He was Peter's only child. She loved the little boy as if he were her own. And now that Peter was dead... "I won't leave Frankie here in this war-torn country. I'll take him back to the United States with me. He'll be safe there. Surely King Julio understands—"

Captain García issued orders quickly. Before Rorie realized what was happening, two of the soldiers ripped a screaming Frankie from her arms.

"Tía Rorie! Tía Rorie!" The frightened child cried out for her.

Rorie ran toward him. Captain García blocked her path. When she tried to move past the man, he drew back his hand and struck her across the face. The force of his blow knocked her backward into the wall.

Shaking her head and protectively crossing her arms in front of her, Rorie cried out as the three soldiers stalked toward her. One of them held a hypodermic needle in his hand. While two soldiers held her down, the third one injected her with the drug. Within minutes she crumpled to the floor, her body weightless. She watched helplessly while Captain García carried a screaming Frankie out into the dark, tropical night.

Chapter 1

"A missionary!" Gabriel Hawk shouted. "Are you out of your mind? You want me to take a missionary into San Miguel? I wouldn't lead a troop of trained soldiers into that godforsaken country, and you're asking me to take some naive, Bible-toting woman right into the middle of a bloody civil war!"

"Aurora Dean served as a missionary for only one year in San Miguel," Dane Carmichael said. "Right now, she's teaching high-school Spanish in Chattanooga."

"Oh, yeah, there's a big difference between a spinster missionary and a spinster schoolteacher. Neither would be prepared for a secret mission into San Miguel. Get somebody else to lead this crazy woman to her death."

"You're the best man for this. The man who can make sure Ms. Dean doesn't wind up dead." Dane Carmichael leaned back in his plush swivel chair and crossed his arms over his wide chest. "The way I see it, considering your background and your firsthand knowledge of San Miguel, you're the only one for the job."

"This woman—" Hawk glanced down at the file Dane had given him "—this Aurora Dean has to be nuts if she thinks she can waltz into San Miguel, kidnap King Julio's grandson and return with him to the United States. That kid is probably being guarded like Fort Knox.''

"Ms. Dean wouldn't be kidnapping the boy," Dane said. "She has copies of her brother's and sister-in-law's wills naming her legal guardian of Francisco Dean, in case of their deaths.''

"In San Miguel, those wills aren't worth the paper they're written on, and you know it. King Julio is a law unto himself in that country, and he's outlawed every U.S. citizen. Hell, we don't even have an embassy there anymore.''

"I'm well aware of that fact." Narrowing his gaze, Dane frowned. "Ms. Dean has spent over three years going through every diplomatic channel available, but with no results.''

"If she knew what we know, she never would have tried getting help from Washington.'' Hawk tossed the file folder down on Dane's desk. "With the U.S. secretly backing the rebels, our government has no interest in saving the young prince's life, despite the fact that his father was a U.S. citizen.''

"All the more reason to help Ms. Dean get her nephew out of the country before General Lazaro's rebels take over down there.'' Dane grimaced. "Even if Lazaro allows the boy to live, we have no guarantee that Emilio Santos or one of his renegades won't take it upon himself to eliminate the only remaining heir to the throne.''

Hawk nodded. "Lazaro won't execute a child, but Santos would butcher his own mother if he thought she was a threat to the revolution.''

"Ms. Dean knows enough to realize that, with the civil war escalating and the odds in favor of the rebels, time is of the essence. If she doesn't get the kid out of the country soon, it'll probably be too late.''

"It would be a suicide mission to take the woman along,'' Hawk said. "If I accept the assignment, I'll go into San Miguel alone. Murdock is still there, working with Lazaro. I can contact him and—''

"Ms. Dean made it perfectly clear that she intends to go to San Miguel,'' Dane interrupted. "Dundee's isn't the only game in town. She can take her money and go elsewhere. But you and I know that if anyone other than you takes her into San Miguel, she'll never come back alive.''

"Dammit!'' Hawk speared his fingers through his hair, loosening the heavy black mass from the band that held his long ponytail in place. "You knew when you gave me that file—'' he glanced meaningfully at the manila folder on Dane's desk ''—that this is an assignment I wouldn't want…but one I couldn't refuse.''

"It's been over three years since you came back from San Miguel. Since you broke ties with the CIA. And in all that time, you haven't been able to put that last job behind you. You couldn't save Cipriana and Peter Dean. But if you accept this assignment, you might be able to save their son.''

"The redemption of Gabriel Hawk, huh?'' Hawk picked up the folder. "Call Ms. Dean. Tell her that I'll go into San Miguel and get her nephew. But she stays here.''

"She won't agree.''

"What the hell's wrong with the woman? Is she suicidal?''

"She's desperate,'' Dane said. "And desperate people are willing to take drastic measures. You know that as well as I do. Ms. Dean has spent the last three years working two jobs—teaching and tutoring—to save enough money to hire someone to take her into San Miguel and help her rescue her nephew.''

Hawk didn't reply. Clutching the file in his hand, he turned and gazed out the windows that overlooked a busy downtown Atlanta street.

Dane eased out of his chair and walked over behind Hawk. He laid his hand on the Hawk's shoulder. "Just go talk to her. You can be in Chattanooga in two hours. Maybe you can make her understand why you should go into San Miguel alone.''

The wind whipped through the end of Hawk's ponytail as he flew along Interstate 75. Dark glasses shaded his eyes from the glare of the late-afternoon sunshine. The black leather jacket shielded him from the chill of the October day. And the black-and-silver helmet protected his head in case of an accident. His long, lean legs straddled the FXDL Dyna Low Rider—his most treasured possession.

Hawk wasn't the type of man who placed any sentimental value on material objects or on human relationships. He lived his life without attachments. Alone. No ties. As long as he could remember, he'd lived on the edge. Even now, at thirty-five, he still lived for the moment. No plans for his future. No hopes and dreams for tomorrow.

When he'd left San Miguel over three years ago, he'd known he had to get out of the business. Infiltrating Emilio Santos's renegade faction of the rebel army had been his last job for the CIA. Finally, after years of covert operations, of murder and destruction, he'd had enough. The brutal slaying of Cipriana and Peter Dean had gotten to him in a way nothing else ever had.

The man and woman had been young and scared—and totally innocent. And Hawk had been unable to prevent their deaths. What would Aurora Dean think of him if she knew that he had not only been a witness to her brother's and sister-in-law's murders, but had been considered a member of the ruthless, renegade gang that had executed the couple?

He had relived that day over and over again. If he had it to do over again, what could he have done differently? No matter how hard he tried to justify what had happened, he couldn't. Guilt and remorse ate away at his soul.

If he could save Cipriana and Peter's son, could go into San Miguel and bring the boy safely to the United States, then maybe his soul would find redemption. Maybe he would be able to forgive himself. And maybe his conscience would finally give him some peace.

But no way in hell was he going to take a woman with him. Any woman. And most especially, not Peter Dean's saintly sister. He would just have to find a way to convince Aurora Dean that this was a one-man mission.

Rorie Dean closed the songbook and placed it in the built-in holder on the back of the wooden pew. The congregation ended the last stanza of "Sweet Hour of Prayer," an old hymn that had been Rorie's favorite since childhood.

The moment the vocal music ended, Ronald Dean led his small congregation in prayer. Before her father said amen, Rorie added her own amendment to the supplication.

Please, dear God, send me a man capable of helping me bring Frankie safely out of San Miguel. Send me a strong, powerful guardian angel. And please, please, keep Frankie safe until we can get there.

When echoes of amen followed Brother Dean's petition to the Almighty, Rorie opened her eyes, picked up her coat and purse and slipped out of the pew. Before she reached the church door, her mother caught her by the arm.

"Your father and I want to talk to you, Rorie." Short and plump, fifty-five-year-old Bettye Lou Dean blocked her daughter's exit.

"Mama, you and Daddy have said it all. There's nothing left to discuss," Rorie told her mother. "I have to go home. I'm expecting Mr. Hawk this evening."

Bettye Lou clung to her daughter's arm while she smiled and nodded to members of the congregation as they passed by on their way out of the church.

"Mr. Hawk? Is that the man from the Dundee Agency in Atlanta?"

"Yes, Mama."

"Isn't there anything your father and I can say to change your mind?" Bettye Lou removed her hand from her daughter's arm.

Bowing her head, Rorie avoided direct eye contact with her mother. They'd had this conversation before, more than once, and it always ended the same. She understood her parents' fears and respected their concern for her safety. But she knew what she had to do—what her heart and soul demanded of her.

Ronald Dean walked down the aisle toward his wife and daughter, looking beyond them to wave goodbye to the last of the parishioners leaving the Wednesday-evening Bible-study meeting. When he reached his wife's side, he halted.

"What's wrong?" he asked.

"That man from the Dundee Agency is coming to see Rorie tonight," Bettye Lou said.

"As much as I want Frankie safe here with us, I simply

do not understand why you feel it is necessary for you to go back to San Miguel,'' Ronald said. ''Send this man. This trained agent. Let him bring Frankie to us.''

''Why can't you understand how I feel, Daddy?'' Rorie looked into her father's sad brown eyes. He had aged a great deal since Peter and Cipriana's execution, as had her mother. They were both such gentle, loving people that cruelty and murder were alien concepts to them.

''You know how much we love you, how much you mean to us.'' Ronald reached out and lifted Rorie's hands, grasping them in his. ''We've already lost Peter. Your mother and I can't bear the thought of losing you, too.''

''If you go to San Miguel, then there's every chance that we will lose both you and Frankie.'' Tears gathered in Bettye Lou's pale blue eyes.

''I have to go, Mama. You know I must. Peter left Frankie in my care. He was my responsibility, and I let those soldiers take him. I should have fought harder. I should have found a way to keep Frankie safe.''

''Don't do this to yourself.'' Ronald drew his daughter into his arms. ''There was nothing you could've done to have stopped King Julio's armed guard.''

Rorie laid her head on her father's shoulder, succumbing to the need for his comfort. ''Please, Daddy, give me your support in what I must do. I believe that Mr. Hawk may be the answer to my prayers.''

Ronald stroked his daughter's head as he'd done to comfort her when she was a small child. ''What do you know about this man?''

Rorie lifted her head and looked directly at her father. ''He worked for the government once. A few years ago. Mr. Carmichael, who is the head of Dundee's, told me that Mr. Hawk has extensive knowledge of San Miguel. It seems that he lived there once, while on an assignment of some sort.''

''A government agent?'' Bettye Lou asked. ''Just what branch did he work for, dear?''

''Mr. Carmichael didn't say. But he didn't work in an office. I understand that Mr. Hawk is quite adept at self-defense. I'm sure his training was extensive. After all, he makes his living as a professional bodyguard now.''

Rorie wondered if her mother knew the difference between an agent who worked behind a desk and an operative who worked in the field, the latter, often little more than a mercenary hired for a specific dirty job. From the information Dane Carmichael had given her, Rorie felt certain that Mr. Hawk had an unsavory past.

But the man's past made no difference to her. If he had the skills necessary to get them into San Miguel, rescue Frankie and get them safely back to the United States, she really didn't care if he was the devil's own. Of course, she could hardly admit that to her parents.

Rorie gave her father a hug, then turned to her mother. "I'll call y'all as soon as I've met with Mr. Hawk and we've made our plans."

"Promise me that you won't leave without coming to say goodbye." Tears trickled down Bettye Lou's round, rosy cheeks.

Rorie embraced her mother, then withdrew and reached into her pocket for a tissue. She patted her mother's cheeks dry. "Once my plans are finalized, I'll come over and tell you and Daddy all the details. I promise."

Rorie pulled her ten-year-old Mercury into an empty parking space near her apartment building. The first thing she noticed was the big, black motorcycle taking up one of the slots. She didn't know of anyone in Building Nine that owned a motorcycle.

She got out of her car, locked the door and fumbled with her key chain, searching for her door key. The cool night wind chilled her. She turned up the collar on her coat and hurried toward the outside stairwell that led to her third-floor apartment. Within seconds she reached the top landing. She glanced down the well-lit open hallway. A lone man stood outside her door, one knee bent, his foot braced against the wall. Blood rushed through Rorie's veins. The drum of her accelerated heartbeat thundered in her ears.

There was nothing to be afraid of, absolutely nothing. If the stranger was dangerous, all she needed do was scream and her neighbors would come running. Chip and Gloria, in

9-A1 were at home. So was Mr. Hicks, in 9-A2. Or she could use the pepper spray in her purse. Or even try out one of the self-defense maneuvers her friend Debbie, a fellow school-teacher, had shown her.

Of course, it was possible that Mr. Hawk had arrived early. The stranger lurking in the shadows could be the guardian angel for whom she'd prayed so fervently. When she neared her apartment door, the man stepped out of the shadows. Rorie gasped. This couldn't be Gabriel Hawk, could it?

The man towered over her five-foot-four-inch frame by a good ten inches. He was big, dark and deadly-looking, with piercing ebony eyes and long, silky black hair secured in a ponytail. Dressed all in black—leather jacket, cotton shirt and jeans—he blended into the night like a prince of darkness. Rorie shuddered at the thought. Whoever or whatever this man was, he was danger personified. She sensed the aura of unholy power that surrounded him.

"Are you Aurora Dean?" he asked, his dark face a somber mask as he gazed directly into her eyes.

"Yes, I am," she replied, transfixed by his mesmerizing stare. "You—you aren't Gabriel Hawk, are you?"

He smiled—a wickedly charming smile—and Rorie immediately sensed that this devilishly handsome stranger was dangerous on more than one level, in more than one way. Everything feminine within her responded to all that was masculine in him, and she cursed herself for being so susceptible to pure sexual attraction.

"I'm afraid I am Gabriel Hawk. I'm not what you were expecting, am I?"

"I—I— No. You aren't what I was expecting." She couldn't take her eyes off the tiny gold ring glistening in his left ear. "You don't look like my idea of a security agent."

He surveyed her from head to toe and chuckled. "You're not my idea of an old maid missionary turned schoolteacher."

Rorie blushed, somehow knowing that his comment was a compliment. Even though she'd often been told—by her parents, her brother, her friends—that she was beautiful, she was unaccustomed to compliments from men.

Quickly turning her back to him to hide her embarrassment, Rorie inserted the key into the lock and opened her front door.

"Please, come in, Mr. Hawk."

Flipping on a light switch, she illuminated the small, cosy living room of her three-room apartment. After following her inside, Hawk closed and locked the door behind him.

"Please, make yourself at home." Rorie slipped off her coat and hung it on the hall tree just inside the door. "Take off your jacket. I'll make us some coffee."

"Don't go to any trouble."

"No trouble." She didn't look back at him when she scurried into the open kitchen area, separated from the living room by a small bar.

He removed his jacket, glanced around the tidy room and sat down in a tan-and-gray plaid recliner. He watched her as she prepared the coffee machine.

So this was Aurora Dean. Former missionary. High-school teacher. Woman with a death-wish mission.

She certainly wasn't what he'd been expecting. He had envisioned Peter Dean's sister as a plain, skinny, unattractive prude. The woman was neither plain nor skinny.

She was beautiful, if you liked voluptuous, full-figured women with perfect facial features and long, golden blond hair. In her simple black skirt and beige sweater, she looked as neat as her apartment. She was a little too plump for his taste, but there was something about her—an ultrafemininity—that unwittingly drew him to her. He couldn't help but wonder just how sweet and innocent she really was.

He knew one thing for certain: he couldn't take this woman into San Miguel with him—she wouldn't last a day.

"Do you want cream or sugar, Mr. Hawk?" she called out from the kitchen.

"I take my coffee black," he told her. "And drop the Mr., okay? Just call me Hawk."

She walked into the living room, handed him a white ceramic mug and sat down on the sofa opposite his chair. "Well, Hawk, how soon can we leave for San Miguel?"

He took a sip of the hot, rich coffee, then held the mug in both hands and gazed down into the dark liquid. "I haven't agreed to take the job, Ms. Dean."

The large, curling snake emblazoned on Hawk's left hand caught Rorie's eye immediately. Squinting to try to make out the word tattooed beneath the snake's belly, Rorie glared at his hand. Cobras. The word was Cobras. What did it mean? When and why had Hawk gotten his hand tattooed with such a vile symbol?

"I thought that was why you were here—to accept the job," she said. "I understood from Mr. Carmichael that once you came to Chattanooga, everything would be set into motion for our trip to San Miguel."

"Things have been set into motion, but not for us to make the trip. Only for *me* to make the trip."

"No!" Rorie set her mug on a coaster on the coffee table in front of her. Easing to the edge of the sofa, she balled her hands into fists and placed them on her knees. "The deal was for you to take me into San Miguel and act as my guide and bodyguard, to help me find Frankie and bring him safely back to the United States."

"San Miguel is no place for a woman, especially not a lady like you. Things have gotten a lot worse since you were down there. We can't just fly in, get our passports checked and stay at a hotel in La Vega." He watched her closely, noting the tension radiating from her body, the glint in her blue eyes and the barely suppressed anger she held in check. "We'll have to go in at night, by boat, and swim ashore. Often we'll have to hide in shacks and caves and maybe even sleep outside in the jungle. We'll have to meet and mix with some pretty rough people. Our lives would be constantly threatened. We couldn't trust King Julio *or* the rebels. The experience would be far too grueling and far too dangerous for you."

"I'm well aware of the conditions in San Miguel." Rorie spoke slowly, each word enunciated in a carefully controlled tone. "I know that I'll be risking my life. But it's a risk I'm willing to take to save my nephew."

"There's no reason for you to take any risks, Ms. Dean. You stay here in the States and let me go into San Miguel alone and bring out your nephew. It's the best solution all the way around. You'll be safe and sound. Besides, I work best alone. Finding and rescuing your nephew will be easier for me without having to worry about you."

"I'm afraid you don't understand." Rorie stood and looked

down at Hawk. Their gazes met and held. "I'm going to San Miguel. If you don't want to accept the assignment as my guide and bodyguard, then I'll find someone else."

"Dammit, lady, are you crazy?" He shot up out of the recliner.

"There's no need for you to curse, Mr. Hawk. Whether or not I go to San Miguel isn't your decision. It's mine. And I am going. With you—or with another protector."

No need for him to curse? Was she kidding? If she called saying "Dammit" cursing, then heaven help her if she ever heard him really let loose with the full extent of his vocabulary. If she went with him to San Miguel, he would have to put up with her naive, innocent sensibilities.

"Look, lady, nobody tells me how to talk."

"Not even your employer?"

"Nobody."

"Then perhaps we've both made a mistake," she said. "I would expect my employee to follow my orders."

"If I were to take you into San Miguel—and I'm not—I'd give the orders and you'd follow them to the letter."

"I'm sorry I've wasted your time, Mr. Hawk." Rorie glanced at the front door. "I'm sure I can find someone else to take me into San Miguel. Someone willing to follow my orders."

A dark foreboding swirled around inside him, tightening his gut. The very thought of her putting her life into someone else's hands bothered Hawk greatly. He hadn't been able to save Peter and Cipriana Dean, but if he allowed Peter's sister to go into San Miguel without him, he would be signing her death warrant.

"Any man stupid enough to follow your orders would lead you to certain death," Hawk told her. "Regardless of what you think, you don't have any idea what you'll be getting yourself into if you go to San Miguel."

"Are you implying that you're the only person capable of keeping me safe once I get to San Miguel? Do you honestly think that no one else is qualified for this assignment?"

He grabbed her by the shoulders. His big, long fingers sank into the plush material of her sweater and bit into the soft flesh beneath. "I'm probably the only man available to you

who knows San Miguel on a firsthand basis and who has
contacts in the country who can help find your nephew.''

She trembled beneath Hawk's big hands. He looked into
her pure blue eyes and wondered if Aurora Dean was frightened or aroused. Or both? As she breathed deeply, in and out,
her full breasts rose and lowered—their voluptuousness, pure
temptation.

Rorie stared him directly in the eye, calling on every ounce
of her willpower not to show him any weakness. His nearness
both aroused and frightened her. He was big and dark and
dangerous. He was gloriously, intriguingly male. And suddenly she knew that he *was* the one man on earth capable of
helping her rescue Frankie. Gabriel Hawk *was* the powerful
guardian angel for whom she'd prayed. She just hadn't expected her protector to be a fallen angel—a dark and deadly
man whom neither she nor anyone else could control.

''Will you take the assignment, Mr. Hawk?'' she asked.

''You're damned and determined to go, aren't you?'' He
felt a twinge of satisfaction when she winced at his use of
the word *damned*.

''Yes. And I want you to take me.''

The air sizzled between them. He ran his hands up and
down her arms, then released her. A closed-mouth smile
spread across Hawk's face. ''All right, lady. I'll take you. On
two conditions.''

''What two conditions.''

''One is that you follow my orders, without question. After
all, you're paying me for my expertise.''

Rorie bit down on her bottom lip. ''All right. I agree to
follow your orders.''

''Without question?''

''Yes,'' she said reluctantly. ''Without question.''

''And the second condition is that you allow me to put you
through a month of physical training, to get you in shape for
our mission.''

''What?''

''Lady, you're not trained for this kind of endeavor. Besides being totally inexperienced, you're soft and plump. In
the shape you're in, you couldn't hold out for very long.
You'd wind up putting both our lives in danger.''

She glared at him, unable to believe the way he'd just insulted her. He had all but called her fat! "I may not be skinny, with a lot of toned muscles, but I'm hardly out of shape just because I'm plump."

"I wasn't trying to be insulting," he said. "I'm just being honest. You're in no condition for the rigorous mission we'll be undertaking. Either you agree to a month's training or we don't have a deal."

He was a devil. She'd known it the minute she saw him. He thought she would back down, refuse his second condition and allow him to go to San Miguel alone. Well, he'd better think again.

"I'll agree to two weeks of training."

"You need at least a month."

"We don't have a month to waste." She walked across the room, lifted his leather jacket from the hall tree and held it out to him. "Two weeks of training and then we go to San Miguel."

Following Rorie to the front door, he reached out and took his jacket from her. When their fingers brushed in the exchange, she jerked away from him as if his touch had burned her. He knew he was making the biggest mistake of his life, but he couldn't let this woman get herself killed. He owed it to Peter Dean to protect his sister, if at all possible.

And he owed it to himself to pay penance for his sins. Maybe, in the process, he would find out whether he still had a soul or if he had lost it—more than three years ago, in San Miguel.

"All right, Ms. Dean. Two weeks of training and I'll take you into San Miguel."

"Call me Rorie." She smiled. "I'll be ready to leave first thing in the morning, right after I say goodbye to my parents."

"I'll pick you up around nine." He opened the door and stepped outside, then paused and turned around to face her. "Pack light. We'll be taking my motorcycle."

When her eyes rounded into big blue circles and her mouth parted into a soft, pink oval, Hawk reached out and gripped her chin.

"Get ready for two weeks of hell."

She glared at him. "What else would I expect since I'll be spending those two weeks with you?"

Rorie decided then and there that she was willing to do anything—absolutely anything—to save Frankie. Even spend two weeks in hell with a fallen angel.

Chapter 2

Hawk stored his motorcycle in Biloxi and they took a boat out to Le Bijou Bleu. He told Rorie that the island belonged to the owner of the Dundee Agency, Sam Dundee, and his wife, Jeannie.

"It's the perfect place for you to train during the next two weeks." He sat beside her in the speedboat, the fierce autumn wind whipping around him, loosening stray tendrils of his long, black hair. "Sam and Jeannie are leaving for vacation today, with Sam's niece and her husband. So we'll have the island to ourselves. Except for Manton."

"Manton?"

"He's been with Jeannie's family for years," Hawk said. "He's the caretaker for Le Bijou Bleu, and from what Sam tells me, he's a second father to Jeannie."

Rorie sighed, a sense of relief spreading through her. She didn't like the idea of being all alone with Gabriel Hawk on an island for two weeks. At least now she knew that if she needed a reprieve from hell, she would have someone other than the devil himself to ask for a pardon.

"Sam has a gym, with a complete workout room in the

house and a scaled-down obstacle course on the back side of the island," Hawk said.

When Rorie eyed him quizzically, he grinned—a devilishly seductive grin that had no doubt lured many a woman to sin. "Sam likes to keep in shape," Hawk explained. "They also have a pool where you can practice your swimming before we try the ocean."

"You've already figured out all the details of my torture, haven't you?"

"Ms. Dean, you have no idea what torture is. Not yet."

"Since we're going to be living together as master and slave for the next couple of weeks, why don't you call me Rorie?"

"Rorie, huh?" He chuckled. "Not Aurora?"

"I was named in honor of my paternal great-grandmother, but Peter had a difficult time pronouncing my name when he was little. He shortened Aurora to Rora and somehow it wound up Rorie."

"Cute little story," Hawk said. "Sounds like you had an idyllic childhood with Mommy and Daddy and big brother."

He hadn't meant to sound so sarcastic. But when people reminisced about their families, he had a tendency to close down and stop listening.

"Sorry if my cute little story bored you."

"Let's just say that childhood memories aren't high on my list of favorite topics."

This was the man with whom she was going to—willingly—spend the next weeks. Disagreeable. Unfriendly. Hateful.

Rorie had never dreaded anything as much as she dreaded having to take orders from Hawk. It wasn't that she was more willful than the average woman; it was just that she'd always hated taking orders. That specific aspect of her personality had been a trial to her parents and occasionally an embarrassment. But despite her aversion to following orders, she was willing to obey Hawk's commands. She was willing to do anything in order to rescue Frankie—even allow Hawk to torment her for the next two weeks.

She still couldn't believe that she'd ridden with him on his motorcycle all the way from Chattanooga to Biloxi. Her backside was sore, her face chapped by the wind and her disposition less than agreeable.

They'd ridden into Mobile late last night, after leaving Chattanooga that afternoon. They'd gotten a late start because he had insisted on her obtaining an okay from her personal physician before he started her on any type of physical-fitness regime. Once in Mobile, Hawk had checked them into separate rooms at a local motel.

Rorie knew that Hawk thought he would break her during the fourteen days of physical training on the island. He was counting on her giving up, returning to Chattanooga and allowing him to go on to San Miguel alone. Well, he didn't know her. Although her idea of rigorous exercise was taking a brisk walk, she was prepared to suffer through whatever torturous exercises he devised.

Hawk watched the woman sitting at his side as they rode out into the Gulf waters, away from Biloxi and toward the small, secluded island that Sam and Jeannie Dundee called home. Rorie was already showing signs of discomfort at having to follow his instructions. But he had to hand it to her; so far, she hadn't mouthed one complaint or questioned one order he'd given. He knew she'd hated making the long trip from Chattanooga on his motorcycle. Rorie didn't exactly seem either the athletic or outdoors type to him—not with her round, plump body and her pale, flawless skin.

He could have rented a car for their trip, but he'd made a split-second decision to use his bike. Using the bike as their means of transportation had been the first of many tests he would put Rorie through over the next fourteen days—or less. He doubted she would last the entire two weeks. He gave her five days—seven at most—before she called it quits and accepted defeat.

They'd made a bargain, one he knew she would keep. If she couldn't make it through two weeks of training, then she would let him go to San Miguel alone. But if she survived his two weeks of "boot camp," he would take her with him.

He didn't doubt for a minute that he would be making the trip alone. Rorie wasn't tough enough for this dangerous mission into a country torn apart by civil war. Few women would be tough enough. He could think of only one he would even consider taking along—Ellen Denby, a fellow Dundee agent. But then, Ellen was no ordinary woman. She was hard as nails and as tough as any man he knew.

But Aurora—correction, Rorie—was soft and sweet and completely unprepared for the physical rigors of the mission. And to make matters worse, she was emotionally involved. In his experience, people in general and women in particular didn't always act rationally when they were personally involved in a dangerous situation.

"Here we are, folks," the boatman told them. "This is Le Bijou Bleu. Looks like the Dundees were expecting y'all. There's Manton waiting on the pier."

The morning sky spread out above them like a pale blue canopy, interspersed with fluffy white clouds. The October sun beamed down on them, its warmth at war with the cool breeze.

Shading her eyes from the glare of the sun, Rorie glanced at the pier. She gasped. A gigantic, brown-skinned man, with a shiny bald head, stood onshore. With his arms crossed over his enormous chest, he looked like a bronze statue.

"That's Manton?" she asked, her gaze transfixed on the seven-foot giant.

"That's Manton. He's a deaf-mute, but he reads lips perfectly."

Hawk lifted their small canvas bags onto the pier, then helped Rorie out of the boat. The minute they were ashore, the boatman waved goodbye and headed back to Biloxi.

Without any gesture of greeting, Manton lifted the two canvas bags and began the climb up the curving set of rock steps that led from the beach to the hilltop above.

"After I whip you into better shape, I'll let you try climbing that rocky hill without using these steps," Hawk told her. "It'll be good practice, just in case we have to go ashore close to the limestone cliffs in San Miguel."

Rorie groaned inwardly, but didn't respond to his taunt. They had just arrived on Le Bijou Bleu and already he was trying to scare her away.

When she stood there glaring at him, the sunlight turning her long, windblown hair to gold, Hawk grinned. "Come on, *la dama dorado*, you're safe for today. We won't start training until the morning. Today, we'll accept the Dundees' hospitality.''

Rorie turned abruptly and quickly followed Manton up the steps. A pink flush spread over her neck and highlighted her cheeks. What had prompted Hawk to call her *golden lady*—and in Spanish? The words were practically an endearment. He knew she spoke Spanish, didn't he? Of course he knew.

Rorie had known the first moment she saw Gabriel Hawk that he was a dangerous man, but now she realized that possibly the most lethal thing about him was his deadly sex appeal. Most women probably fell into his arms after one exposure to his wicked smile.

She didn't have to look behind her to know that he followed her up the steps. She felt his nearness. When she hesitated at the top of the steps, he came up behind her, so close that she felt the warmth of his breath.

"Beautiful, isn't it?" He gripped her shoulder.

Willing herself not to respond to his touch, Rorie held the shivers inside as she looked out over the expanse of green grass in front of them. Huge live oaks, heavily laden with Spanish moss, mingled with palm trees. Circling the island, the sky and ocean met, blue on blue, one shade fading into the other on the distant horizon.

"You haven't seen anything yet," Hawk said. "Wait until you get a good look at the house."

They continued following Manton on the seemingly endless trek through the ankle-high grass. When Rorie saw the Dundees' home, she slowed and then stopped. The huge, two-story French cottage had been built on the top of a rise, allowing all four sides of the island and the Gulf waters to be viewed from the wide verandas that surrounded the house.

"It's like something out of a movie." Rorie sighed deeply.

Hawk nudged her. "Get a move on. We're expected for lunch and I'm sure you'll want time to freshen up first."

"We're expected for lunch?"

"We sure are. When I called Sam this morning to let him know we were in Mobile and were headed for the island, he told me that Jeannie insisted on our having lunch with the family before they leave for the mainland later this afternoon."

A menagerie of cats and dogs came out to meet them as they neared the house. Rorie counted six mixed-breed dogs as they greeted Manton and then raced past him to sniff the new arrivals. Cats of various colors and sizes lounged on the veranda, two curled into furry balls in wicker chairs.

A woman with flowing brown hair stood on the veranda, a warm and welcoming smile on her face. Despite the roundness of her body and the pink glow of her cheeks, Rorie thought the woman seemed fragile and delicate.

"Welcome to Le Bijou Bleu." The woman braced herself with a cane. She held out her free hand to Rorie, who stepped up on the porch and accepted the cordial greeting. "I'm Jeannie Dundee."

The moment the two women's hands touched, Jeannie sighed. "You mustn't worry about your stay here on my island," Jeannie whispered as she drew Rorie to her. "I sense that you are a very strong, determined woman. You will prove yourself to Gabriel."

Stunned by her hostess's insight, Rorie stared questioningly at Jeannie. "How did you—"

"I have empathic abilities," Jeannie said. "The moment I touched you, I felt your worry...your great concern."

A shiver of apprehension rippled along Rorie's nerve endings. She had been taught since childhood about the uniqueness of the human spirit, that the soul was eternal, but she'd never met anyone with an unearthly power.

Holding open the front door, Manton waited. Jeannie hurried Rorie and Hawk inside, through the spacious foyer and into the front parlor—a huge white room with floor-to-ceiling windows and French doors leading to the veranda.

"Take the bags downstairs to the ground level," Jeannie told Manton. "I've given Ms. Dean the Sunlight Room that Elizabeth and Reece have been using. And put Mr. Hawk's bag in the small bedroom."

"Where's Sam?" Hawk asked.

"Oh, he and Reece are out back playing with the children. You should see Samantha now that she's nearly two. She runs us ragged, but her little cousin Jamie gives her a run for her money. Jamie's three and he thinks he's the boss."

"Would you mind if I interrupt Sam for a few minutes?"

Hawk asked. "I'd like to go over a few details of this assignment with him." Hawk glanced at Rorie. "Why don't you go on to your room and freshen up before lunch?"

Jeannie smiled at Hawk. "Go right down the hall. It'll lead you to the back porch. And don't worry about Ms. Dean. I'll take her downstairs, help her get settled in and introduce her to Elizabeth."

"Please, call me Rorie. And I don't want to be any trouble. If you'll just tell me—"

"No trouble at all." Jeannie laced her arm through Rorie's and led her out into the foyer. Rorie slowed her pace to accommodate Jeannie's hampered gait as they descended the stairs to the ground level of the huge, old cottage. "I want to introduce you to Elizabeth, Sam's niece. She's eager to meet you."

"She is?" Rorie couldn't imagine why the woman, someone she'd never even heard of before today, would be eager to meet her.

"I'm afraid you're going to think you've fallen through Alice's looking glass," Jeannie said. "You see, where I have empathic abilities, Elizabeth is clairvoyant. Hawk should have told you before you met us. Of course, he probably had no idea that we would reveal ourselves to you. We usually don't. But Elizabeth and I agreed that you were a special case and that we should warn—no, not warn, prepare—yes, prepare you for what lies ahead."

"Mrs. Dundee—"

"Jeannie, please."

"Jeannie, I'm afraid I don't understand. I have to admit that you're unnerving me just a little."

"I'm sorry. But if you'll come and meet Elizabeth, she can explain everything. You see, she's been having—uh—er...visions about you, ever since Dane Carmichael called Sam and told him about your situation. About your nephew."

As a general rule Rorie wasn't a believer in the supernatural, other than a God in heaven and his host of angels; but on the other hand she wasn't exactly a skeptic, either. She'd always had an open mind, and as a spiritual person, she did believe in the power of miracles. So, who was she to say that

Jeannie and Elizabeth did not possess special gifts? Perhaps God was using them to help her in her quest to save Frankie.

Jeannie led Rorie into a large, airy suite that extended the width of the ground floor, with windows facing east, west and south. When Rorie entered the suite, she realized that it consisted of three rooms. The sitting room in which they were standing led to a bedroom just beyond the French doors. To her left, the door to a private bath stood partially open.

Rorie wasn't accustomed to such luxury, such splendor. Antique furniture. Mansions on private islands. A suite of rooms for guests. She'd been raised as the daughter of missionaries, her father now a country minister. They had never had much money, and what her father earned, he often used to help the less fortunate.

An incredibly beautiful woman walked out of the bedroom and into the sitting area. Her sable-brown hair was French braided and the plait hung to her waist. The empire-cut dress she wore hid her pregnancy, until she sat down on the green wicker sofa. She laid her hand on top of her swollen belly.

"You must be Aurora...Rorie," the woman said. "I'm Elizabeth Landry. Please, come and sit with me." She held out her hand to Rorie.

"Don't be afraid." Jeannie gave Rorie a gentle shove. "We truly want to help you."

Uncertain whether she should accept these women at face value, Rorie cautiously crossed the room and sat down on the sofa beside Elizabeth.

"I'll leave the two of you alone for a while," Jeannie said. "I'll let y'all know when lunch is ready."

Rorie almost cried out for Jeannie not to leave her. Instead she turned to face Elizabeth and found instant assurance when she gazed into the woman's kind blue eyes.

"You have nothing to fear from me," Elizabeth said. "However, there is great danger in your future. But I see great happiness also, if you are courageous enough to reach out and grab it."

"Are you telling my fortune?" Rorie tried for joviality, but the quiver in her voice revealed her anxiety.

"The gift of clairvoyance is a great burden," Elizabeth said. "And I don't make a habit of sharing my visions with others. Gabriel Hawk is one of Sam's friends. He is a man tormented by demons. He is plagued by a past he cannot undo. I sense a true goodness in you. A goodness that can cleanse Gabriel's soul.''

"Look…Elizabeth… I hardly think that I'm Hawk's salvation. I don't even know the man. We met only the day before yesterday. And we don't really like each other all that much. I've hired him for a mission to rescue my nephew, and that's all there is to our relationship.''

"I know about your nephew. Frankie is alive and well and safe…for the time being.''

Rorie grabbed Elizabeth's arm. "You've had a vision about Frankie?''

"My visions are of you and Gabriel and of the boy being rescued.'' Elizabeth laid her hand over Rorie's where she grasped her arm. "Prepare yourself for what is to come, for what you must do. Gabriel will take you to San Miguel and he will rescue your nephew. But in the end, it will be you who must save both Frankie and Gabriel—if you have the courage. If your love is strong enough. If it is not…''

Rorie gazed into Elizabeth's eyes and saw only the truth. "If not? Are you saying that Frankie could die and so could Hawk, unless I save them?''

"Prepare yourself,'' Elizabeth repeated. "And open your heart to a new and glorious wonder, for only love can give you the strength you will need.''

"My love for Frankie will give me strength. I *am* prepared to do anything to save him.''

"'Anything' covers a great deal of territory, Rorie. You say you would do anything, but the woman you are now is not prepared for what must be done. When the time comes, you will have to find the strength to do what your heart tells you is necessary.''

Elizabeth patted Rorie's hand, then pulled away and rose from the sofa slowly, awkwardly. Steadying herself when she stood, Elizabeth smiled at Rorie. "I will think of you in the weeks ahead. And Jeannie and I will pray for you.''

As Elizabeth walked out of the room, Rorie sat on the sofa, momentarily spellbound. For several minutes, she couldn't move, couldn't even think. But suddenly, emotions washed over her, like the pounding surf at high tide. Fear greater than any she'd ever known spiraled through her. Her fear subsided, making way for anger. And then anger was replaced by uncertainty.

Should she believe Elizabeth Landry's dire warnings? Could she trust the woman's visions? If she dared to believe, if she did trust, then she would have to accept her destiny.

She was destined to save Frankie. She accepted that responsibility wholeheartedly. But cleansing Gabriel Hawk's soul and saving him was a task for which she was unprepared.

Prepare yourself. If you have the courage... If your love is strong enough...

Hawk stood on the back veranda watching Sam Dundee and Reece Landry frolicking like a couple of kids. Sitting on the grass, Sam tossed a large, red ball to his daughter, a petite, toddler-size replica of himself. Her blond curls bounced up and down around her angelic face as she caught the ball, hugged it to her chest and then threw it back at her big, rugged father. Sam then threw the ball to Jamie Landry, his three-year-old nephew, who caught the ball high above his head and quickly tossed it to his father. Glancing toward Hawk, Reece missed the ball, much to his son's dismay.

"Daddy! Watch the ball," Jamie said.

"Sorry, little man." Reece picked up the ball from where it had landed at his feet and pitched it to his son.

"I didn't mean to interrupt playtime." Hawk walked down the steps leading off the veranda and into the backyard. "But Jeannie said it would be all right to come on out here."

When Sam stood and lifted his daughter onto his hip, she laid her head on his chest and snuggled against him. For the life of him, Hawk couldn't understand the ease with which a man like Sam Dundee had taken to fatherhood. Sam's background had no better prepared him for domesticity than Hawk's had him. And yet here was Sam happily married, a father, and obviously loving every minute of it.

"Is Jeannie getting Ms. Dean settled in?" Sam asked.

"My guess is that with three women alone together, they're plotting something," Reece Landry said.

"Did you need to see me about anything in particular?"
Sam looked directly at Hawk.

"Yeah. If you can spare a few minutes," Hawk said.

Sam kissed his daughter's forehead. "Samantha, sweetheart, you go to Uncle Reece and play ball with him and Jamie, while I take a walk with Mr. Hawk."

Going reluctantly to her uncle, Samantha crinkled up her nose and pursed her lips in a spoiled little pout.

"Daddy will be right back," Sam assured the child.

Oh, how the mighty have fallen, Hawk thought. Sam Dundee was a slave to his love for his wife and daughter. Hawk had never allowed his emotions to enslave him, to make him weak and vulnerable. A man who didn't love remained strong and invincible. He could never be disappointed, never be hurt.

Hawk had learned long ago not to want what he couldn't have.

"Reece, give us a holler when lunch is ready." Sam turned to Hawk, then nodded toward a path leading from the yard to the beach. "Let's take a walk."

They remained silent until they were out of earshot of the children. Sam paused briefly.

"So you took the assignment," Sam said. "I figured you would."

"I'm not taking her with me. She thinks I am, but I talked her into agreeing to undergo two weeks of training. If she fails the training, she doesn't go to San Miguel."

"And you're sure she's going to fail."

"I'm sure."

"Never underestimate a determined woman."

"Hell, wait until you see her," Hawk said. "She's plump and soft. And she's young, naive and my guess is she's as innocent as your little Samantha."

Widening his eyes and raising his eyebrows, Sam looked questioningly at Hawk. "There's innocent and then there's innocent. Are you saying Ms. Dean—who is what, twenty-seven?—doesn't know anything about the real world? Dammit, Hawk, the woman lived a whole year in San Miguel. She saw, firsthand, what the ugly side of life looks like. Her brother and sister-in-law were executed, she was drugged and put on a plane out of the country and her nephew was kid-

napped by his grandfather's goons. I don't think the woman
is naive.''

"All right. So maybe she's not totally naive, but she's a
damn do-gooder. That's why she was in San Miguel to start
with. She was a missionary. Her brother was a minister. Her
old man is a minister. She may not be naive, but she's…
Well, she's…''

"Innocent?'' Sam supplied the word.

"She's sweet. Syrupy sweet. She corrects me every time I
use a curse word.''

Sam Dundee burst into laughter. "I know what's wrong
with you.'' Sam slapped Hawk on the back. "Aurora Dean
is a virgin and you're going to be stuck alone here with her
on Le Bijou Bleu for two weeks and possibly longer, if she
goes to San Miguel with you. You've never spent that much
time with a woman without having sex with her, and you
know that Ms. Dean isn't going to give you the keys to her
kingdom.''

"You're crazy! I don't want Rorie Dean. I wouldn't take
her virginity, if she begged me to take it.''

Sam eyed Hawk skeptically. "You're protesting a little too
vehemently.''

"Hell! The woman's not my type. I told you, she's plump
and soft and sweet. And she's inexperienced. I like 'em long
and lean and mean. When I take a woman to bed, I expect
her to know what she's doing.''

"So, considering the fact that Ms. Dean is totally unsuit-
able—'' Sam cleared his throat "—for the mission, you're
going to sabotage her plans to accompany you. You're going
to make her training so difficult that she'll have no choice but
to give up and let you win.''

"I'm going to do it for her own good as well as mine. If
I took her into San Miguel, she'd only wind up getting herself
killed and probably me along with her.''

"How honest have you been with her about your past?''
Sam asked. "Does she know about your connection to Emilio
Santos?''

"All she knows is that I used to work for the government
and that I spent some time in San Miguel on an assignment.

Since she's not going with me, I didn't see any need for her to know."

"And if somehow she passes your test and you have to take her with—"

"That won't happen."

"All right." Sam walked toward the beach.

Hawk followed alongside Sam. "Is everything set? The boat? The supplies? Has Murdock been contacted? Will he be ready for me?"

"Everything is ready. All you have to do is say when. Murdock's put out feelers. He's trying to find out where young Prince Francisco is and what it'll take to—"

"What do you mean? Isn't the kid living with his grandfather?"

"Murdock said his informers tell him that no one has seen the prince for nearly a month, that there's a good chance King Julio has sent the boy into hiding to protect him."

"Damn! Now, not only will I have to figure out a way to get the boy, I'll have to find him first. Does Murdock have any idea where Frankie is now?"

"Not a clue, but Murdock says King Julio made a smart move, sending the kid away. It looks as if everything is about to blow sky-high. The rebels will probably take La Vega within the next few weeks."

Hawk kicked the sand beneath his feet. "I need to get into San Miguel now, find the kid and get him out. And I could, if I didn't have to deal with a damn, irrational woman!"

"Take her with you and you can leave tomorrow."

"I am not taking her with me!"

Rorie knew what couples in love looked like and how they acted. She'd been around Peter and Cipriana for nearly a year before their deaths. And even after more than thirty years of marriage, there was still a magical quality to her parents' relationship. But she had never felt so left out, so totally separate and apart from the wonders of love, as she felt sitting through lunch with the Dundees and the Landrys. The unguarded touches. The lingering glances. The tender smiles.

And she had the strangest notion that Gabriel Hawk felt as out of place as she did—perhaps even more so.

"Make yourselves at home," Jeannie told Rorie and Hawk as she bade them farewell on the veranda.

"If you need Manton for anything, let him know," Sam said. "Otherwise, he'll stay out of your way. You'll hardly know he's around."

Elizabeth waved goodbye, her gaze locking with Rorie's for one brief instant. She mouthed the words, "Be strong."

Jeannie reached out, took Rorie's hand and squeezed gently. "It can be yours, too."

Rorie gasped, realizing that Jeannie had sensed her desire for love—the passionate, earth-shattering love Jeannie shared with Sam.

"Have a safe trip," Rorie said.

She prayed that no one else had guessed what Jeannie's cryptic statement meant. But in the hustle and bustle of departure, she doubted that even Hawk had overheard. She wasn't ashamed of the longing she had kept buried deep within her heart for such a long time; it was just that she didn't want to appear weak and vulnerable—perhaps even romantically foolish—to others. Especially not to Hawk. She doubted he would understand. He didn't seem the type to whom love and marriage and a family meant a great deal.

Hawk stood on the veranda behind Rorie, watching while the Dundees and Landrys headed for the docks to load into the Dundees' big cruiser. It was a family holiday to take the little kiddies to Walt Disney World—and Sam and Reece acted as if they really were looking forward to spending two weeks trapped in fantasyland with their wives and children. The very thought of it made Hawk shudder. He had never been on a family vacation, even as a kid. Hell, he'd never had a family. Not a real one. Just a succession of foster homes.

All this idealistic happily-ever-after was a crock. No! For Sam and Jeannie, as well as for Reece and Elizabeth, it *was* the real thing. But for the life of him, he couldn't understand how a guy like Sam Dundee had let one soft, delicate woman wrap him around her little finger. Of course, Jeannie wasn't just any woman. She was nothing like the women he and Sam had known over the years. Special women like Jeannie, women who knew how to give instead of take, to love one man till the day they died, the ones who wanted marriage and kids—those were the ones a smart guy stayed away from.

"Well, they're gone," Rorie said.

Hawk glanced at the woman standing beside him. The late-afternoon sun bathed her in a shimmering gold light, creating a transparent nimbus around her entire body. Aurora Dean looked radiant. Her yellow hair hung about her shoulders like a spun-sugar cloud and her lush, womanly body filled out—to perfection—the simple, little blue cotton dress she wore.

La dama dorado, he thought for the second time that day. Rorie was a golden lady. Hawk shook his head to dislodge such ridiculous notions. Thinking that there was something undeniably unique about a woman was what got a man in trouble. Rorie Dean wasn't the kind of woman he could take to his bed and then dismiss.

Clearing his throat loudly, Hawk looked away, out at the ocean. He didn't want to have sex with Rorie! She wasn't his type.

"So, what do we do for the rest of the day?" she asked.

If you were just about any other woman, I know exactly what we'd do for the rest of the day. "I suggest you enjoy yourself doing whatever you want. Today will be your last day of freedom for the next two weeks."

"Then I think I'll take a long walk on the beach before it gets dark," she said. "I have a great deal to think about."

"All right. I'll see you in the morning." He turned toward the front door.

"Aren't we eating supper together tonight?" she asked.

"There's no reason why we should, is there? After all, we'll spend more than enough time together over the next fourteen days."

"Fine, then. I'll see you in the morning."

"Five o'clock sharp," he told her. "For a run on the beach and a swim in the pool before breakfast. Then we'll really get to work on trimming you up and training you for action."

Glaring at him, she smiled, hoping to disguise her irritation. She wanted to tell him that she knew what he was trying to do. But she kept silent. The moment Hawk opened the front door, she turned and rushed down the steps and out into the yard.

As she walked along the beach, she kept remembering every word that Elizabeth and Jeannie had said to her. The success of the mission for which she'd hired Hawk as a guide and bodyguard would depend on her. On her strength. She could not fail. Frankie's life depended on her. And if Elizabeth Landry was right, so did Hawk's.

Chapter 3

When Rorie marched into the house, after her long walk on the beach, she felt fortified, confident and prepared for whatever happened tomorrow. Times of solitude, meditation and prayer always helped her to focus and return to her daily life energized and ready to conquer the world. She had been called an optimist, a dreamer, even a Pollyanna. And perhaps she was all these things; but beneath the happy smile and the can-do attitude, existed the heart of a realist. Just because she preferred to look on the bright side, didn't mean she wasn't aware that a dark side existed.

"Hawk," she called out when she entered the foyer. No response. "Hawk?"

She heard only the sound of the ocean waves mating with the shore in the distance and the distinct tick-tock of the giant grandfather clock in the front parlor.

"He's probably holed up in his room, plotting my torture," she said aloud to herself, as she made her way down the hallway and into the kitchen. "I don't know why the Good Lord couldn't have sent me a more gentlemanly guardian angel."

The big sunny-yellow kitchen boasted an array of modern

appliances, yet still maintained the charm of yesteryear. An antique table and chairs had been strategically placed so that diners could view the sunset through the French doors leading to the back veranda.

When she started to open the refrigerator door, she saw a note attached with a magnet. She read the message without removing the paper. *Eat whatever you want tonight and enjoy it. It'll be your last supper, so to speak. In the morning, I'm putting you on a diet. Get a good night's sleep. Remember, wakeup is at five o'clock.*

"'I'm putting you on a diet!'" She grabbed the note off the refrigerator and crumbled it into a wad. "There is no end to his means of torture. Strenuous exercise. Dieting. Up at the crack of dawn. Gabriel Hawk is a bully...a tyrant...a devil...and the man who is going to take me to San Miguel to rescue Frankie."

She tossed Hawk's note into the garbage, then opened the refrigerator and found a prepared plate of chicken salad, surrounded by slices of tropical fruit. She removed the plate and a pitcher of iced tea and placed them on the table. No doubt, Manton had set aside her dinner. She couldn't imagine Hawk preparing the delectable plate of food for her.

After dinner, Rorie explored her suite of rooms and got the oddest sensation that she was dreaming. That she had dreamed her trip to the island with Hawk. Had dreamed her conversations with Jeannie and Elizabeth. And now she was dreaming that she was a guest in this beautiful paradise.

Maybe today and tonight were dreams, but tomorrow those dreams would turn into nightmares. Hawk would see to that.

Rorie took a bubble bath in the luxurious whirlpool tub and used the scented toiletries Jeannie had left in a basket for guests. After putting on her gown, Rorie read for a while, then turned out the lights and went to bed.

Tormented with memories of the day Frankie was stolen from her arms, thoughts of her parents' worried faces when she'd said goodbye to them yesterday and images of a big, dark and imposing taskmaster, her mind refused her request to sleep. If only she could turn off her mind the way she could flip off a light switch. If only she could stop thinking, stop worrying, stop torturing herself with doubts. Would she be able to survive Hawk's two weeks of training? And if she did, would he keep his word and take her to San Miguel? Would they be able to find Frankie and bring him safely back to the United States?

Tossing and turning endlessly, Rorie finally flung back the covers and got out of bed. Switching on a table lamp, she nestled on the window seat and looked outside. Countless tiny, sparkling stars studded the ebony night sky like diamond chips on black velvet. The quarter-moon cast a minimum of light. The ocean's heartbeat drummed rythmically every time the waves kissed the beach.

Hawk rolled up the maps of San Miguel that Sam had left for him and tossed them into a stack in the corner of the room. From the most recent information Murdock had sent, Hawk knew there were now only two possible ways to get into San Miguel undetected. Both meant going by boat, at night. One meant scaling the fifteen-hundred foot-high limestone cliffs on the windward coast. Hawk remembered the thicket wreathing those bluffs, where ceaseless winds and ocean spray shaped the terrain. Considering that route risky and time-consuming, he decided his best bet was the other alternative—anchoring a boat at least five miles off the coast, then taking a raft past the coral reefs and swimming the last half-mile to the deserted, scalloped stretch of volcanic sand-covered beach still patrolled by the king's army. Murdock could take care of the patrol and have a jeep waiting for them.

If it weren't for Rorie Dean's irrational stubbornness, he would set his plans into motion and be in San Miguel by tomorrow night. Instead, he was stuck here on Le Bijou Bleu, with a woman he couldn't take to his bed. And he faced a possible two weeks of going through the motions of training the woman for a mission that, come hell or high water, he was not going to allow her to undertake.

Retrieving his shave kit from his canvas bag, he headed for the bath across the hall—the bath his room shared with the third downstairs bedroom. He glanced up the corridor and noticed a light under Rorie's door. She was still awake. It was nearly midnight. He was used to getting by on a few hours' sleep when he was on an assignment, but he was sure she was accustomed to eight hours of rest. What the hell was she doing still up?

Maybe she was already having second thoughts about this ridiculous training routine and was prepared to go home and let him handle the job alone. Opening the bathroom door, he tossed his case on the vanity, then walked down the hall to Rorie's closed door. He hesitated momentarily, then knocked. When he received no response, he knocked again, louder.

"Yes? Who is it?" Rorie possessed that slow, syrupy drawl many Southern women had, a seductive-yet-unintentional invitation in the tone.

"It's Hawk. May I come in?"

She opened the door cautiously and peeked out into the hallway. He grasped the edge of the door, not completely sure she wouldn't slam the door in his face.

"You're up awfully late, aren't you?" he asked.

"So are you," she said.

She didn't move out of the doorway and indicate for him to come in, so he took a step toward her and grinned when she backed up and out of his way.

He tried not to notice the way she looked, all soft and feminine in her floor-length pink cotton gown, edged with lace. He tried to ignore the way she smelled, all sweet and fresh and flowery. And he tried to pretend that he didn't find this plump little Southern belle a delectable temptation. But his body couldn't ignore the seduction of hers. He damned his own uncontrollable reaction when his sex hardened.

Get yourself under control, he warned himself. You don't really want this woman. She's not your type. You can live two weeks without having sex. You won't have any trouble finding a willing woman in San Miguel. La Vega, the capital city, has an abundance of Latin lovelies.

Hawk eyed the rumpled covers on the bed. "Couldn't sleep?"

"No. I was restless."

"Something wrong?" he asked.

"I had too much on my mind."

"Not having second thoughts about our deal, are you?" He wished she would move over a couple of feet and get out of the direct line of lamplight that silhouetted her form through her modest-but-thin cotton gown. He could see every round, luscious inch of her body. The contours of her broad hips. The curve of her firm, womanly rear end. The ripe swell of her full breasts. The outline of her shapely legs.

"Second thoughts?" Rorie's breath caught in her throat. Moisture coated the palms of her unsteady hands. Her heartbeat thumped a little too loudly in her ears.

She wanted him to leave, to go back to his room and out of her sight. She wasn't used to having a man in her bedroom late at night, with her wearing nothing but a gown. Actually, she wasn't used to a man being in her bedroom at all. And to make matters worse, Gabriel Hawk wasn't just any man. He was overwhelmingly, dangerously attractive in the most basic, primitive way a man could be.

He stood there, only a few steps away from her, his feet bare, his unbuttoned shirt hanging loosely around his hips, and a thick strand of his long, black hair falling over his shoulder, the tips brushing one tiny male nipple. Rorie deliberately avoided looking any lower than his waist or higher than his knees. She couldn't ogle this man simply because he was good-looking.

A pink flush rose up her neck and onto her face. Turning from him, she glanced away, out the windows, hoping he wouldn't notice her embarrassment. She didn't want Hawk to think she was interested in him—in that way. She wasn't. But if he thought she was, he would probably laugh in her face. A man like Hawk wouldn't want a woman like her any more than she wanted him. If ever two people were from different worlds, with opposing sets of morals and life-styles, those two people were Gabriel Hawk and herself.

Rorie heard his footsteps on the wooden floor as he walked up behind her. She drew in a deep, calming breath and held it. *Please, dear God, don't let him touch me.*

"There's no need for you to put yourself through days of torture, when we both know I can't whip you into shape, into fighting form, in two weeks." Hawk gripped her shoulder, then wished he hadn't. Her skin was silky soft yet youthfully firm. Being this close, he could smell not only the flowery scent of the toiletries she'd used, but the sweet, inviting aroma of the woman herself. "I can put you on a bus or a plane for Chattanooga tomorrow," he told her. "And I can be in San Miguel by tomorrow night."

Rorie tensed. His hand was big and hard, and although his touch was gentle, she sensed the lethal power in his grip. This man probably could break her in two with very little effort. She didn't doubt that he was capable of snapping her neck like a twig. But the fear she felt when his flesh touched hers was not fear for her physical safety, but a deep, primordial, woman's fear of man. He could take her if he wanted and she would be powerless to stop him. And she had to admit that the thought that she might not want to stop him was what scared her more than anything.

She pulled away from him, moving directly in front of the big windows that overlooked the ocean. "Are you trying to back out of our deal, Hawk?"

"No, I'm not trying to back out," he said. "I'm just giving you a chance to change your mind before we waste both your time and mine."

She gazed out the windows at the barely visible ocean, illuminated by only the faint glimmer of pale moonlight.

"You promised me that if I could survive two weeks of training, you'd take me to San Miguel." She squared her shoulders and turned to face him. "I have to go to San Miguel, so I will find a way to survive the next fourteen days. No matter what you put me through, I won't give up. If you think that just because my body isn't sleek and lean and toned to perfection, I'm going to fail your fitness test, then think again. When a person wants something as badly as I want to get to San Miguel, she will do whatever is necessary."

"If all you needed was stubbornness and determination, then you'd be prepared right now. But it's going to take physical stamina to swim ashore at night. And depending on what we find when we get to La Vega, we could well end up on foot, in the jungle, climbing up the mountain or just running for our lives in some out-of-the-way village."

She pointed her index finger at him. "I'll diet, I'll exercise, I'll follow every one of your commands in order to get in shape. All I want is for you to keep your promise to me."

"It would be so much easier if you'd let me go to San

Miguel and get your nephew. You wouldn't have to risk your life—or maybe my life—if you screw up."

In the end it will be you who must save both Frankie and Gabriel. If you have the courage... If your love is strong enough... Rorie heard Elizabeth's voice predicting the future. Elizabeth couldn't be right, could she? How was it possible that, in the end, it would be up to her to save not only Frankie, but Hawk, as well?

"I have to go with you to San Miguel. I— You don't understand how I feel," she told him. "Peter and Cipriana trusted me to keep Frankie safe. They left him in my care and I let King Julio take him from me. I have to be the one to rescue him. I have to—'' Her voice cracked with emotion. She swallowed the unshed tears trapped in her throat.

"There was no way you could have stopped the king's men from taking Frankie."

Grasping her shoulders, Hawk forced her to face him.

She lifted her chin and glared defiantly into his dark eyes. What would he say if she told him about Elizabeth's prediction? How would he react if she told him that, in her heart of hearts, she believed the prediction?

He tightened his hold on her and drew her closer, looking down into her beautiful face. She glared at him boldly. Suddenly he noticed that the eyes he'd thought an ordinary blue were, in reality, an azure blue as brilliant and bright as the Caribbean waters surrounding San Miguel.

"I've known some stubborn women in my time, lady, but you take the cake."

Her chin quivered. Her eyes misted. Dammit, she was going to cry. He hated weepy females. He didn't tolerate tears. Other men might hang around and put up with a blubbering woman, but he made sure his relationships were so brief that a woman didn't have time to get emotional on him. The few times he'd been caught off guard by a woman's tears, he had walked away. He'd never cared enough to stay.

Rorie clenched her teeth, refusing to give in to the tears threatening to reveal her weakness to Hawk. Why was he looking at her like that? As if he wanted to strangle her and kiss her at the same time?

From above them, on the upper level of the house, rose a

throbbing, avalanche of musical emotion, so powerful that it took Rorie's breath away. The melody wrapped around her heart as if tying it with a ribbon to present it as a gift.

A tear dropped from Rorie's eye and trickled down her cheek. She bit down on her bottom lip in an effort to control the feelings raging inside her. Gazing at Hawk, her eyes questioned him.

He chose to answer the least provocative of her silent questions. "That's Manton playing the piano."

"The baby grand in the parlor? But how is that possible, if he's deaf?"

Hawk loosened his tenacious hold on Rorie's shoulders, but did not release her. Instead he slid his hands down her arms to her wrists and slowly eased upward again, stopping at her elbows. When she sucked in her breath, he released her. "Jeannie says he feels the music. That it's inside him. A part of him. A vital part, like his heart or lungs."

A second tear cascaded down Rorie's cheek. Reaching out, Hawk wiped the moisture from her face. She gasped. Involuntarily, their bodies swayed toward each other. The magical piano concerto enveloped them in its spell, drawing them closer and closer. Almost touching. A hairbreadth separating their straining bodies.

Rorie had never felt anything so powerful, so absolutely compelling. She could not look away, could not break the hypnotizing eye contact with Hawk. His black gaze devoured her, consuming her with its heat.

Hawk wanted to pull this woman into his arms and drink his fill of her sweetness. He wanted to lay her down in the big, soft bed and take her with all the wild passion that was riding him so hard.

The crashing melodic crescendo reached its peak just as the ocean waves burst onto shore. Then the tide washed back out to sea and the music's tone mellowed to a sweet, quiet tenderness.

"Gabriel?" Why she had used his given name, Rorie would never know. It was as if she had known this man forever, since the dawn of time. As if his name had been the last name on her lips in lifetime after lifetime.

Hawk forced himself to break the spell, to release them

both from the enchantment of Manton's music. What the hell was going on? What was happening to him?

He stepped backward, putting some distance between Rorie and him. Then he glanced away from her. Get the hell out of here now, he told himself. Turning around, he rushed toward the door, not pausing a second in his flight from her room.

During his hasty departure, he mumbled, "Good night."

For several seconds, Rorie stood frozen to the spot, unable to move as Manton's piano recital ended and Hawk slammed her bedroom door in his abrupt departure. Finally she willed herself to move. She walked slowly over to the bed and sat down, then grabbed a feather pillow. Curling into a ball, she clutched the pillow to her stomach and cried silently, not quite sure exactly why her heart was breaking.

Down the hall, Hawk stormed into the bathroom, stripped off his clothes and turned on the shower. Stepping beneath the warm spray, he threw back his head and allowed the water to drench him thoroughly.

He was hot and hard and aching. He hadn't wanted sex this badly since he'd been a teenager and unable to control his raging hormones. He had no idea what had just happened between Rorie and him. All he knew was that it had scared the hell out of him, that he couldn't get away from her fast enough—and that he didn't dare let it happen again.

Tears didn't affect him. Not *anyone's* tears—man's, woman's or child's. And yet Rorie's tears *had* gotten to him. When he'd seen those tears falling down her cheek, all he'd been able to think about was wiping them away—of comforting her. Gabriel Hawk neither gave comfort nor accepted it. Not in the past. Not in the present. And not in the future.

Rorie Dean didn't mean anything to him. And she never would. Hell, just because he wanted to take her to bed, didn't mean he cared about her.

As the water covered his body in prickling rivulets, he tried to erase Rorie from his mind. But as the image of her standing there in her thin cotton gown, the outline of her lush body visible in the lamplight, flashed through his mind, his sex hardened painfully. While thinking of a woman he could never have, he gave himself the relief he dared not seek in her virgin body.

* * *

The alarm broke through the haze of sleep cocooning Rorie in its peaceful warmth. She lifted her eyelids slowly, then closed them again. When the clock continued its piercing wail, she opened her eyes and focused on the illuminated face of the offensive object. Darkness surrounded her. Reaching out, she punched the Off button on the alarm and sighed sleepily after she'd silenced the deafening beep.

Ten till five. Oh, Lord, she had ten minutes to get up, use the bathroom and dress before Hawk took control of her life. She threw back the covers, flipped on the bedside lamp, got up and rushed to the bathroom. Hurriedly, she went through her morning routine, except for the eye-opening shower she usually enjoyed. No time for a shower. She threw cold water on her face and peered into the mirror. Her eyes were swollen and puffy and her hair looked like a rat's nest. Running her tongue over her teeth, she grunted.

Just as she squirted toothpaste on her brush, Rorie heard a loud knock on the outside door. She groaned. Oh, no. Hawk already?

"It's five o'clock," Hawk yelled. "Up and at 'em. I want you ready for our morning run in five minutes."

Rorie pulled the toothbrush out of her mouth. "I'll be there!"

Eight minutes later, she rushed into the foyer. Hawk waited impatiently, his arms crossed over his broad chest. He looked great, Rorie thought, as if he'd gotten a good night's sleep and was ready to take on the world. On the other hand, she realized that she looked like a woman who had slept less than four hours and was ready for a nap.

"Have you ever done any running or jogging?" Hawk asked.

Rorie hated the way he surveyed her plump body. She knew that she looked even fatter in the baggy sweatpants and shirt, which she usually wore when she lounged around the house alone.

"I walk," she told him. "I've never had any desire to run or jog."

"Why not? Don't you like to sweat?"

"As a matter of fact, I don't." She smiled. "Besides, Southern ladies never sweat. We don't even perspire."

"Then what the hell do you do?"

"We glow."

"Damn!" This wasn't going to work, trying to whip some some soft, little, *glowing* Southern belle into shape. He would be fighting a losing cause to try.

A sudden, unbidden image appeared in his mind. Rorie Dean naked beneath him, her lush body damp and glowing after they'd made passionate love.

"We'll walk this morning." He sounded too gruff, even to his own ears. *Don't take it out on Rorie, just because you need a woman.* "We will make as many rounds as you're able to make in an hour, then we'll do some laps in the pool. You can swim, can't you?"

"Yes, I can swim, thank you very much! I was born in Chattanooga, and whenever we weren't in the mission field, we lived there. Swimming and boating on the Tennessee River are a way of life back home."

"All right. Let's go. I want to return to the house by six o'clock, then do our laps in the pool and have a quick breakfast. After that, you can take an hour to shower and change before I introduce you to Sam's private gym."

"Goody, goody. I can hardly wait."

She'd known she would hate walking with Hawk, if you could call his fast-paced canter walking. It was more like a low-speed jog. Time after time, he moved ahead of her, then stopped on the beach and waited for her to catch up. Out of breath, her chest aching and her calves throbbing, Rorie glared at Hawk, who wasn't even breathing hard. The man was in such superb physical condition, she suspected he wasn't human at all—he was some sort of humanoid with circuits and wires inside him instead of blood and bones.

Standing on a rise above the beach, Hawk shook his head, the look on his face mocking sadness. "Lady, you are one pitiful sight. I suggest you call it quits now, before you kill yourself."

"No way am I quitting!" She panted as she climbed the knoll to reach him. "Have you ever considered the possibility that one of the reasons I can't keep up with you—besides the fact that I'm not accustomed to this—is that my legs are a lot shorter than yours? You've got to be at least eight inches taller than I am.''

Hawk grinned. ''You know, you're crazy. But I must be even crazier to have made such a ludicrous bargain with you. You're going to put yourself through hell with this training program for nothing. There's no way you'll last two whole weeks.''

She wanted to scream at him, to shout that she knew he was trying to break her. That despite the bargain they'd made, he'd never had any intention of taking her to San Miguel. He was so sure she would give up before the time limit expired, so sure she didn't have what it took to withstand his brutal punishment.

''I'm ready to continue,'' she said, still slightly out of breath.

He looked at her. Yellow strands of hair that had escaped from her ponytail stuck to the side of her damp face and neck. Her cheeks glowed rosy pink. Her breasts lifted and fell with each labored breath she took.

''We've been at it for nearly an hour,'' he said. ''It's time to head back to the house for our swim.''

Oh, thrill, thrill! she thought. Now I'm going to get to change into my bathing suit and let him get a good look at my fabulous figure. It wasn't that she disliked her body. A hundred years ago her form had been the ideal. A Lillian Russell hourglass shape. But in today's world, waiflike models and skinny-legged, silicone-breasted actresses were the ideal of beauty. And she didn't have a doubt that Hawk was the type who would appreciate the current trend in long, lean, toned bodies. After all, he himself possessed a rugged, muscular, hard-as-nails body.

Once back at the house, Rorie took her time changing into her one-piece black swimsuit. The suit wasn't overly revealing or the least bit sexy, but somehow with it on, she felt completely naked. Grabbing one of the huge bath towels from the stack on the wicker wall shelves, she draped it around her hips and overlapped it on one side.

Bracing her shoulders, she marched out of her room, along the hall, up the stairs and through the house. Hawk waited for her by the pool. She took a really good look at him and wanted to run back to her room and lock the door. He was, without a doubt, the most magnificent man she'd ever seen. Tall and muscular, with a to-die-for body. Sleek bronze skin over finely toned muscles. Long, powerful arms and legs. Jet-black hair that hung loosely down his broad back, like the mane of a stallion.

And he was naked, except for a pair of tiny black briefs that did absolutely nothing to disguise the well-endowed proportions of his lower body.

"What took you so long?" he asked. "I thought I was going to have to come and drag you out here."

"You're exaggerating," she said. "I wasn't gone more than fifteen minutes."

"I've been waiting at least twenty minutes." His gaze traveled the length of her body, as if taking inventory. "Get rid of the towel and come over here."

Reluctantly, she loosened the towel, pulled it off and tossed it onto a nearby lounge chair. She felt as naked as the day she was born. Move it, she told herself. Get your behind over there and do what you have to do. It doesn't matter what Hawk thinks of your body. You don't care whether or not he thinks you're fat. You're not here to impress him with your beauty. You're here to fulfill the stipulations of a bargain.

Hawk watched her walk slowly toward him. "Get the lead out, lady. We're running behind schedule as it is."

She marched over to him, her chin held high, her cheeks slightly flushed. She stopped directly in front of him and narrowed her gaze, focusing on his face.

He wasn't quite sure what he had expected Rorie to look like in a bathing suit. Fat and soft and unattractive, maybe. Well, if she'd been in a skimpy bikini she might have looked fat. But in the black one-piece she wore, she looked voluptuous. Flawless, pale-ivory skin. Soft flesh covering a surprisingly firm body. Large breasts swelling out of the top of the modestly-cut swimsuit bodice. And a mane of golden blond hair that cascaded over her shoulders.

"I'm ready," she said.

After they'd done several laps, Hawk dragged himself up

onto the edge of the pool. Rorie halted in the middle of her
lap and swam over to him, but stayed in the water.

"What's wrong?" she asked.

"You're a damn good swimmer," he said. "Not quite fast
enough, but with practice..." What the hell was he saying?
With practice, she would become fast and strong enough to
swim the distance from a raft a half-mile offshore to the secluded beach on San Miguel?

"I'm surprised that you'll admit I'm not a total flop in the
physical-fitness department."

"All I said was that you're a good swimmer," Hawk told
her. "That alone doesn't prepare you for making this trip with
me."

"Give me the next thirteen days and I'll prove to you that
I'll be able to go on this mission." She smiled at him.

Hawk hated the way she smiled. With warm, genuine welcome. A friendly, happy smile. He was used to women whose
smiles were coy and flirty and cunning. And usually fake.
There was nothing fake about Rorie or her smile. She was
the genuine article. A good woman. No, not just a woman—a
sweet, old-fashioned lady, with an innocence untouched by
cruel, ugly reality.

Angered by his own feelings, Hawk pushed Rorie to make
as many laps in the pool as she possibly could; and then he
demanded that she make one more. If he was going to break
her, he couldn't allow his admiration for her determination or
his respect for her as a person to interfere with his plans.

Rorie hated Hawk. He was a Machiavellian monster. How
could he sit there and devour a plate of bacon, eggs and toast,
while she scraped the bottom of her yogurt container and eyed
the carrot sticks on the table with disgust? He'd done it deliberately—fed her rabbit food while he feasted on a real
breakfast. It was part of his plan to make her give up. She
slammed the empty yogurt container down on the table and
picked up a carrot stick.

"Take the carrots with you up to your room, if you'd like,"
Hawk said. "You've got less than an hour before we start
our morning workout in the gym."

His smile was more wicked than ever, which tempted Rorie to wipe that sinister grin off his face. But she was a believer in nonviolence, in a peaceful solution to every problem. She smiled weakly at him, snatched up a handful of carrot sticks and stormed out of the kitchen.

During the next thirty minutes, she ate all the carrot sticks while she rested on the bed in her room. Noting how quickly the time had passed, she jumped up and ran into the bathroom. After a rushed shower, she secured her wet hair with an elasticized hair ribbon, pulled on her shorts, T-shirt, socks and sneakers, then raced out of her room and down the hallway.

A somber Hawk, arms folded over his chest, waited for her. "Maybe we need to synchronize our watches. Yours seems to be running a little slower than mine."

"Lighten up, will you? Five or ten minutes one way or another isn't going to matter, and you know it!"

Hawk grabbed her chin between his thumb and index finger and tilted her head upward so that she was forced to look directly at him. "You're right. Here on Le Bijou Bleu, five or ten minutes doesn't matter. But on San Miguel, being just a couple of minutes off could mean the difference between life and death."

"Oh." Rorie had to admit that she'd never considered Hawk's obsession with timing a part of her training. She'd thought he was just being mean.

"Yeah, oh." He released her chin. "Come on. Sam's gym is down here on the ground level of the house."

She followed him past what he told her were Manton's private quarters and on to a set of double doors on the opposite end of the house.

Hawk opened the doors to reveal a state-of-the-art gym, with a variety of exercise equipment that included a treadmill, stair stepper, cross-country skier and a stationary bicycle, as well as numerous weight machines. One whole wall was mirrored.

"Before I start you on any of the equipment, we'll do some warm-up exercises," Hawk said. "We'll wait until tomorrow to start your practice on the obstacle course. But this afternoon I'll introduce you to aerobic exercises and some power yoga.''

"Power yoga? Isn't that an oxymoron? I thought yoga was supposed to be a calm, relaxed form of exercise.''

"Power-yoga techniques help release the shoulders for activities like swimming, and it's good for opening up the hip joints and buttocks for running.''

"Sounds like a lot of fun,'' she said sarcastically.

"But before we do anything, I need to take your measurements and weigh you.''

"What!''

"I expect you to lose a few pounds and inches, if you stick with this training for the entire two weeks. I want to be able to check your progress.''

Rorie poked Hawk in the chest with her index finger. "Now, let's get one thing straight. Only I, my doctor and God know how much I weigh. And my measurements are top secret.''

"Don't act so silly about this. I can look at you and pretty much guess your measurements—about 38-28-38, I'd say. And as for your weight—''

Rorie covered his mouth with her hand and glared at him. She felt his lips twitching beneath her palm. "You're not going to weigh me and you're not going to take my measurements.'' He licked her palm. Gasping, she jerked her hand from his mouth.

"What if I told you that if you don't agree to being weighed and measured, you'll be breaking the terms of our deal by not following my orders?''

"I'd say your weighing and measuring me has nothing to do with our deal—that you just want to embarrass me in the hopes I'll run away and cry.''

"Will you be embarrassed?'' he asked. "Will you run away and cry?''

"I'll be embarrassed, but I won't run away and cry.''

"Then go hop up on the scales, while I find the tape measure.'' He didn't think she would do it. He knew how vain women were about their weight and measurements. Women usually lied about their weight as often as they did about their age.

If looks could kill, he would be a dead man. Rorie glowered at him with pure, undisguised loathing. But she stomped across the gym and stepped up on the scale. Well, I'll be damned, he thought.

He rummaged in a corner desk, retrieved a tape measure, pad and pencil and walked over to where Rorie waited for him. She didn't look at him or acknowledge his existence in any way while he weighed her.

"Hmmm. You weigh more than I thought," he said. "It must be because you're so solid." He scribbled her weight on the pad and stuck the pad in the pocket of his shorts.

"May I step down now?"

He took her by the arm. She jerked away. He chuckled. "Angry with me?"

"I'm so mad I could spit...right in one of your evil black eyes." She spoke slowly, enunciating every word.

"Now, let me get your measurements." Hawk didn't know when he'd enjoyed anything quite so much as irritating the hell out of Rorie Dean. She was fit to be tied and would like nothing better than to scratch his eyes out. But despite the steam rising inside her, she retained a calm, controlled facade.

One thing was certain—by encouraging her anger and hatred, he was making sure she didn't get any foolish, romantic notions about him. After last night, during Manton's mesmerizing piano concerto, he'd worried that Rorie might mistake plain old lust for something else.

Hawk whipped out the tape measure, eased it around her waist and clicked his tongue. "Twenty-eight inches." Removing the tape, he pulled out the notepad, wrote down the figure and then stuck the pad back in his pocket.

He measured her hips. Forty inches. He let out a long, low whistle. Rorie stood perfectly straight and still. Not moving a muscle. Barely breathing. He wrapped the tape around her back and brought it across her breasts. His knuckles scraped across her nipples. She sucked in her breath. Her nipples puckered to diamond-hard points.

Hawk swallowed hard. "Forty inches." He hadn't meant to touch her intimately, to arouse her or himself. But the damage had been done. Her nipples were tight, and so was his sex.

"Upper arms and thighs, now." He measured her arms, then knelt before her and slipped his hand between her legs, parting them.

She shivered involuntarily when he measured her. His big hand was warm and hard against the tender flesh of her inner thigh.

Standing quickly, Hawk pulled out the notepad. His hand shook so badly, he had to wait a couple of seconds before he wrote down her other measurements.

He had thought of weighing and measuring her as a scare tactic—one that might put an end to this ridiculous bargain they'd made. But all his "scare" tactic had done was make her dig her heels in, more determined than ever to prove herself to him.

And his actions had also given him a royal hard-on.

If Rorie thought she'd made a pact with the devil, she was right. He was the kind of man who did whatever was necessary to win, no matter who got hurt.

But what he hadn't counted on was that it bothered his conscience to hurt Rorie Dean.

Chapter 4

Hawk hesitated outside Rorie's door. He glanced down at his wristwatch. Ten minutes after five. Lifting his hand, he formed a fist and knocked softly. For the life of him, he wasn't quite sure why he hated disturbing her. He thought he had talked himself out of feeling sorry for Rorie Dean. After all, she was the one who had agreed to this bargain, who had insisted on being stubborn and unrelenting. It wasn't his fault if she didn't have sense enough to know she wasn't capable of undertaking a dangerous mission that required the kind of physical stamina she didn't possess.

He had put her through a fairly rigorous routine yesterday, especially for someone unaccustomed to daily physical exercise. She had panted and heaved and grunted and sweated. But not once had she begged for mercy. Not once had she refused to do what he asked. She'd been so exhausted that she'd almost fallen asleep during dinner and had gone to bed immediately following the meal. He'd been tempted to check on her before he went to bed, but he hadn't.

He knocked again. No response. Maybe her alarm hadn't gone off. Or maybe she'd turned off the alarm and gone back to sleep. She was probably irritable since every muscle in her body was bound to be sore from yesterday's workout.

"Rorie? Are you awake?"

"Yes," she groaned.

"Are you decent?"

"If you're asking if I have on any clothes, then yes, I'm decent. I'm still in my gown."

He opened the door and walked in. Frowning when he looked into the bedroom and saw her still in bed, he marched through the sitting room and straight to her bedside. He flung back the covers. Rorie screeched.

"Get up and get ready. I thought you understood the importance of being punctual."

"If I could get up, I would." She lay on her side, her gown bunched up around her hips, her full, shapely body exposed from upper thigh to bright red toenails. Instinctively, Hawk leaned over and swatted her on the behind. She cried out in pain.

"I didn't hit you that hard," he said. "What's wrong with you?"

"For your information, Mr. Hawk, my body is in agony. There isn't one inch of me that isn't aching and so sore I can barely move."

"It's only natural that you'd be sore from all the exercise you did yesterday. The best thing for you is to get up and work the soreness out of your body." When he grabbed her hands and pulled her up into a sitting position, she screamed. He released her immediately. "Dammit!"

"Don't you curse at me, you…you…slave driver, you! If you hadn't pushed me so hard, expected me to jump through hoops for you, I wouldn't be in this shape."

"Why the hell didn't you tell me you'd had enough, that you couldn't take any more? I'd have slowed down." He noted how pale her face was since he'd forced her to sit. "All you had to do was say the word and we could have stopped."

"And have you call me a quitter?" She glared at him, her blue eyes focusing on his face. "No way was I going to give you an excuse to call off our deal."

"Stubborn idiot female," Hawk said, then lowered his

voice and grumbled a few choice imprecations. "Just stay where you are. I'll be back in a minute."

When he went into her bathroom, she called out to him. "What are you doing?"

"Drawing you a hot bath. You need to soak those tired muscles. Then, after your bath, I'll give you a massage and work out some of the soreness."

"How do you suggest I get to the tub? Crawl?"

Hawk chuckled. "That sore, huh?"

"You're being a total jerk about this, you know. But I shouldn't have expected anything else from you, should I?"

He walked out of the bathroom and hovered in the doorway. "Don't be so glum. You'll live."

"I'm not so sure. There's not one spot on my body that isn't sore. Even my hair aches."

"After a good hot soak and a massage, you should be able to go for our morning trek around the island and then do a few laps in the pool." He grinned wickedly. "After that, you can take the morning off. We'll check out the obstacle course this afternoon and get in a little target practice, too."

Rorie groaned. "You're too kind. I can hardly wait to see the scene of my future torture. And the very thought of handling a deadly weapon excites me no end."

"Get your fanny in motion, lady." Crossing his arms over his chest, he surveyed her from the top of her tousled blond hair to the tips of her round, pink toes. "I'd carry you to the bathtub if I didn't think I'd throw my back out doing it."

He'd made the statement as a joke, but the moment he saw the stricken look on her face, he wished the words back. He'd hurt her feelings. He saw it in her misty eyes, her clenched jaw, her flushed cheeks.

Why the hell should you care that you hurt her feelings? The meaner, the more rotten you treat her, the more likely she is to give up this insane notion of training for a mission into San Miguel. The more she hates you, the better. If she hates you, she won't get any romantic notions about you.

When Rorie tried to crawl out of bed, she gasped, then bit down on her bottom lip and continued the effort. By the time she was on her feet, her face was as pale as chalk, sweat coated her forehead and tears trickled down her cheeks.

Suddenly Hawk felt like the jerk she had accused him of being. Rorie was in terrible pain. Any fool could see how badly she was hurting. He had done this to her. Pushing her beyond her limits in his effort to make her cry uncle. He had convinced himself that she had sense enough to tell him when she'd had enough. Obviously her stubbornness and determination had overruled her common sense. And his own stubbornness and determination had endangered someone he had been hired to protect.

Without saying another word to her, he rushed across the room, lifted her into his arms and headed toward the bathroom. She cried out when he swept her off her feet. Hastily, she threw her arm around his neck.

"What are you doing?" she demanded, her startled, tear-filled eyes fixed on his face. "Put me down. I'd never forgive myself if you threw your back out."

"Shut up, will you? You might not be a featherweight, but in case you haven't noticed, I'm a big, strong man."

When he reached the bathtub, filled with steaming-hot water, he eased her feet down to the floor and felt a twinge of sympathy when she gasped in pain.

He undid the top button on her gown. She slapped away his hand. "Now what do you think you're doing?"

"Helping you undress."

"I think I can manage," she told him. "Go away and leave me alone."

"Maybe I should wait outside, just in case you need me."

"I won't need you."

"Okay. I'll go down to the kitchen and get breakfast ready and bring it up here. We can eat before I massage the kinks out of your sore muscles."

He was gone before Rorie could reply. She stood on wobbly legs, her stomach queasy, her hands shaky. Unbuttoning her gown proved to be easy compared to easing her sore arms through the sleeves. Why had she been such a fool yesterday? Why had she allowed Hawk to goad her into over-exerting herself the way she had? She blamed him for being such an overbearing taskmaster, for pushing her beyond her limit. But she had to take at least partial blame for allowing him to drive her so hard.

After dropping her gown down her hips and onto the tiled floor, she lifted one leg over and into the tub, testing the water. Groaning as pain sliced up her calf, through her thigh and into her hip, she cautiously lifted her other leg, slid down into the whirlpool and immersed herself in the hot water.

Twenty minutes later, Hawk knocked on the bathroom door. "Time to get out. Just wrap yourself in a towel and come on in here. Coffee's hot."

Rorie shook her head. No. Absolutely not. Hawk was nuts if he thought she was going to parade around in front of him in nothing but a towel. By nature and upbringing, she was a modest woman. Exposing herself to Hawk in her bathing suit had been unnerving. The very thought of presenting her body to him for a massage was unthinkable, especially if she was covered with only a towel.

She eased up and out of the tub, wrapped a towel turban-fashion around her wet head and dried her body slowly, being careful not to stretch too much in the effort. After slipping into her gown, she walked out of the bathroom. The hot whirlpool bath had helped ease her sore muscles a little, but she was still aching so much that she doubted her body would ever fully recover.

Standing in the sitting-room doorway, Hawk held a cup of coffee out to her. She accepted the black coffee. She preferred sweet, creamy, mild coffee, but Hawk had pointed out yesterday that sugar and cream were not on her diet.

"Thanks." Lifting the mug to her lips, she sipped the strong brew. "The hot bath helped some. I don't think a massage is necessary."

"Let's eat breakfast." He nodded to the round, cloth-covered table where he had placed their meal.

She followed him to the table. Acting gentlemanly for the first time since she'd met him, Hawk pulled out a chair and seated her. "Thank you."

"Eat up." He removed the cover from the breakfast tray, revealing two bowls of dry cereal, a pitcher of milk and two glasses of orange juice.

"Don't tell me that you and I are actually going to eat the same thing for breakfast this morning. You can't test my willpower if you don't eat something tempting, the way you did yesterday."

Hawk sat opposite her, lifted the pitcher of milk and doused his cereal. "All right, I admit that I went a little overboard yesterday, in every respect. It was cruel of me to eat bacon and eggs in front of you, while you had to eat non-fat yogurt."

"Yes, it was cruel. And petty and mean and—"

"Let's just agree that I acted like a real bastard yesterday and leave it at that." When he noted the disapproving frown on her face, he groaned. "Lady, I am not going to clean up my language for you."

Glancing away, she set down her coffee cup and picked up her juice glass. They ate in silence, each avoiding eye contact with the other. The minute she finished the last bite of cereal, Hawk scooted back his chair and stood.

"Go lie on the bed, facedown," he said. "A massage should get out enough kinks so you can get in your morning walk and swim."

"I don't need a massage. I'll be all right without it."

"This is a perfect example of why I don't want to take you into San Miguel." Hawk jerked her chair away from the table, grabbed her arms and drew her to her feet. "In a dangerous situation, I couldn't afford the time to argue with you, to try to convince you to follow my orders. Your stubbornness could cost us both our lives."

"We aren't in San Miguel and this is hardly a life-or-death situation." She glared down at his big hands tightly holding her arms.

"No, but this is a part of your training. Obedience to my commands and punctuality are as crucial as your physical training."

"Oh, all right." Rorie pulled away from him. "Give me the darn massage." She whirled around and stomped off into the bedroom.

The sound from Hawk's throat was a combination of groan and chuckle. *Darn*. He supposed that was the closest Rorie ever came to cursing.

She flopped, facedown, on the bed. "Well, what are you waiting for? Let's get this over with."

Hawk hesitated momentarily as he braced himself for what was to come. Rorie needed this massage. But it wouldn't be easy putting his hands on her body and remaining unaffected. Usually, when he touched a woman, it was for one reason and one reason only—foreplay. His sex stirred to life just at the thought.

He retrieved a bottle of lotion from the bathroom, then crawled onto the bed and straddled Rorie's hips. She didn't move a muscle or say a word, but her breathing accelerated and deepened. Removing the towel from around her hair, he lifted the long, blond mass off her back, separated it into two sections and laid them across the bed on each side of her head.

"Unbutton your gown and ease it down to your waist," he told her.

"Is that necessary?" Cocking her head to one side, she craned her neck and looked up at him.

"No, it's not necessary." Reaching behind him, he clutched the hem of her gown and lifted it. "If you'd rather, I can pull your gown up to your neck and—"

"No!" She wriggled beneath him, her hips brushing his thigh. "I'll unbutton my gown."

After she undid her gown, he helped her ease the garment to her waist. She lay beneath him, her breasts flattened into the mattress, and held her breath, waiting for him to touch her.

Hawk squirted some of the honeysuckle-scented lotion into his hands, spread it across Rorie's naked back, then grasped her shoulders. The moment he encompassed her shoulders, she tensed.

"Relax, Rorie."

"I'm trying."

Within five minutes, Rorie was prepared to concede that Hawk's touch was pure magic. He rubbed and kneaded her neck, shoulders, back and arms. With each stroke, the pain intensified and then subsided, leaving her weak and relaxed. He lifted her gown to her upper thighs and began working on her feet and legs. She had never experienced anything quite so gloriously hedonistic. She sighed when he massaged her thigh, one hand between her legs, his fingers biting into her flesh. Quivers of awareness spiraled out and over her nerve endings. Pinpricks of sensual pleasure alerted her to danger.

Her nipples tightened. Her feminine core clenched and unclenched.

This shouldn't be happening, she thought. This is wrong. This is sinful. But if she made him stop, would he taunt her, telling her that she was weak and not capable of seeing a job through to the finish?

You don't want to stop him. Admit the truth to yourself. You are enjoying this, enjoying the way he makes you feel. And you want more—so much more—from him.

Hawk knew he should put an end to the massage. He'd been a fool to think he could touch this woman and not want to make love to her. During the past fifteen minutes, he'd gotten hard as a rock. The more he touched her, the more he wanted to touch her.

What would it be like, he wondered, to teach this sweet innocent about the pleasures of the flesh? He'd never had sex with an inexperienced woman, not even when he'd been an untutored boy with raging hormones. His first time, when he was fifteen, had been with a buddy's older sister, Rita, and she had been a talented teacher.

If he softened his touch, turned the massage from therapeutic to sensual, would Rorie protest? Or would she succumb to the pleasure?

Hawk fought a war within himself. His libido urged him to discover the unknown, to take what was before him—and his conscience be damned. But his mind warned him that if he pursued this any further, he would regret his actions.

If he made love to Rorie Dean, she would expect more from him than he was willing to give. More than he had in him to give.

No matter how much he might enjoy the experience of seducing a virgin, he had no right to take away Rorie's innocence and give her nothing in return—nothing except a few fleeting moments of pleasure. She was the kind of woman who would want and need and expect love and a commitment. He could offer her neither.

Hawk yanked her gown down to cover her legs, then lifted the bodice and pulled it up her back. "That should do it."

He slapped her behind. "Get dressed while I clear away our breakfast." He shot up off the bed. "Meet me on the veranda as soon as you're finished."

Rorie lay on the bed for several minutes, stunned by the abrupt cessation of the pleasure Hawk had given her. She had wanted to protest, to cry out and beg him not to leave her, to continue touching her, caressing her.

Moaning into the covers, she curled up into a ball. "Idiot," she mumbled into the sheet. Hawk was giving you a massage, not making love to you. You don't interest him in the least. Remember that. He could have his pick of women. Why would he want you?

"Yes, Mama, I'm fine." Rorie preened in front of the mirror as she braced the telephone between her ear and her shoulder. "I've lost eight pounds in twelve days. And I've trimmed a half-inch off my hips, a quarter of an inch off my waist and off my thighs."

"You aren't starving yourself, are you? You know that crash dieting is dangerous to your health," Bettye Lou Dean warned her daughter.

"No, Mama. I told you that Hawk has me on a low-fat diet. But the intense physical activity is what has trimmed the pounds and inches off me."

"Are you and Mr. Hawk getting along any better? When you called a few days ago, you disliked him intensely."

"I think I said that I hated him."

"And I reminded you that we must not hate a person, only the things that person does."

Rorie laughed. "I can assure you that I love and treasure Hawk's soul, but I hate almost everything the man does. For a while, I thought he might be human, but now I know he isn't. He's an unfeeling machine. All he wants to do is wear me down so that I'll give up and he won't have to fulfill his agreement to take me to San Miguel."

"I would give anything if you'd change your mind and let Mr. Hawk go alone. There's no need for you to—"

"Please stop trying to talk me out of doing what I know I

must do. If I can survive Hawk's brutal regime just two more days, he'll have to take me to San Miguel.''

"Your father told me that it's useless to keep trying to change your mind." Bettye Lou sniffled several times. "Please call us, before you go away.''

"I promise I will.''

Rorie hated to hear her mother cry, but she couldn't allow her parents' concerns to stop her from fulfilling her destiny. For over three years, she had tried, by every legal means possible, to get Frankie out of San Miguel. Now she knew, in her heart of hearts, that she had to be the one to rescue her nephew. Since Elizabeth Landry's prediction that Rorie would have to save both Frankie and Hawk, she had come to have faith in her own strength and power.

"We love you, Rorie,'' Bettye Lou said.

"I love y'all, too, Mama.'' Rorie hung up the receiver, then surveyed her body from head to toe. She was still plump, but not quite as plump. And she was physically stronger than she'd ever been in her life.

She had survived twelve days of torment; twelve days of a bullying, surly, demanding Hawk. The glimpse of kindness she'd seen in him their second morning on Le Bijou Bleu had been the only indication that Hawk was human. After abruptly ending her massage that morning, he had reverted back into the same unfeeling monster he'd been the day before. But no matter what he'd said or done, no matter how much he had punished her body and hurt her feelings, she had endured. She had accepted every challenge. She'd even learned to use a gun, as much as she detested the thought of ever firing it at another person.

And now triumph was close at hand. Only two more days and Hawk would have to admit defeat. He would have to adhere to the terms of their agreement and take her with him to San Miguel.

"Hell, no, I haven't been able to break her.'' Gripping the telephone in his hand, Hawk paced back and forth in Sam Dundee's den. "When I first brought her here, I didn't think she'd last a week. After our second morning here, I figured she'd give up. But she's taken everything I've dished out.''

"You don't think she'll give up within the next two days, do you?'' Dane Carmichael asked.

"Dammit, man, I can't believe she's lasted this long. But I've found out one thing about Rorie Dean—she never gives up when she wants something.''

"So what are you going to do about the bargain you made with her?''

"Well, one thing's for certain—I'm not taking her into San Miguel with me.''

"And if she won't let you go on the mission without her, what then?''

Hawk huffed loudly. "I'm sick and tired of trying to pound some sense into that woman's head, so if she won't listen to me, I have one last tactic to use—one I think just might convince her that she's better off staying here in the States, while I go into San Miguel alone.''

"Dare I ask what?''

"Let's just say that I'm going to ask the lady for something I don't think she's willing to give.''

Dane chuckled. "The lady has surprised you once. She just might surprise you again.''

A foreboding chill radiated up Hawk's spine. He sure as hell hoped Dane was wrong.

"Well, when do we leave for San Miguel?'' Rorie looked across the dinner table and smiled at Hawk.

She had survived fourteen days of training—training that he had made as difficult as possible for her, without endangering her life. Despite his best efforts to break her physically and emotionally, she had met the challenge. She had followed his orders, to the letter, despite a lot of dirty looks and mumbled death-wishes for him.

As much as he hated to admit it, he admired Rorie's grit and resolve. He'd never met a woman so damned and determined to put her own life at risk because she truly believed in what she was doing.

It shouldn't matter to him if she wound up getting herself

killed. He wouldn't be at fault. He'd done everything he could
to prevent her from acting irrationally, hadn't he? So, why
was he so damn worried about her?

"I know we had a bargain, but—"

"But you didn't think I'd stick it out the whole two weeks,
did you?" Her smiled widened. She tilted her chin triumphantly.

"I'll give you credit for taking everything I dished out.
You're a lot tougher than you look. But the fact remains that
I can do this job better without you."

Abruptly standing, Rorie knocked over her chair. She threw
her napkin down on the table. "We made a deal. I expect
you to live up to your part of our bargain. I'm going with
you to San Miguel and that's that!"

She stormed out of the kitchen. Hawk jumped up and ran
after her, catching her in the hallway. Grabbing her, he
whirled her around. She faced him defiantly.

"All right, honey, I'll take you with me to San Miguel—"

"Oh, Hawk, I knew you wouldn't break your promise to
me." She threw her arms around his neck and hugged him.

Holding the back of her head with one hand, he let his
other hand sweep downward to her hips. "You'll follow my
orders, no questions asked?"

"Yes. I've already said that I would."

"You'll do whatever I tell you to do, give me whatever I
want?"

"Yes, of course, I... What do you mean, give you whatever
you want?" She dropped her arms from his shoulders and
tried to step backward, but he tightened his hold around her
neck and drew her body up against his.

"We'll be two people, alone on a dangerous mission,
counting on each other every minute." He lowered his head
until his lips were only a hairbreadth from hers. "We'll eat
together, sleep together, bathe together."

Her face flushed scarlet. She squirmed, trying to free herself from his masterful hold. "Are you saying that when
we're in San Miguel, you expect us to—me to...?"

He took her mouth in a devastatingly passionate kiss, planning to frighten her with the intensity of his desire. He would
show her what he could do to her with only one kiss.

She fought him, shoving against his chest, thrashing her head from side to side in an effort to break the kiss. But he held fast, pushing his tongue inside her mouth, taking her against her will. She whimpered. He explored her mouth, deepening the kiss. She went limp in his arms. Releasing her neck, he cupped her buttocks in both of his hands and pulled her up against his crotch, allowing her to feel how hard and hungry he was.

Suddenly she slid her arms around his waist, holding on to him with a fierce possessiveness. Tentatively, shyly, she began responding to his kiss. She touched her tongue to his and sighed when he groaned.

Hawk hardened painfully. Hell, this wasn't supposed to happen. She wasn't supposed to respond. And he wasn't supposed to like it. If he didn't put a stop to this immediately, he would be backing her up against the wall and taking her where she stood.

He broke the kiss. She clung to him. His breathing was labored. Sweat dotted his forehead.

He grasped Rorie's shoulders and shoved her away from him. They stood there in the semidarkness of the hallway and stared at each other for an endless moment.

He had only one shot left, only one last chance to make her back out on their deal. It might be a cheap, dirty, unfair shot, but he'd never let that stop him before.

"Well, honey, this mission could turn out to be more interesting than I thought."

He gently pressed his index finger to the hollow of her throat, then ran it down between her breasts. Rorie sucked in a deep breath. He glided his finger over one breast, circled the nipple, then repeated the process on her other breast. She stood there, transfixed, holding her breath, gazing into his eyes.

"I've never had a fat little virgin before." He scanned her from breasts to hips and grinned wickedly. "But a man needs new experiences from time to time."

She slapped his face. Her blow stunned him. He didn't know how he had expected her to react, but he certainly hadn't expected her to hit him.

"You *are* a real—" she hesitated "—bastard, Mr. Hawk."

"You've got that right, lady. I am a real bastard, in every sense of the word. I have no idea who my old man was." Hawk laughed loudly. "Hell, I don't even know who my old lady was." He continued laughing.

Tears welled up in Rorie's eyes and threatened to overflow. She turned and ran down the hall.

Hawk watched her as she escaped from his laughter. He couldn't ever remember feeling so ashamed of something he'd done. He'd hurt her in order to be kind, in order to prevent her from making a monumental mistake, hadn't he? So why did he feel like such a son of a bitch? Why did he want to go after her and tell her that he was sorry, that he hadn't meant what he'd said?

Downstairs in her bedroom, Rorie sat on the window seat and cried. She cried loud and long and hard, even screaming a couple of times. She pounded her fists into the cushioned seat beneath her, pretending it was Gabriel Hawk. She hated him! Hated him! Hated him! He was the vilest, cruelest, most despicable man on God's green earth.

It was his own fault that she'd slapped him. She hadn't thought about it, hadn't even realized that she intended to do it, until she'd already struck the blow. She had never hit anyone in her life. But Hawk had brought her to this, making her act like a heathen.

She should have known he wouldn't keep his promise, wouldn't uphold his end of their deal. So what was she going to do now? She had to go to San Miguel, and if Hawk wouldn't take her, she would have to find another way.

But how could she fulfill Elizabeth Landry's prediction, if she didn't go with Hawk?

She tried to ignore the repetitive knocking on the door. Let him knock. Let him stand outside and wait.

He flung open the sitting-room door and blew into her bedroom like an ill wind from the sea. "Pack up. I've contacted Murdock. He's expecting us to arrive in San Miguel tomorrow night."

"Us?" She wiped the tears from her face with her fingertips.

"Yes, dammit. *Us.*"

"You're taking me with you?"

"Yes, I'm taking you with me. Heaven help us both."

She scooted to the edge of the window seat. "Do you expect me to... I mean will I have to..."

Hawk clenched his jaw tightly. The pulse in his neck throbbed. "Lady, I wouldn't touch you if you were the last woman on earth."

Chapter 5

Hawk had hoped for clouds to cover the stars and blacken the night sky. Instead, the moonlight seemed unusually bright and the stars twinkled mockingly overhead when the captain of the Buccaneer dropped anchor several miles off the coast of San Miguel.

This was an insane mission, one that might easily end in death for him and for Rorie. He'd been a fool to let his emotions get in the way of his logic. He should have insisted on leaving her behind. But he knew what returning to San Miguel to rescue her nephew meant to her. He understood all too well feelings of guilt and remorse, the gut-wrenching wish that you could go back in time and do that one thing over again.

Hawk checked his watch. He'd told Murdock that they would come ashore around ten o'clock, to secure the perimeter for him. If anyone could give them safe conduct from the beach landing to a night's hideaway in Cabo Verde, Murdock could. The guy was the smartest, toughest man that Hawk had ever known. His old comrade was a loner with no past and no future, living always for the present.

"This is the last chance to change your mind," Hawk told Rorie. "Once we're in the water, there's no turning back."

"I understand," she said.

"You're going with me?"

"Yes."

He hadn't doubted her answer, but he had needed to give her that one last chance to change her mind. He already had enough blood of innocents on his hands without adding Rorie's. He hadn't been able to save her brother and sister-in-law, but by God, he was going to do everything in his power to keep Rorie safe—to protect her, no matter what the cost to himself.

Hawk motioned for Captain Bernard to have the rubber raft lowered to the sea. Grabbing Rorie's arm, he led her to the ladder hanging over the side of the cruiser.

"I'll go first," he said, then climbed down into the raft and steadied it with his weight.

Rorie took a deep breath, willing herself to be strong and in control. She joined Hawk in the raft and took her place in front of him. She thanked the good Lord that she wasn't prone to motion sickness. If she had been, this mission would have been impossible for her.

She was as physically and mentally prepared for this mission as she would ever be. But emotionally, she teetered precariously on the precipice of hell. When she had planned for this rescue, she had expected to risk her life to save Frankie. What she hadn't counted on was risking the principles by which she had always lived. She'd never considered the possibility that her heart and her morals could be in danger. But Gabriel Hawk posed a threat to her; the consequences of succumbing to him were as devastating as any other danger she would face in San Miguel.

Hawk rowed the raft farther and farther from the cruiser. One mile. Two. Three. Rorie didn't look behind her when Hawk issued orders. Obeying his every command, she remained silent as she focused straight ahead on the looming mountain peaks of San Miguel. A volcanic mass rose steeply to a crater at the center of the mountain range, the plug of the crater hidden by dense, boggy moss. Rorie remembered her one trip into the mountains with Peter, when she'd first arrived on San Miguel for her year of missionary work. They had visited the Catholic Sisters who lived at the Blessed Virgin Mission atop La Montana Grande. On their return down the mountain the following day, they had been caught in the daily noontime drenching from the lowering rain clouds.

"Get ready." Hawk issued the command in a deep, dark whisper when they were less than a mile from shore. He drew in the paddles and waited.

Moisture coated Rorie's palms. Her heartbeat drummed in her ears. She could just make out the shoreline in the moonlight.

A light flickered in the distance—a signal from Murdock that it was safe for them to come ashore. She waited for Hawk to tell her when to dive into the water. The plan was for him to dispose of the raft and them to swim the last half-mile.

"Now," Hawk said.

Without question, Rorie slid over the side of the raft and into the shark-infested ocean. She treaded water, waiting. Joining her quickly, Hawk eased up beside her. "Start swimming. Head straight for shore. No matter what, don't look back. Go directly to the beach. Murdock will be waiting."

"Hawk?"

"I'll be right behind you," he assured her.

She sliced through the dark water, pacing herself as Hawk had taught her during two weeks of fitness training and tutoring in survival techniques. She still couldn't believe that she had actually learned how to use a gun. She despised violence. She abhorred any and all kinds of weapons. But learning to handle a gun had been one of Hawk's requirements for bringing her along on this mission.

She sensed Hawk behind her, silently gliding his big body through the waves heading toward the shoreline. As she neared the shore, she saw that crumbling limestone boulders edged a large section of the beach.

"We're going ashore on a small, isolated stretch of beach that's patrolled by King Julio's army," Hawk had told her. "Murdock says that there's usually only a lone soldier at this point, day or night."

Hawk swam up beside Rorie as they neared land, guiding her away from the rocky, morning-glory-infested boulders and toward a smoother section where the heavy waves washed a sandy surface.

Side by side, they rose from the ocean and ran onto the beach. Rivulets of water dripped from their soaked bodies. Winded from the mile-long swim, Rorie dropped to her knees and gulped in huge swallows of recuperative air.

A tropical breeze wafted through the enormous fronds on the coconut palms. Moonlight shimmered across the land, turning the dark, volcanic sand to ebony-diamond particles. Sheathed in thick, abundant vegetation, towering hills flanked each side of the narrow beach.

Grasping Rorie under her armpits, Hawk swiftly lifted her to her feet. "You can't rest here." He draped his arm around her damp waist.

"Just for a minute," she pleaded.

"Not here!" he told her in a whispered growl. "You're too close to that damn manchineel tree. The leaves and fruit on the tree are poisonous to touch. Even dewdrops falling from the leaves can cause very painful blisters."

He dragged her away from the tree and up the beach. She tried to pull away from him. "Will you stop manhandling me?" Defensively she added, "I couldn't see well enough to identify the tree."

Hawk shoved her forward toward the thicket of trees that blanketed the land. The ground lifted upward directly behind the beach to form a knoll overlooking the sea.

Guiding Rorie, Hawk rushed up the rise, toward the area from where he'd seen the all-clear signal. Once they were cocooned in the frond cloak of dozens of palms, he slowed their pace, then brought them to a standstill.

"Now what?" Rorie whispered.

"We wait."

Suddenly a rustling from the tangle of surrounding growth alerted Hawk and Rorie that they were not alone.

"Señor Hawk?" a heavily accented voice called out in the darkness.

"Carlos?" Hawk asked.

"*Sí, señor.*" A scrawny, dark-skinned man appeared before them, barely visible in the moonlight. "Murdock, he waits for you and the *señorita. ¡Data prisa!* Hurry! Hurry!"

Carlos led them into the darkness of the hillside, climbing forever upward, through the thick cover of trees and tangled greenery. Never venturing out of Hawk's grasp, Rorie realized that someone—Carlos?—had cut a path through the growth. She traipsed along behind Carlos, her feet squishing inside her soaked socks and shoes. When she felt as if she couldn't climb another foot, they came to a clearing that opened onto a dirt road.

The moonlight flickered off the metal body of an old, battered jeep. Behind the wheel sat a mountain of a man, only his huge outline visible in the shadowy darkness.

Carlos jumped into the front seat beside the driver. Hawk assisted Rorie into the back seat, then crawled in beside her.

"You're a damn fool for coming back here," a deep, gravelly voice roared from the front of the jeep. "And you're an even bigger fool for bringing the woman with you."

"We're in agreement on that," Hawk said.

The man, who Rorie assumed was Murdock, laughed, the rumble from his chest like a roll of thunder.

With the headlights off, the jeep lurched forward in the darkness. Rorie prayed that the driver could see the road better than she could.

"We'll drop you and the lady off in Cabo Verde for tonight," Murdock said, his accent decidedly Southern. "There's some blankets, fresh water and food waiting for you in the basement of the old hotel. Since the war has escalated and the tourist trade died out completely, the place is deserted. Y'all will be safe enough overnight."

Hitting a huge hole in the road, the jeep bounced, tumbling its passengers. Rorie cried out. Hawk draped his arm around her shoulders and drew her to his side.

"It's all right," he told her. "Despite what you think, Murdock will get you to Cabo Verde in one piece."

"I'm beginning to wonder," Rorie said. "How can he see where he's going without any headlights?"

"The moon is pretty bright tonight. Besides, knowing Murdock, he's sniffing his way. Anyone who knows him will tell you that he's part animal." Hawk squeezed Rorie's shoulder. "Just sit tight, close your eyes and relax."

Relax? Was he kidding? She didn't relax, but she did close

her eyes and pray. Lord only knew that someone needed to pray for Mr. Murdock. Pray he wouldn't drive them into the ocean or off into a ravine. As they neared the village, the dirt road turned into a gravel one that led to a paved street.

The quiet little fishing village of Cabo Verde slept peacefully for the night. Only dim lights, hidden behind the shutters of one or two homes in the distance, advised them that anyone was still awake. Murdock eased the jeep off the gravel road that led directly to the narrow main street. He zipped the jeep onto a rutted trail that led them to the back of the two-story hotel.

Hawk helped Rorie out of the Jeep. Carlos tossed Hawk a canvas bag that he caught in midair.

"Go in that door." Murdock shone a flashlight toward a faded green door. "Go straight down the hallway, turn right and the first door will lead to the basement. There's a kerosene lamp you can light. We placed it on the floor, directly behind the stairs. There are no windows in the room, so the light can't be seen from the outside."

Rorie noticed the peeling pink paint on the hotel's outer walls and the broken panes in the windows. Murdock held the flashlight beam on the door until she and Hawk had scurried inside the building. The resonant throbbing of the jeep's motor quickly disappeared.

"I can't see a thing," Rorie whispered.

Hawk shoved Rorie behind him. "Hang on to me."

She followed his slow, cautious movement down the pitch-black hallway. When he stopped abruptly, she rammed into his back. He mumbled a curse.

"Sorry," she said. "You should have warned me."

When Hawk turned the rusty knob, the basement door creaked loudly. Shoving it wide open, he extended his foot outward, feeling for the first step. With cautious precision, Hawk led Rorie down the moaning wooden staircase. When they reached the cool, dank, underground level, he halted.

"Stay right here. Don't move an inch until you see a light," he said. "I'm going to find that lamp."

"I promise I'm not going anywhere," Rorie told him.

Hawk grappled around in the darkness for several minutes until the toe of his boot encountered the lamp. Dropping the canvas bag to the floor, he rummaged inside until he found a box of matches. Bending down on one knee, he lifted the globe off the lamp, struck a match and lit the wick.

A muted yellow-white glow illuminated the dreary, cobweb-infested basement. Glancing around, Hawk spotted a pile of old blankets in the corner of the room. Atop the blankets lay an assortment of local fruit.

Rorie gasped. Hawk's gaze followed her line of vision. A large roach scurried across the concrete floor.

"Ah, *la cucaracha*." When he saw Rorie crinkle her nose and frown in disgust, Hawk grinned.

"I thought I wanted to be out of the darkness." Rorie made her way toward him. "But now that I've seen this place, I'm not so sure I wouldn't prefer to be in the dark again."

"Come on. We need to get out of our wet clothes. We'll lay them out and hope they'll dry by morning." Hawk picked up the lamp and handed it to Rorie. When he lifted the partially open canvas bag from the floor, Rorie glanced inside and saw two handguns.

"One for you and one for me?" she asked.

"You knew in advance that I'd expect you to carry a weapon. It would be suicidal for us to go into La Vega tomorrow unarmed."

Rorie walked across the room, placed the lamp on a dusty wooden table and glanced down at the pile of blankets. She picked up the melons and bananas and laid them beside the the lamp, then lifted one of the blankets. She frowned. The small blanket looked clean enough, but it was obviously part wool and would feel scratchy to her skin.

She tossed the blanket to Hawk, who caught it up against his chest. "You go behind the stairs to undress," she told him. "And don't come out until I tell you that it's all right."

Hawk chuckled. "Lady, before this little adventure of ours is over, you and I are going to become so intimately familiar with each other's bodies that your show of modesty right now will seem ludicrous."

"Well, we aren't going to become intimately familiar tonight, so go change clothes behind the stairwell!"

Rorie crossed her arms over her chest and stamped her foot

on the floor. Hawk grinned wickedly, then turned and walked across the room and behind the stairs.

Undressing hurriedly, she removed her boots, soggy socks and damp khaki pants. After taking off her cotton shirt, she laid the articles of clothing out across a couple of rickety wooden chairs. She hesitated before unhooking her wet bra, and when she tried to remove her moist panties, they stuck to her skin. But she peeled off the nylon underwear, then reached down, grabbed a blanket and wrapped it around her body. Just as she had suspected, the rough material felt scratchy.

She doubled the blanket around her, overlapping the ends securely above her left breast. The hem of the makeshift garment hit her just below her knees. Due to the width of her hips, the blanket didn't quite double around her lower body, leaving a gap that revealed a glimpse of her left thigh. Despite the itchy, woolen cover, she felt naked and vulnerable. Spearing her fingers through the sides of her hair, then running her hand down the long braid that hung past her shoulder blades, she tested for dampness. Apparently the windy jeep-ride had partially dried her hair, as it had her clothes.

"Aren't you a fashion plate in that outfit," Hawk said.

Gasping silently, Rorie jumped at the sound of his voice, then turned to face him. He stood a couple of yards from her, halfway across the small, musty room. He had draped his blanket around his hips, leaving his chest bare. Trying to avoid looking directly into his face, Rorie glanced downward and the sight of his muscular chest took her breath away. She swallowed hard.

"You look pretty cute yourself." She forced the playful words from her mouth.

Taking inventory of Hawk proved to be a visual delight. His broad shoulders and big arms bulged with sleek, fine-toned muscles. His skin gleamed a pale, mellow copper in the lamplight. While she stared at him, he snapped the band that held his ponytail in place, then bent over and shook loose the vibrant black strands of his long hair.

Rorie glanced away, unable to continue her perusal without melting into a pool of pure sensual lust. Warning herself once again about the dangers a man like Hawk presented to a woman like her, Rorie busied herself by turning away and picking up the other blankets.

"There are two more apiece," she said, her back to him. "But no pillows. I suppose I can use one for cover and roll the other one up to put under my head."

"Don't you want to eat before you make our bed?" he asked teasingly.

"What?" She whirled around, her mouth gaping, her eyes as round as saucers.

"Aren't you hungry? Those melons look delicious. If you'd like, I can slice one open."

"You go ahead and eat," she said. "I'm really not very hungry. I'm just tired. I think I'll make my bed for the night."

"Lay mine out beside yours, and don't give me any arguments. It's cool and damp down here and it'll get even cooler toward morning. We'll appreciate each other's body heat."

She glared at him, but didn't say a word. She prepared two blankets side by side, then rolled up two to use as pillows.

Hawk knew she was deliberately ignoring him, pretending that she'd forgotten his threat to claim her body as part of their bargain. Of course, it was possible that she had actually believed him when he'd later told her that he wouldn't touch her if she was the last woman on earth. His guess was that she was uncertain about his intentions. He thought she deserved to worry about if and when he would take her. Her stubbornness and determination had put him in a position he didn't like. He had allowed his feelings to cloud his judgment; he'd brought a female civilian along on a deadly mission.

In his peripheral vision, he saw her lie down and lift one side of the blanket up and over her. Let her lie there and squirm, he thought. Let her wonder if tonight is the night I'll ask for the use of her body.

Retrieving a knife from the canvas bag Murdock had stocked for him, Hawk sliced one of the melons and bit into it with gusto. The juice ran down the corners of his mouth and dribbled over his chin.

"Sure you don't want some?" He held up the other half of the ripe fruit.

"No, thank you. Maybe in the morning I'll eat something." She turned over toward the wall.

Hawk finished off the whole melon, then peeled a banana. Wiping his sticky hands on the blanket, he glanced around the filthy basement room. A safe little hideaway. Maybe the last one they would have until they left San Miguel.

He flung the knife blade into the tabletop. Morning would come too soon. He needed rest as much as Rorie did. There might be nights ahead of them without the comfort and safety of an abandoned hotel.

When he stood over her, gazing down at her still form, Hawk removed the blanket from around his waist and dropped down on his knees behind her.

The moment he lifted her long, damp braid, Rorie stiffened. "What are you doing?"

With nimble fingers, he began unbraiding her hair. "You shouldn't sleep with your wet hair plaited."

"Oh." She lay perfectly still, her back to him, and allowed him to unbraid her hair.

Was that all he intended to do? she wondered. If he tried to force himself on her, how would she react? She should have made it perfectly clear to him that she had no intention of having sex with him. To her, sex was not some bodily function for releasing tension and deriving physical pleasure. When she made love with a man, it would be because she loved him with all her heart and soul.

When Hawk finished the unbraiding, he thrust his big fingers through the yellow strands, lifting her hair off her bare shoulders. He released the thick mass slowly, allowing it to fall through his fingers. In the soft lamplight her hair looked like shiny silken threads—threads of pure gold. *La dama dorado*. Golden lady.

His knuckles brushed her naked back. Rorie drew in her breath. He stretched out beside her, his body almost touching hers, then drew his blanket up and over them both. He nuzzled her neck. She moved away from him, toward the wall. He threw his arm over her waist and drew her back to him, fitting their bodies together, spoon-fashion.

His hardened sex pulsated against her buttocks. Rorie trembled. Hawk smiled.

"Such a skittish little virgin," he mocked. "Don't you ever wonder what it would be like to have a man make love to you?"

Lying in his arms, her body shivering with fear and desire as he held her, Rorie knew she had to be strong. Now was the time to set him straight, to let him know she was not his for the taking.

"I'm not going to have sex with you, Hawk. I'll take orders from you without question, but I draw the line at giving you my virginity."

He slipped his hand inside the blanket wrapped around her body and covered one of her breasts. Her nipple blossomed against his palm. She struggled to free herself. He squeezed her breast gently. She shivered. Then he removed his hand and turned over, facing the opposite direction.

"Go to sleep, Rorie. I won't ask you to give me your virginity, since you seem to prize it so highly. But…"

"But what?" Her voice quivered ever so slightly.

"If you ever decide you want me to make love to you, all you have to do is ask. And I'll make sure your first time is unforgettable."

His statement left her speechless. Her stomach flip-flopped nervously. Her nipples puckered and tightened, almost painfully. Her feminine core clenched and released, spreading a fierce tingling sensation through her lower body.

She had no doubt that he could make sure her first time was unforgettable. But what Hawk didn't understand was that, despite her desire for an unforgettable first experience, she wanted more—so much more. She wanted love and commitment and the hope of "forever after." She was a woman with a great deal to give the right man. She hadn't saved herself just to squander her love on a man to whom she meant nothing.

Hawk awoke with a hard-on. A soft, female body lay draped over his. When he turned his head to see who the lady was, golden blond hair tickled his nose. Then suddenly he remembered where he was and with whom. Rorie Dean. The plump little virgin was all but lying on top of him. Her head cuddled on his chest. One arm rested across his belly. And the apex of her thighs pressed against his hip.

He had never taken a woman who didn't want him, but he was sorely tempted at that precise moment. With the right kind of seduction, she would be begging him for it. All he had to do was— No! Hell, no!

The last thing he needed was to have sex with Rorie and for her to decide that she was in love with him. This mission was dangerous and complicated enough as it was, without the added risk of having a lovesick female on his hands.

Easing his body away from hers, Hawk stood and stretched.

He checked the clothes he'd spread out under the stairwell last night and found them completely dry. Picking up the wrinkled garments, he shoved them under his arm and headed for the bathroom in the basement. Not wanting to leave Rorie alone in the dark, he didn't take the lamp. Feeling his way around in the gloomy hallway, he found the toilet, which was a room no bigger than a broom closet. When he flung open the bathroom door, bright morning sunshine flooded through the dirty, cracked windowpanes.

He turned the chipped porcelain faucets and breathed a sigh of relief when a thin stream of cold, dingy water trickled out and into the filthy sink. Cupping his hands, he filled them and splashed the water on his face.

He used the commode, washed his hands and dressed hurriedly, then checked his watch. It was nearly six-thirty. Murdock would be here soon.

When he returned to the area of the basement he had shared with Rorie last night, he found her awake, sitting at the table and hungrily devouring a banana.

"I found a bathroom," he said.

Gulping down the last bite of fruit, she wiped her mouth on the back of her hand. "A bathroom? That's wonderful. Where?"

"Don't get too excited. There's no shower or tub. Just a sink with cold water and a commode that actually works."

"Beggars can't be choosers." Standing, she held the edges of the blanket securely around her body. "Where is it?"

"Straight down that hallway. Turn right and you'll see daylight through the bathroom window."

Grabbing up her clothes from the chairs, she smiled at Hawk. "Thanks. I'll be back in a few minutes."

"Make it snappy, honey. Murdock should be here any minute."

"I'll hurry."

Rorie had no more than disappeared down the hallway when Hawk heard footsteps overhead. Heavy, booted footsteps. One man. Probably Murdock. But he would be a fool to take any chances. Retrieving the XM4 Springfield pistol from the canvas bag, Hawk eased up the L-shaped stairway. Waiting on the landing, he held the 9-mm weapon in his hand.

The door flew open. "Hawk?"

Hawk slipped the gun under his waistband. "Yeah. Down here." He retreated to the basement hideaway.

Murdock clumped down the stairs. Glancing around, he grunted, "Where's the woman?"

"Freshening up," Hawk told him.

Murdock tossed Hawk the Thermos he'd brought with him. "Here's some coffee. Where you're going, you'll need to be wide-awake and alert."

Hawk caught the Thermos, unscrewed the lid and poured the black liquid into the lid cup. "Any word at all on Prince Francisco's whereabouts?"

"All I know is that the kid's not at the palace with his grandfather. And like I told you before, he hasn't been seen for over a month."

"Any chance that he's been kidnapped or killed? Or do you still think the king sent the boy into hiding?" Hawk sipped the warm, bitter coffee.

"Information on the young prince is top secret. I don't think anyone except the king and maybe those closest to him know the truth about what happened to the boy."

"So that means I'll have to talk to King Julio if I want to find out where his grandson is." Hawk downed another swallow of coffee. "Dammit, Murdock, what'd you put in this coffee—your old boots?"

Laughter rumbled from Murdock's chest. "What's the matter, aren't you man enough for my super brew?"

Rorie cleared her throat loudly. Simultaneously he and Murdock turned toward the sound. She stood just inside the room, staring bug-eyed at Murdock. Her cheeks were rosy from a cold-water wash. She had freshly plaited her hair into one long braid and put on her wrinkled pants and shirt.

"Excuse me. I heard voices and I wondered if—"

"Murdock, this is Miss Aurora Dean." Hawk set the cup on the table. "Miss Dean's brother was the missionary, Peter Dean, the guy who was married to Princess Cipriana." Hawk took a few steps toward Rorie, his gut instincts urging him to protect her, even from his old friend. "Rorie, this is Murdock. You met him last night."

Murdock gave Hawk a knowing glance, one that held no meaning for Rorie. But Hawk understood that Murdock was questioning him on the wisdom of keeping the truth from Rorie. Without saying a word, Murdock warned him that not telling Rorie about his part in her brother's and sister-in-law's executions was a mistake that he would live to regret.

"Hello, Mr. Murdock," Rorie said. "Thank you very much for everything you've done to help us."

Rorie couldn't stop staring at the big mountain of a man. She didn't think she'd ever seen a man as large as Mr. Murdock except for Manton. Hawk was tall—about six-two—and muscular, his body sleek, toned perfection. But beside his friend, Hawk didn't look so big.

Mr. Murdock had to be at least six-five, with massive shoulders and huge, granite arms. If she had to guess his age, she would say well over forty. Maybe close to fifty. There was a hard, rugged, almost-ageless quality to his suntanned features. Not a handsome face, but a strong, compelling one. He wore his brown hair a little too long, the shaggy tips just brushing the collar of his khaki shirt. She caught a glimpse of the sadness in his hazel eyes—a sadness that he seemed to think he kept well hidden.

Murdock surveyed Rorie from head to toe, studying her so thoroughly that he made her blush. When he looked directly into her face, he laughed.

"Lady, I don't know who's the craziest—you, for wanting to come back to San Miguel, or Hawk, for bringing you."

"I am," Hawk admitted. "No point in discussing it. We're here and there's no turning back now."

"Are you two ready to leave?" Murdock asked.

Hawk glanced at Rorie. She nodded.

"We're ready," Hawk said.

"Then you'd better head straight for La Vega this morning. You don't have any time to lose." Murdock glanced at Rorie and shook his head. "Damn! Look, it's like this—the capital city is on the verge of falling to Lazaro. The rebels have mounted an all-out attack. Word is that the king is preparing to flee to Puerto Angelo and set up a new, temporary capital there."

"Is there any chance that Frankie might be waiting in Puerto Angelo for King Julio?" Rorie asked.

"The odds are against it. My bet is that your nephew won't be with his grandfather at any time. The king knows the boy is safer as far away from him as possible," Murdock told Rorie. "And your only chance to find out where the prince is will be to confront the king himself. Only that old reprobate and maybe his most trusted comrades know what happened to the boy."

"That means we have to get to La Vega before King Julio leaves, doesn't it?" Rorie knew the answer to her question, even before Murdock replied.

"Yeah. Once the king is in Puerto Angelo, even I won't be able to get to him, without an army of my own," Murdock admitted.

"Then we have to go to La Vega now." She looked to Hawk for agreement.

"If we do that, it will mean walking right into the middle of the battle," Hawk said. "You could stay here and—"

"No! King Julio won't tell you anything, but considering the situation in San Miguel now, he might realize that Frankie's only hope for survival depends on my taking him back to the United States."

"She's right," Murdock said. "Julio Francisco loves his only grandchild as much as he hates anything American. There's a chance that he'll actually put the boy's safety first, if he realizes he's not going to be able to protect him indefinitely."

"Can you get us through the rebel lines and into the city?" Hawk asked Murdock.

The corners of Murdock's mouth lifted just a fraction, into a quirky, self-satisfied smile. "Can Superman fly?"

Chapter 6

Rorie's stomach growled, reminding her that she hadn't eaten anything except a banana since noon yesterday before they left Miami. She'd tried Murdock's coffee, but one sip had been more than enough. It had been all she could do not to spit out the putrid liquid the minute it hit her tongue. But she had forced herself to swallow that small taste, while Hawk watched in amusement.

Sitting in the back of the jeep, she felt every bump and jostle as Murdock maneuvered the vehicle along the only road between Cabo Verde and La Vega. She squirmed about on the ragged seat, trying unsuccessfully to settle her body into a semicomfortable position. The gun holster Hawk had forced her to strap on felt larger and heavier than it actually was—probably because she loathed the very idea of carrying a weapon. Hawk had assured her that it was now commonplace in San Miguel to see both men and women wearing their weapons openly. She adjusted the brim of the hat Murdock had given her to hide her blond hair. The big man had also advised her to wear the sunglasses he had provided.

"Hawk can easily pass as a native, but we'll need to disguise you, at least until y'all get in to see the king," Murdock had told her.

They made the first few miles out of Cabo Verde quickly, seeing no one in transit. The scenery along the route would have captivated her, if she hadn't been so worried about the lifesaving mission that had brought her to this tropical paradise. The farther north they traveled, the less mountainous and smoother the terrain. Occasionally she caught glimpses of the ocean through the thicket of verdant growth—coconut palms, mangroves and greenery she couldn't readily identify.

Halfway to their destination, when the road from Cabo Verde merged with a two-lane highway, they began meeting an unusually large flow of traffic coming from La Vega. Within ten minutes, the narrow roadway was clogged with cars, trucks, jeeps and donkey carts. People on foot covered both sides of the road.

Cursing loudly, Murdock slammed his fist down on the jeep's horn. When only a few women and children moved out of the way, he revved the motor and charged forward. His bold move cleared the right-hand lane.

"They're fleeing the city in a big hurry," he said. "Getting out before Lazaro's army takes over the capital. I expected as much, but not so many people so soon. Things must be falling apart fast."

Rorie leaned forward, clutching the back of Hawk's seat. "Do you think King Julio will have left La Vega before we get there?"

"Let's hope not," Hawk said, then glanced at Murdock. "How long will Nina wait for us?"

"As long as she can," Murdock replied. "But when old Julio leaves the city, she'll go with him. Let's just hope I can get y'all through in time to put our plan into action."

"Are you talking about Nina Hernández?" Rorie asked. "King Julio's mistress?"

Hawk turned halfway around in his seat and looked at Rorie, who stared back at him, her eyes filled with questions. "Nina and Murdock are old acquaintances. She occasionally does favors for him."

"For the right price." Murdock chuckled, the deep, throaty sound like the beat of a bass drum.

"And you paid Nina to help us get through to see the king?" Rorie remembered King Julio's young mistress, a raven-haired beauty with a seductive body, a viper tongue and a hot temper. Cipriana had disliked the woman intensely and refused to acknowledge her father's relationship with the former prostitute.

"Nina is a smart girl," Murdock said. "She knows that gold can help her more than the king can, if the rebel forces win this war. Besides, Nina said that she doesn't want to see the kid get killed. She became fond of your nephew during these past few years."

"But she doesn't know where Frankie is?" Rorie asked.

"She says she doesn't. She told us that one day the kid was at the palace and the next day he wasn't. And when she asked the king about the young prince, he told her that she was better off not knowing."

Rorie shuddered to think what kind of influence King Julio, his mistress and his corrupt officials might have had on Frankie. "Whatever her reasons for helping us, I'm thankful."

"Other than Captain García, old Julio's personal goon-squad leader, Nina has more influence with the king than anyone." Murdock kept the speeding jeep far to the right of the congested left lane, running the vehicle completely off the road when pedestrians blocked his path.

"Captain García is the one who took Frankie away from me." Rorie had relived that horrible day a thousand times, and every time, she had tried to think of something—anything —she could have done differently. "He had me drugged and put on a plane back to the United States. But I'm sure he was following the king's orders."

Hawk grabbed Rorie's hand that clutched the back of his seat. She gasped. "Did that bastard do anything else to you?"

"What do you mean—? Oh. No! No, they didn't. I vaguely recall, before I blacked out, one soldier warning another that he'd better not touch me because of King Julio's orders."

Hawk let out a deep, painful breath. "Then they didn't *touch* you?" Hawk ran the tip of his thumb across her wrist.

"Not in the way you mean. But Captain García did hit me, when I refused to let them take Frankie." Absently, Rorie rubbed the side of her face. "He hit me so hard, he knocked me down."

"God damn son of a bitch!" Hawk released his hold on Rorie and turned sharply, facing forward. He didn't want her to see the murder in his eyes, the raging desire to break Captain García's neck.

Rorie leaned back in the seat. The racket from the vehicles and people congesting the road blocked out the sound of Hawk's and Murdock's voices.

"You can take care of this García after you finish your business with old Julio," Murdock said.

"What makes you think—"

"Don't try to lie to me. We've known each other too long, been through too much together for you to feed me a line of bull. The very thought that anybody touched her has got you totally bent out of shape."

"So? Nobody would want to see an innocent like her brutalized by the likes of García and his men."

"It's more personal than that," Murdock said. "I understand. If I found out somebody had hit my woman, I'd bash his head in."

"She's not my woman."

"Not yet. But it's only a matter of time, isn't it?"

Rorie leaned forward, irritated that she couldn't hear Hawk and Murdock's conversation. "What are y'all talking about?"

"Just going over some details," Hawk said.

"What sort of details? Something I should know?" she asked.

"I was just telling Hawk that a couple of soldiers, who are very loyal to Nina, will meet us right outside the city and personally escort y'all to the palace."

Murdock honked the horn at a scattering of natives who littered the road, many toting their possessions in baskets balanced on their heads and in cloth wraps strapped to their backs. "The soldiers will take you directly to Nina, and she'll get you in to see the king."

Ten minutes later, they entered the outskirts of La Vega, the capital city. Cloud-shadowed hills cradled the town and the once-busy harbor.

The streets leading out of the city were jammed with fright-

ened citizens trying to flee before their town was captured.
Horns honked. Men cursed obscenities at one another.
Women screamed in terror as they ran from their homes. Chil-
dren wept as their parents snatched them from their yards.
The roar of battle rumbled like thunder in the distance. Bil-
lows of smoke darkened the inland sky.

Murdock eased the jeep off the main road, onto a side road
that led down to the docks. He pulled to a stop in front of an
old warehouse.

"Wait here." Murdock jumped out of the jeep, went over
to a metal door at the side of the building and knocked a
rhythmic beat.

The door opened and Murdock disappeared inside, then
returned in a couple of seconds and motioned for Hawk and
Rorie. They climbed out of the jeep. Two armed soldiers
emerged from the warehouse.

Murdock spoke rapidly in Spanish to the two men. They
nodded agreement and then took their positions behind Hawk
and Rorie, relieving them of their exposed weapons.

"You're going to pose as a couple of captives," Murdock
said. "Once y'all get within sight of the palace, put your
hands over your heads and act scared."

Rorie glanced nervously at Hawk, who gave her a reassuring nod and smile.

"If anything goes wrong and you can't meet me back here
in three hours, try to make your way to Papa Joe's." Murdock
grasped Hawk's shoulder. "Dulcina will know how to contact
me."

The soldiers led Hawk and Rorie along the back streets,
avoiding as much of the escape pandemonium as possible.
Chaos reigned in the city. Deserting soldiers and civilians
alike ran amok, scurrying like rats fleeing from a sinking ship.

The palace loomed ahead of them—an enormous Spanish
mission-style building of pale pink stucco, with a red-tiled
roof. The palace had formerly been a convent, but King Julio's father had restored the abandoned structure, which con-
tained forty-seven rooms, and turned it into a magnificent
landmark.

When they neared the entrance to the palace, Hawk nudged
Rorie, then raised his hands and entwined his fingers across

the back of his head. Rorie followed his lead as they began their prisoner act.

"We are to take these two directly to Captain García." Speaking in Spanish, the younger soldier explained to the guards. "Orders of Colonel Yago."

The guards made no protest. Rorie let out a deep breath once they passed through the palace gates. Inside the king's personal domain, the flurry of activity was as frantic as it had been in the city's streets. Even with her untrained civilian eye, Rorie could tell that the palace staff was preparing for a hurried exodus.

They entered the palace by the arched doorways on the west side. Rorie recalled that the king's private quarters were in this wing of the house.

"This way, *por favor.* Señorita Hernández is waiting." The younger soldier pointed the way.

Lowering his hands from his head, Hawk held out one hand to the soldier, who immediately returned Hawk's pistol to him. The man's comrade handed Rorie the gun he'd taken from her holster.

Hawk stepped behind Rorie, sandwiching himself between her and the two soldiers. The young man in front of Rorie, knocked softly on the heavily gilded double doors. One door eased ajar slightly and a pair of dark eyes peeped through the crack. The door opened wider and Nina Hernández extended her hand outward and motioned for her guests to enter.

The soldiers flanked the doors. After removing her sunglasses, Rorie took a tentative step forward. Hawk gave her a gentle shove. She stepped over the threshold and into Nina's bedroom. Hawk followed her and closed the door behind him.

Wringing her hands together, Nina paced the floor. Her waist-length black hair swayed from side to side, shimmering like a rich sable pelt in the muted light. She looked like a magazine ad for a Caribbean holiday in her hot-pink suit and enormous straw hat with a matching pink flower adorning the rim.

Rorie thought Nina looked older and plumper than she remembered—more overripe than voluptuous in her skintight clothes and heavy coating of makeup.

"We are leaving La Vega within the hour," Nina said.

"García has gone to double-check the limousine. I must get you in to see Julio before *el capitán* returns." Halting abruptly, Nina rushed forward. She reach out and grasped Rorie's hands. "Señorita Dean, you must get little Francisco out of San Miguel before he is captured by that animal, Emilio Santos. He will kill our sweet child, just as he murdered the boy's *madre y padre*." Nina spoke rapidly, mixing her Spanish and English.

"Where is King Julio?" Hawk asked.

Nina glanced toward a door to her left, one that Hawk assumed connected her bedroom to the dictator's. "Come. We must do this quickly," Nina said. "Before García comes back. He will try to persuade Julio to tell you nothing. García hates all *americanos*. He would rather see Prince Francisco dead than taken to the United States."

Nina opened the connecting door and walked into the other room. Hawk and Rorie followed, holding back, waiting in the doorway.

King Julio smiled softly when he saw Nina. "You are ready, my dear? You have packed only what you will need?"

She nodded an affirmative reply to his question. When he held open his arms, she ran into them, hugging him as she cooed soothing words in his ear.

Rorie couldn't believe how much Julio Francisco had aged in three years—far more than either of her parents. His once-steel-gray hair had lightened to a striking white. The lines in his face had deepened. Fat pouches bulged beneath his dark, sunken eyes. And he had lost weight. At least twenty pounds or more.

"Julio, *mi querido*." She kissed him on the cheek, leaving an oval smudge of pink lipstick. "Señorita Dean... Peter's sister... She has come to take little Francisco back to the United States."

"What? How do you know this?" the dictator demanded.

When Nina glanced toward the open doorway, King Julio followed her line of vision and gasped loudly. "How did you get into the palace?"

"I gave them safe passage," Nina told him as she motioned for Rorie and Hawk to enter. When the king glared angrily at her, she explained, "I did it for Francisco. I know you love the child more than your own life and that you worry about his safety here in San Miguel now…now that the time has come when you may not be able to protect him.''

"Your Majesty, please tell me where Frank—Francisco—is.'' Rorie moved slowly toward the king, her fingers braided together in front of her in a prayerful gesture. "If we—'' she looked meaningfully at Hawk "—know where Francisco is, we can go get him and take him out of San Miguel before…before…''

"Before Lazaro takes over the country,'' Hawk finished for her.

"Who is this man?'' King Julio asked.

"This is Señor Hawk,'' Nina said. "He is a friend of Señorita Dean's. He has come with her to find Francisco.''

The king eyed Hawk suspiciously. "You do not look like the sort of man with whom Peter Dean's sister would associate.''

"I'm not,'' Hawk admitted. "I'm a professional bodyguard. She hired me to get her into San Miguel and get her and the boy out safely.''

King Julio turned to Rorie, his dark eyes scrutinizing her. "If I allow you to take my grandson to the United States for safekeeping, you must promise me that if…when I put down this rebellion and all is safe once again in San Miguel, you will return the boy to me.''

"Return him to you? No, I can't make such a promise.'' Rorie looked nervously, pleadingly from Nina to Hawk.

"You cannot have the boy unless you give me your word that you will return him to San Miguel. He is a prince. The heir to the throne. I will not have him live as a commoner in the United States.'' The king crossed his arms over his chest in a defiant manner, as if saying, "Take my offer or leave it.''

"I—I…'' How could she lie to him? Rorie wondered. She had been taught since infancy that lying was a sin. But if she didn't give King Julio her word, he wouldn't tell her where Frankie was. "Please, think of Francisco. If you lose this war—and you know there's a good chance you will—he might be killed. He could die because you are so stubborn that you would—''

"I'll give you my word,'' Hawk said. "If you win this war

and make the country a safe place for Prince Francisco, I'll personally bring him back to San Miguel. Directly to you.''

"No, Hawk, you don't have the right to make such a promise!" Rorie glowered at Hawk.

"She is correct, isn't she, *señor?*" The king said. "Once I allow you to take the prince out of San Miguel, he will belong to Señorita Dean. My foolish daughter and her husband assigned the boy's guardianship to her in their wills.''

"You and I know, don't we, Your Majesty, that wills are simply words written on paper. And to men like you and me, legal documents are worthless, if we choose for them to be.''

King Julio looked at Hawk in a different way, his keen dark eyes inspecting the brash young man. "So, you want me to believe that you could take the boy against Señorita Dean's wishes and return him to me?''

"If I can get the boy safely out of San Miguel, then why should you doubt that I could just as easily bring him back at any time?" Hawk gave Rorie a threatening glare, warning her to keep her mouth shut.

Suddenly Rorie understood what Hawk was doing. He was giving King Julio what he wanted, without the necessity of her having to lie. She stood silent and still, holding her breath, praying that Hawk's tactic would work.

"Please, Julio," Nina pleaded. "Think of the boy. He is such a sweet, innocent little thing. If Santos were to get his hands on Francisco—"

The king crumpled before them—an old, weak man, already defeated, even if he didn't realize it, yet. He nodded solemnly.

"I sent Francisco to the Reverend Mother at the Blessed Virgin Mission.''

"Who else knows where the boy is?" Hawk asked.

"Only Captain García. He took Francisco himself.''

A powerful boom rocked the palace, rattling the windowpanes and shaking the floors. Nina cried out. Rorie gasped. Gunfire echoed in the distance.

The outer doors of the king's bedroom suite swung open and a big, barrel-chested man in a military uniform dashed toward King Julio.

"Your Majesty, we must leave immediately," Captain

García said. "Colonel Yago has been forced to withdraw. As we speak, Lazaro's army is pushing through and has already taken the eastern section of the city."

"Come, *mi querido*." Nina laced her arm through the king's. "We must do as Captain García says and leave immediately."

Captain García suddenly noticed the other two people in the room. When García reached for his revolver, Hawk drew his pistol and aimed it directly at the captain's head.

So this was the man who had ripped Frankie Dean from his aunt's arms, the man whose vicious blow had knocked Rorie into the wall.

"Give me a reason to kill you, García," Hawk said. "Nothing would please me more."

When Rorie gasped, she gained García's attention. "Señorita Dean? But how—"

"She is here to take Francisco back to the United States, until it is safe for him once again in San Miguel," King Julio said.

"Your Majesty, it would be a mistake to give your grandson to this woman," García said. "You know how her brother turned your own daughter against you."

Hawk grinned wickedly as he took several steps toward Captain García. "You're too late. We know where the boy is."

García glared at the king, his eyes filled with disgust. Then he sneered at Nina. "You are responsible for this, you stupid whore."

"Captain García, you forget yourself." King Julio reprimanded his subject by both words and look.

Four soldiers appeared at the open doorway of the king's private chambers. One man marched forward, then halted abruptly when he saw that Hawk held a gun aimed directly at the captain.

"Gentleman, escort King Julio and Señorita Hernández to the limousine," Hawk said, not taking his eyes off García for even a split second. "Your captain will follow in a few minutes, after we settle some unfinished business."

The mortar fire beyond the palace walls intensified, thundering closer and closer, like a nearby storm threatening imminent destruction. Another bomb exploded somewhere to the east, sending the surrounding earth into spasms.

"We are ready to leave," King Julio said. "García will join us later." He motioned for the soldiers to make way, then with Nina at his side, he marched out of his suite and into the hallway. The four guards followed their king.

"Just who are you and what business do you have with me?" García asked Hawk. "We have never met before, have we?"

"Toss your sword and your revolver on the floor," Hawk said. When García hesitated, Hawk steadied his XM4 with both hands, squinted his left eye ever so slightly and drew a bead.

García divested himself of both weapons hurriedly, his thick, fat fingers working nervously to comply with Hawk's wishes. Hawk holstered his pistol.

"What are you doing?" Rorie's voice quivered.

Hawk ignored Rorie completely, focusing his attention on the surly captain. "I'm Señorita Dean's personal bodyguard. And the business I have with you concerns an event that occurred over three years ago. The night you kidnapped Francisco Dean."

"I did not kidnap the prince." García bristled, sticking out his chest and tilting his chin upward. "I acted on King Julio's orders to bring the boy to the safety of the palace."

"Did King Julio also order you to strike Señorita Dean?"

"She resisted my command. She refused to hand over Prince Francisco!" García smirked. His small, beady eyes glistened.

"Hawk, we don't have time for this," Rorie told him. "Let him go. We need to get out of La Vega while we can."

"Be patient. This won't take long." Hawk glanced at Rorie for just a fraction of a second. Long enough for García to make his move.

Hawk whirled around just as García lurched forward. Blocking the captain's hard right fist, Hawk landed a breath-robbing punch to his soft belly, then delivered a powerful blow to his jaw. García bounced backward, landing with a resounding thud on the floor. He moaned once, twice, and then passed out.

"You didn't kill him, did you?" Rorie grabbed Hawk's shirtsleeve.

"He's still alive." Hawk pulled away from Rorie, knelt over García and shook him soundly.

Coming to suddenly, García moaned, then glared up at Hawk.

"You'll think twice before you hit a lady again, won't you, Captain, now that you know how it feels?"

Hawk dragged Rorie in front of him and gave her a gentle shove toward the door. When they reached the hallway, García yelled out, cursing Hawk. García tried unsuccessfully to stand. He flopped down on the floor, landing on his back end.

"Pray you never see me again, *señor*," the captain shouted.

"No, García," Hawk shouted back. "You pray you never see me again. You're damn lucky I didn't kill you this time!"

Hawk ushered Rorie down the stairs, through the hallways on the lower level of the palace and out into the courtyard. The repetitive gunfire grew closer and closer. Shouts of fear and agony reverberated all around them. Another explosion rocketed through a building on the opposite side of the street.

Hawk removed his pistol from the holster, shoved Rorie behind him and peered around the gate. "Stay right with me. We're going to make a run for it, down the alley."

"Are we going back to the warehouse to meet Mr. Murdock?" Rorie asked.

"If my calculations are correct, Lazaro's army has already sealed off the harbor," Hawk told her.

"Does that mean—?"

"It means we're heading for Papa Joe's."

"What is Papa Joe's?"

"It used to be the hottest nightspot in town," Hawk said. "Now there's a seedy bar downstairs and a three-whore brothel upstairs."

"A brothel? You're taking me to a brothel?"

"Yes, I'm taking you to a brothel…if we're lucky enough to make it through the city alive."

Chapter 7

The farther up the alley Hawk and Rorie fled, the more difficult it became to avoid other people—frightened, angry,
armed citizens of La Vega, who were ready to shoot anyone
on sight. But Hawk seemed to possess a sixth sense for danger
and an innate ability to avoid confrontations. He led; she followed. Twice they took refuge. Once behind a huge garbage
bin and once behind a wooden fence.

A wild-eyed, middle-aged man flew out of a building's
back door and chased them for nearly a block, taking potshots
at them. Hawk flung Rorie behind a tree in an open yard,
took aim and hit their pursuer in the leg. The man crumpled
to the ground, screaming in pain. Hawk grabbed Rorie's arm.

"Don't think about helping him," Hawk said. "He tried
to kill us."

When Hawk tugged on her arm, she turned quickly and
followed him. Adrenaline raced through her body like a swollen river rushing over deadly rapids.

Rebel soldiers flooded the main streets, confronting the rag-
tag remains of the king's army, whose mission was to slow
General Lazaro's takeover of the capital long enough for King
Julio and the majority of his forces to escape to Puerto An-

gelo. Heated battles pursued them everywhere throughout the city. No matter how far or fast Hawk and Rorie ran, they were never more than a stone's throw away from the fighting. Never more than a heartbeat away from danger and death.

A small band of loyalists, rifles in hand and ammunition strapped across their chests, retreated from the street into the alley. Hawk jerked Rorie into a recessed doorway.

"What are you—" she protested.

He slammed the palm of his hand across her mouth. "Shh." Lowering his lips to her ear, he whispered, "Keep quiet."

She opened her mouth to mumble a complaint, then heard the booted footsteps of several running men and suddenly understood Hawk's actions. She reminded herself once again that she wasn't supposed to question his orders, and she assumed that that now included not questioning his actions, as well.

Hawk was so close that she smelled his perspiration and tasted the sweat on his palm. When her tongue touched his skin, his hand jerked.

The king's soldiers fled in the opposite direction. Hawk held Rorie in the doorway, his hand over her mouth, his body pressing hers against the wooden door behind her. As he waited, listening for the echoes of the deserting soldiers' retreat, he looked down into Rorie's face. He tightened his hold around her waist and lifted her up as he lowered his head and removed his hand from her mouth.

"Don't ever question anything I say or do," he whispered against her lips. "The slightest hesitation on your part could get us both killed."

Her heartbeat quickened. Warmth suffused her face. Leaning back, she pressed herself against the door, trying to put even a little space between their bodies. She nodded agreement, then said, "I understand. It won't happen again. But don't you ever put your hand over my mouth!"

Hawk took a step backward, then grabbed her by the arm and pulled her out of the recessed doorway. "We're only a few blocks from Papa Joe's. If there's anyone there except old Guido and his girls, you keep quiet and let me do all the talking. I expect the place to be empty, but you never know.

Some of Lazaro's troops might have decided to stop by for a drink on their way into La Vega.''

"How do you know we'll be safe at this brothel?'' Rorie asked, as Hawk led her up the alley.

"Guido is another friend of Murdock's. He'll get word to him that we're there and—''

"I assume these are friends Mr. Murdock has bought and paid for, also. Just where does Mr. Murdock get all his money and exactly who is he working for, anyway?''

At that instant a bomb exploded in the street. A wooden-bed truck, filled with two dozen people, burst into flames. Bodies sailed through the dark smoke and hit the pavement, some in pieces. Several survivors jumped from the truck, screaming in terror. One woman fell to the sidewalk and rolled over and over to extinguish the fire eating away at her clothes and flesh.

Rorie pulled away from Hawk, heading toward the main street. Her instinct was to rush to those injured people and help them in any way she could. She wasn't a nurse, but she knew basic first aid for burns.

Before she'd gotten three feet away from him, Hawk jerked her back to his side. "Where the hell do you think you're going?''

"To help those people!'' She tugged on her arm, trying to free herself.

"Are you out of your mind? Of course you are! Otherwise, you wouldn't be in San Miguel in the first place. You'd be back in Chattanooga, letting me do this job alone.''

"We can't just do nothing. Those people need our help.'' The harder she tried to escape from his tenacious hold, the tighter he held her.

"Look, lady, this city is filled with wounded, dying people. A team of doctors couldn't save most of them. Our main objective is to save ourselves.''

"How can you be so cold-blooded? So heartless and unfeeling?''

Before Hawk could reply to her charges, a rebel patrol opened fire on the few survivors of the truck bombing. Rorie turned from the sight, burying her face in Hawk's chest. He held the back of her head, pressing her hat against her skull.

She shuddered. Hawk momentarily closed his eyes, blocking out the scene of death, then he slipped his arm around Rorie's waist and hurried her away.

She stumbled several times before she picked up Hawk's pace. Numb from having witnessed slaughter firsthand, Rorie continued following Hawk, her movements as stiff as an automated mannequin's.

Hawk spotted the back entrance to Papa's Joe's—Murdock's home whenever he was in La Vega. When Hawk reached the door, he found it locked. Gently shoving Rorie up against the wall beside him, he cupped her face in his hands. He didn't like the way she looked; all he needed was for her to go off the deep end.

"Rorie?" She didn't reply. "Rorie, you're all right. We're safe. We've made it to Papa Joe's." When she stared at him with sightless eyes he shook her lightly. "Snap out of it, lady. If you can't stomach bloody gore on the streets, how are you going to face what lies ahead of us? How are you going to find the strength and courage to save Frankie?"

Save Frankie. Save Frankie. Her mind swirled with visions of the truck exploding. Of bodies flying through the air. Of the burning woman rolling helplessly on the sidewalk. Of soldiers mercilessly killing screaming civilians.

Rorie heard Elizabeth Landry's voice clearly, reminding her of her destiny. *In the end, it will be you who must save both Frankie and Gabriel. If you have the courage. If your love is strong enough.*

"I'm all right." The words rushed out of her at the end of a long, mournful gasp. Tears clouded her vision. She rubbed her eyes, wiping away the moisture.

Hawk let out a deep breath. He clutched her shoulders as he gazed deeply into her eyes. She's herself again, he thought. Rorie Dean never ceased to amaze him. The woman was a hell of a lot stronger than he ever could have imagined.

Hawk rapped repeatedly on the back door to Papa Joe's until someone called out from the other side, asking who was there.

"*¿Quién está allí?*"

"Murdock sent us," Hawk said.

"Your name, *señor?*" the voice asked.

"Hawk."

The door opened. Hawk pushed Rorie through the doorway and into the shadowy storeroom. She hesitated after entering. Hawk closed and bolted the door behind him, then faced their host.

"Guido, this is Señorita Dean," Hawk said.

"*Señorita?*" The wrinkled, leather-skinned man grinned at her. His two front teeth glimmered with gold caps. "It's good to see you again, Hawk. It's been a long time."

Hawk glanced at Rorie, wondering what she was thinking. She had questioned him about Murdock's background, but the truck explosion had saved him from having to explain. She would no doubt question him again. And the next time, she would undoubtedly want to know more about his past, as well as Murdock's.

"Come with me." The short, potbellied man scratched his scraggly gray beard. "I have locked the front door. There is no one here except me and *las prostitutas*. You and the *señorita* will be safe at Papa Joe's."

"Could you whip us up something to eat?" Hawk asked.

"Omelets? I can make good omelets. Murdock brings me fresh eggs from the villages."

"Omelets would be great. Thanks." Hawk patted Guido on the back.

Guido led them through the storeroom and out into the hot, semidark saloon. Closed, heavy wooden shutters shut out the afternoon sunlight and any breeze that might be stirring. An array of candles placed in the center of the six tables scattered about the room and two kerosene lamps on each end of the bar illuminated the interior of Papa Joe's.

"A thousand pardons, *señorita*, for the darkness and the heat," Guido said. "But we have had no electricity for the past three hours."

Rorie smiled and nodded to their host, uncertain what her reply should be.

"I need to get in touch with Murdock," Hawk said. "He brought us into La Vega this morning—now we need to get out of the city as soon as possible."

"*Sí*, Hawk, I understand. Everyone wants to leave the capital now that General Lazaro is here. Everyone except the citizens who are loyal to the cause, of course.''

Rorie didn't need to ask which side Guido was on. The very fact that he wasn't fleeing from the city indicated that the man thought he had nothing to fear from the rebel troops. If Guido was a rebel supporter, did that mean that Murdock was, too? She already knew that Murdock was some sort of U.S. government agent, someone Hawk had worked with in the past. But was the United States backing the rebel army? If so, that fact was certainly top secret. For the past four years, the official statement from Washington had been that the United States held a neutral position in the San Miguel civil war.

"How long will it take to get a message to Murdock?" Hawk pulled out a chair from one of the tables and motioned for Rorie to sit.

She eased down in the chair and sighed with relief. Her body ached. Her head throbbed. She snatched off her hat, tossed it on the table and flipped her long braid over her shoulder.

"If Murdock brought you to La Vega and told you to come to Papa Joe's when you were ready to leave town, then he will meet you here," Guido said. "He will go see General Lazaro first, I am sure. To congratulate him on this great victory."

Rorie opened her mouth to ask how Murdock could get through to General Lazaro and why he would congratulate the man on all the death and destruction his army had brought to La Vega. But before she could utter a word, Hawk glared at her.

"Don't ask," he told her.

She closed her mouth. She would follow orders like a good little girl. But sooner or later, Hawk was going to have to answer her questions. Questions about Murdock. And questions about himself.

Feminine giggles rippled through the air. Rorie glanced in the direction of the sound. Leaning over the wooden banisters that surrounded the landing at the top of the stairs, stood three young black-haired women, ranging in age from maybe eighteen to twenty-five. They were scantily dressed in thin nylon gowns that clung to their slender curves and left very little to the imagination. The dark areolas of their breasts showed plainly through the sheer fabric.

Guido turned sharply and shook his fist at the three women. He cursed them in Spanish, calling them *las prostitutas* again. Whores. He told the women, whom he referred to by name—Alva, Trella and Dulcina—to go back to their rooms. The two younger women scurried away, disappearing quickly. But the older woman, who might have been in her mid-twenties, slunk down the stairs. She looked straight at Hawk and smiled.

Hawk returned the woman's smile, and Rorie could have strangled him. Guido glanced from Rorie's frown to Hawk's grin to the prostitute's come-hither smile.

"Go back upstairs, Dulcina," Guido said in English. "Can't you see there is a lady down here? She does not want the likes of you around."

Rorie felt a sudden twinge of pity for the woman. She opened her mouth to tell Guido that it was all right, not to send Dulcina away. But once again, before she could say a word, Hawk interceded.

"Go back up to your room," Hawk said. "You're Murdock's woman when he's in town, aren't you?"

"Murdock will share me with you." Dulcina walked farther into the saloon, swaying her hips seductively. The thatch of black hair at the apex of her legs darkened a vee at the front of her gown.

A scarlet flush covered Rorie's neck and face. Moisture coated her body. A trickle of perspiration dribbled down between her breasts.

Hawk laughed heartily. "That would be generous of Murdock, but I'm afraid even if he's willing to share you, my lady isn't willing to share me." He glanced meaningfully at Rorie. "You wouldn't share me with Dulcina, would you, honey?"

It was on the tip of Rorie's tongue to tell him she would be more than glad to share him with the delectable Dulcina or any other woman in La Vega, but instead she said, "You know how possessive I am, darling." Rorie rose from the chair, sauntered slowly over to Hawk and draped her arms around his neck. Then she looked directly at Dulcina. "I'm afraid you'll just have to wait for Murdock. Gabriel already has more woman than he can handle just with me." Acting purely on instinct, not taking time to thoroughly think through her actions, Rorie planted a kiss squarely on Hawk's lips.

In her peripheral vision, she saw Dulcina toss back her head and march up the stairs. When Rorie drew away from Hawk, he pulled her up against him and finished the kiss she had started. When he cupped her buttocks in his hands and pressed her intimately against him, she stilled instantly. But when he thrust his tongue inside her mouth, she melted, clinging to him.

Guido chuckled. "*Mi casa es su casa.* Sit. Rest. Make love. I will bring omelets and coffee. But I will announce myself first." He left the room abruptly.

Hawk ended the kiss. When he released Rorie, she swayed, then grabbed the nearest table. The man certainly knew how to kiss, she thought. But then he'd probably had a lot of practice. With women like Dulcina? Maybe. Maybe not. She couldn't imagine Hawk ever having to pay a woman for her services.

"What are we going to do now?" Rorie asked.

Hawk grinned wickedly. She hated the way his smile made her stomach flip-flop.

"What did you have in mind?"

"Oh, for goodness' sake. I meant, what are we going to do about contacting Murdock?"

"We're going to wait," Hawk said.

"Do you think Murdock really is with General Lazaro?"

"You're not stupid, Rorie." Hawk sat down at a table, then motioned for her to join him. She eased out a chair and sat. "Murdock works for the U.S. government."

"He's a CIA agent?" Rorie gripped the edge of the table.

"Not exactly. The agency contracts him for certain jobs. For the past four years, he's been under contract to help General Lazaro win the civil war, by whatever means necessary."

She balled her hands into fists. "And you? When you worked for our government, were you in San Miguel to help General Lazaro win the war?"

"I was sent to do a specific job, which I did. It was my

last assignment. After that, I went to work for Dundee's.''
Hawk's jaw tightened. The pulse in his neck throbbed.

"Then General Lazaro is an old friend of yours as well as
Murdock's?''

"'Friend' is too strong a word,'' Hawk told her. "Let's
just say he's an acquaintance.''

"You—you wouldn't tell him where Frankie is, would
you?'' Spreading her hand out across the table, she unknow-
ingly asked for Hawk's response.

Grabbing her hand, he rose from the chair, then knelt in
front of her. "I work for you, remember? My only loyalty is
to you. We aren't going to share the information King Julio
gave us about Frankie with anyone.''

"Not even Murdock?'' She searched Hawk's eyes for the
truth. She had put not only her own life in this man's hands,
but Frankie's, too. Despite having spent two weeks on Le
Bijou Bleu with him, he was virtually a stranger to her. Could
she trust him?

Did she have any other choice?

"Murdock is my friend. One of the few I've ever had. I
trust him more than any man I know.'' Hawk released her
hand, then ran his fingers over her cheek. "I would never
betray you. And Murdock would never betray me.''

She swallowed hard, praying that she could believe Hawk,
all the while knowing in her heart of hearts that she could.
That she did.

"So, we wait for Murdock?'' she asked.

"Yeah, honey. We don't have much choice. He's our only
ticket out of town.''

After enjoying Guido's omelet and three cups of his delicious coffee, Rorie spent most of the afternoon watching
Hawk and Guido play cards. The hours dragged by. Two.
Three. Four. Five. Afternoon turned to evening and evening
to night. The sounds of fighting lessened throughout the day,
ending completely when darkness claimed the city.

On her second return trip from the rest room, Rorie heard
Murdock's voice rumbling down the hallway. It's about time,
she thought. She was ready to leave La Vega and begin the

journey up the mountain to the Blessed Virgin Mission high atop La Montaña Grande. Considering the political climate in the nation, Rorie couldn't help wondering how long the usually three-and-a-half-hour trip would take. If she and Hawk left first thing in the morning, surely they could reach the mission by late afternoon. Then by the day after tomorrow, they could leave San Miguel—she and Hawk and Frankie. Within three days she could take Frankie home to Chattanooga. Home to his grandparents. Home to safety.

When she neared the barroom, she heard Murdock say, "Mateo insists that we join him at the palace tonight for his victory celebration. The general is eager to see you again, my friend. And very interested in meeting Peter Dean's sister."

"How does General Lazaro know about me?" Rorie walked into the room.

Three heads turned in her direction; three sets of eyes focused on her entrance.

"I told him, of course," Murdock said. "He's eager to meet you and give you his personal assurance that you have nothing to fear from him. He gave me his word that he doesn't want to harm your nephew. In fact, he's all for your taking the boy to the United States with you."

"You told him I'm here in San Miguel to rescue Frankie?" Rorie stormed across the room, halting in front of Murdock. "Did you tell the general that I went to see King Julio before he left the city?"

"Calm down, Rorie." Hawk headed toward her, but stopped abruptly when she held both hands in front of her to ward off his advance. "All right. Go ahead and get upset. But don't assume the worst. Murdock had good reason to tell the general about your presence here in La Vega."

Rorie crossed her arms over her chest and glared at Murdock. "And just what would that good reason be?"

"Nobody is going in or out of the city without General Mateo Lazaro's permission," Murdock told her. "You and Hawk and I are invited to the palace for the party...and to spend the night. You can have a good meal, a hot bath and a good night's sleep. Then tomorrow morning, you and Hawk can leave La Vega and begin your search for Prince Francisco. Lazaro will give you a jeep and provisions for the hunt.''

"Begin our search? The hunt? What—?" Rorie asked.

"I told Lazaro that King Julio refused to tell you anything about the prince," Murdock said. "So, you and Hawk must search the whole of San Miguel, which could take weeks, even months."

"I'm afraid I don't understand why—" Rorie said.

"Lazaro isn't an evil man." Hawk walked around behind the bar and lifted a whiskey bottle. "He's simply a man who wants his country to be free from the dictatorship of a king whose family has bled the people of San Miguel dry for five generations."

Hawk set up three shot glasses and poured them full to the rim. "Lazaro's done whatever was necessary to achieve his goals. And our government has helped him. He has no reason to kill Prince Francisco, but he would probably sleep better at night knowing the boy wasn't growing up here in San Miguel, possibly plotting to take his rightful place as heir to the throne."

"General Lazaro is a man of his word," Guido said as he reached for one of the shot glasses on the bar. "*Señorita*, if he says he will not harm Prince Francisco, you can believe him."

Hawk lifted his glass, then Murdock walked over and picked up the remaining glass. "Gentlemen," Hawk said. "A toast to General Mateo Lazaro. Man of the people. Savior of his country. Victor in the battle of La Vega."

All three men saluted with their glasses, then downed the liquor. Rorie watched, frustration slowly building inside her. They were acting as if this was some sort of game, instead a matter of life and death. She started to tell them just what she thought when Dulcina came running down the stairs and straight into Murdock's arms.

Dulcina spoke to Murdock in Spanish, telling him with earthy vulgarity how much she had missed him and just what she wanted to do to him and what she wanted him to do to her. Hawk glanced at Rorie and grinned. He knew she understood every word the woman was saying, and he was thoroughly enjoying Rorie's discomfort.

Murdock swatted the young prostitute on the behind. "Dulcina, my sweet, go put on your prettiest red dress. I'm taking you with me to a party at the palace."

Dulcina kissed Murdock so passionately that Rorie wondered if the two weren't going to have sex right there in front of everyone. But Murdock ended the kiss and shooed the woman away, telling her to hurry. Then he turned to Hawk.

"Have a talk with Miss Dean," Murdock said. "Make her understand how this game is played."

"I knew it!" Rorie stomped her foot. "If you big government agents think this is some sort of game, you're wrong. What's at stake isn't some jackpot payoff. What's at stake is my nephew's life!"

Hawk came out from behind the bar and stalked toward Rorie. His eyes turned a searing black as he neared her. Instinctively, she backed away from him. He cornered her before she reached the door to the storeroom. She halted when her behind encountered the wall.

Hawk spread his arms out on each side of Rorie's head, placing his open palms on the plaster wall. "Murdock and I know what's at stake, honey." He leaned his body closer to hers and laughed when she shoved uselessly against his chest. "The games we play always have high stakes."

She looked directly into his eyes, her gaze defiant and bold. More than anything, Hawk wanted to kiss her again, to capture and tame that wildness he sensed in her.

He lowered his voice, so that only she heard what he said. "All you have to do is remember that I'm the trained professional. I know how to play to win. You don't. So, you follow my orders, play the game by the rules I teach you, and if we're lucky, we'll get Prince Francisco out of San Miguel alive." He brushed his lips across hers. "Do you understand?"

She nodded that she did. Reaching behind her back, he grabbed her long braid, snapped the band that held it together and thrust his fingers through her hair. She didn't move, didn't say a word. She just stood there, staring at him, her heart beating like a trapped bird trying to free itself from a snare. He spread her hair over her shoulders.

"We're going to Lazaro's party and you're going to be

sweet and charming,'' Hawk told her. "And you are going to act as if you believe everything he says to you and as if you trust him completely. Understand?''

Rorie nodded again.

"But under no circumstances will you let on that you have any idea where Prince Francisco is," Hawk said. "In this game, we are General Lazaro's friends and he is ours. We want safe conduct out of this city, with a jeep and provisions for a bogus search. We don't know for sure what Lazaro wants in return, but whatever it is, we're going to give it to him. Understand?''

"But what if he—'' Rorie began.

"If he asks us to bring Frankie to him when we find the boy, then we will promise him that we will do as he asks. Am I making myself clear? Do you understand?''

She understood, all right. She understood that Hawk had once been a part of a world that specialized in lies and deceit; in espionage and counterespionage. He hadn't been a CIA agent. He'd been something far worse. He'd been a contracted operative. She had read once that those men were little more than mercenaries, hired soldiers and assassins.

"You're right," she said. "You are the trained professional. And I understand that unless I'm willing to—'' she took a deep breath ''—play the game by the rules, we won't be able to rescue Frankie and get him out of this country alive.''

Hawk stepped back, separating their bodies, then grabbed her wrist and tugged her forward. "Come on, honey. We're going to a party."

Chapter 8

On the jeep ride from Papa Joe's to the king's palace, now occupied by the rebel forces, Rorie tried to prepare herself, both mentally and emotionally, for her first meeting with General Mateo Lazaro. The U.S. government officials with whom she'd spoken, after Peter and Cipriana's execution, assured her that General Lazaro had played no part in the brutal murders. But she wasn't sure she believed them—not now that she knew her own government had a secret agenda, that they had been backing the rebel army since the beginning of the civil war.

Hawk had convinced her that she must play the game—to pretend, to act the part he had assigned her. Pretense and lies went against her nature, against every good and honest instinct she possessed. She wasn't a very good liar. The few times in her twenty-seven years when she had lied, her dishonesty had shown plainly on her face. Her father had told her that her facial expressions were very revealing. That had been after the one and only time she'd ever tried to lie to him. She had fibbed about going with her friends to see an R-rated movie.

Murdock drove through the palace gates, waving to the

guards and hollering greetings in their native language. He parked the jeep directly in front of the palace, then got out and opened his arms for Dulcina. Laughing giddily, the young woman jumped into Murdock's waiting embrace. Her dress swirled up around her thighs, exposing a long expanse of slender dark leg and three layers of stiff red-and-black petticoats. As the two entered the palace, Murdock called out greetings to the soldiers, addressing several by name.

Rorie shivered at the thought of how familiar Hawk's good friend was with these brutal men—General Lazaro's soldiers. They were part of the same army as the men she had seen gun down innocent civilians earlier in the day.

"Try not to look like that when I introduce you to the general," Hawk told her. "Smile and be gracious. Use your Southern charm. And just keep telling yourself that being friendly to Lazaro is a means to an end. He can help us rescue Frankie."

"I'll do my best, but I'm not a practiced liar." The words, *Not like you,* hung silently between them. But she could tell by the way he looked at her that he knew what she'd left unsaid.

"Remember, this is a party." Hawk stepped down out of the jeep, then assisted Rorie. He kept his hands around her waist after her feet hit the ground. "Force yourself to eat the general's food and drink a little of his wine. Accept his hospitality tonight and tomorrow morning we'll be able to leave La Vega with the conquering hero's blessing."

"I don't feel much like a party." Rorie swung her head from side to side, disgusted by the unkempt condition of her hair. "My hair is a mess, my clothes are wrinkled and I need a bath."

"All in good time." Hawk wrapped her arm though his and escorted her into the palace.

She tensed every time Hawk spoke to one of the rebel officers. She could tell that he knew them and they him. What exactly had Hawk's assignment in San Miguel been three years ago? And just how closely had he worked with the rebel army?

The banquet hall was filled with soldiers of every age and physical description. From boys in their teens to old men in their seventies. From handsome, dashing officers, who had apparently bathed and changed clothes for the celebration, to dirty, bloodstained, heavily bearded ruffians, who looked as if they'd come directly from battle. And female soldiers— some young, some middle-aged; some attractive, some decidedly unattractive. And at least three dozen women like Dulcina, attired in bright, shiny dresses that revealed their undeniable physical charms.

Rorie wasn't surprised to see so many prostitutes hanging on the arms of various officers. But she was surprised to see so many women wearing battle fatigues, with gun belts strapped to their hips.

A band played a tune with a hot, Latin beat and many of the guests danced together, their bodies undulating to the sensuous rhythm. Servants paraded in and out, carrying trays of food, while others kept the wineglasses filled.

Murdock shouted a greeting to a tall, slender man walking directly toward him. A path cleared for the man as he approached, and Rorie knew instantly that this had to be General Lazaro. The general grabbed Murdock and hugged him with robust camaraderie. The two exchanged hardy slaps on the back, and then the general eyed Dulcina.

"*¡Muy hermosa!* Very pretty." The general slid a long, lean finger down Dulcina's throat.

"She's yours for the night, Mateo." Murdock released Dulcina, who instantly draped herself on the general's arm.

"*Muchas gracias,* my old friend." Lazaro ran his hand down the girl's back, lifted her dress and petticoats and squeezed her hip. "Now, to more serious business. Did you bring Hawk with you?"

"He's right over there." Murdock motioned to Hawk.

"Ah, I see he has persuaded Señorita Dean to accompany him," Lazaro said.

General Mateo Lazaro was not what Rorie had expected. She had pictured him a hard, grizzled gorilla fighter; ugly, bearded and at least fifty. Instead, the man who stood before her, watching her like a bird of prey, was clean-shaven, handsome, not a day over forty, and filled out his battle fatigues quite impressively. Almost as tall as Hawk and almost as good-looking, Lazaro possessed a thick mane of black hair and large, chocolate-brown eyes.

The general shook hands heartily with Hawk. "It is good to see you again. Murdock tells me that you have accompanied Peter Dean's sister into our country to find her nephew and take him to the United States."

Hawk pulled Rorie forward, placing her at his right side, about a foot in front of him. "General, let me introduce you to Aurora Dean. She's eager to meet the man of the hour."

Lazaro smiled, showing a mouthful of perfect white teeth. He reminded Rorie of an old Latin movie star known for his mesmerizing smile. The general bowed graciously, then reached out and drew her hand to his lips. When he raised his head, he did not release her hand. His gaze spanned the length of her body, lingering first on her breasts and then returning to her face.

"Bella. Bella"

Lazaro lifted a strand of Rorie's hair from her shoulder, and it was all she could do not to cringe. Her cheeks flushed as warmth spread over her face, but she smiled weakly and forced herself to reply to his compliment.

"Thank you," she said, looking away shyly.

Lazaro seemed to approve of her demure response. His smile widened. He released her hair, letting it fall over her shoulder, the tips brushing across her breast.

Hawk moved to Rorie's side and slipped his arm around her waist, drawing her up against him. Instinctively, Rorie leaned on him, thankful for his presence, knowing that Hawk had just laid claim to her. Lazaro glanced at Hawk's possessive hold on Rorie. He nodded to Hawk, silently acknowledging the other man's ownership.

"You are a fortunate man, Hawk," Lazaro said. "A fortunate man, indeed." Lazaro snapped his fingers and a servant came running. "Wine, *por favor!* We will toast my victory today. And we will also drink to the success of Señorita Dean's quest to find her nephew."

Hawk tightened his hold around Rorie's waist, warning her to keep quiet. The servant returned quickly with a tray of filled wine flutes. Those assembled around the general lifted their glasses.

Murdock proposed the first toast. "To the rebel army's victorious takeover of the capital!"

Beaming with narcissistic delight, Lazaro hugged Dulcina to his side as cheers filled the banquet hall. When the cheers died away, Lazaro lifted his glass again and nodded to Rorie.

"To the success of Señorita Dean's search for her nephew. May she find him unharmed and safe." A hush fell over the room. The general narrowed his gaze, hooding his eyes with his thick, black lashes. "And may Francisco Dean live a long and happy life in the United States." A boisterous round of cheers and applause rocked the banquet hall.

Rorie shuddered involuntarily when she downed half a glass of wine in a show of support for the general's toast.

"Come, my friends, and eat with me at my table." Lazaro led the way to the head of the enormous banquet table.

Rorie remembered dining here only once before—a few months after she had arrived in San Miguel for her year of missionary work with Peter. She had been invited to attend King Julio's sixtieth birthday party, a lavish affair that had ended for her after Cipriana and her father had quarreled bitterly.

The general led the group to his table, then took his place in the king's elaborately carved chair. Already sitting to his right was a young female soldier, whose heated glare raked over Dulcina as Lazaro seated the prostitute on his left.

"Hawk, you remember Major Santiago, don't you?" Lazaro asked, signaling to the proud young woman at his right.

Rorie watched the visual exchange between Hawk and the major. Closed-mouth smiles. Friendly nods. Two pairs of dark eyes that glimmered with memories.

"Congratulations, Consuela, on your promotion to major," Hawk said. "When I left San Miguel, you were Captain Santiago."

"Consuela is one of my most valued officers," Lazaro said. "She has become my right hand. No soldier has been more loyal to me or more devoted to the cause."

Rorie wondered if the general had any idea that Consuela was in love with him. Probably not. But if he did, he obviously didn't care.

All during the meal, Mateo Lazaro laughed and drank and

kissed Dulcina repeatedly. By the end of the feast, he had dragged the giggling prostitute onto his lap. And all the while the general enjoyed himself with Murdock's "gift for the night," Consuela Santiago flirted outrageously with Hawk, who sat between the sexy major and Rorie.

When Consuela led Hawk onto the dance floor, Rorie tried to pretend indifference. But even a partially intoxicated Lazaro noticed her discomfort.

"Do not worry, beautiful Aurora." While the general turned his attention to Rorie, Dulcina clung possessively to his neck, squirming about in his lap. "Hawk and Consuela are old friends. He dances with her to be polite. He knows that she is trying to make me jealous."

When Rorie didn't reply, the general laughed loudly, tossed Dulcina onto the floor as he stood and held out his hand to Rorie. "You will dance with me."

Shocked by the general's request, Rorie only stared at him for a moment, then when he approached her chair, she rose slowly and accepted his arm.

"You and I will make Hawk and Consuela jealous. *¿Sí?*"

"*¡Sí!*" Rorie went willingly into the general's arms.

He waltzed her across the dance floor as if she were as light as air, then when they neared Hawk and Consuela, Lazaro pulled Rorie very close and nuzzled her neck.

"If you were not Hawk's woman, I would ask you to stay the night with me."

Rorie shuddered. "General, I—"

"My name is Mateo." He brought her hand to his lips, opened his mouth and glided the tip of his tongue over her hand.

Rorie gasped. "Mateo...I have risked everything—my very life—to come to San Miguel to find my nephew. Help me, and I promise that I will take him to the United States and he will never come back to San Miguel."

"I have heard that your brother was a fine man. I am sorry that he and his wife met such a terrible fate at the hands of Emilio Santos." Lazaro grinned at Hawk when he whirled Rorie past the other couple. "I do not condone anything that that butcher does. He calls himself my comrade, but he is not. He and his followers are renegades. They do not love San

Miguel and the people of this country the way I do. Santos is not fighting for freedom. Santos is fighting for the love of killing.''

"I've been led to believe that Emilio Santos will kill Francisco, if he finds him."

"You must find the boy first and get him out of the country. I will provide you and Hawk with whatever you need."

"You're most generous, Gener—Mateo."

"When this war is over, I want peace and prosperity for San Miguel. I am tired of the bloodshed." Lazaro looked directly into Rorie's eyes. "I would never harm Prince Francisco. I am not a murderer of children. But I do want the royal line to end with King Julio. For this reason, once you have found the young prince, I will help you and Hawk get the child safely out of San Miguel."

"I believe you." Rorie stopped dancing, stood on tiptoe and kissed Mateo Lazaro's cheek.

As Lazaro propelled Rorie across the dance floor, Hawk watched and listened when he heard the general and his partner laughing. What the hell was Rorie laughing about? He had told her to be friendly to Lazaro, but he hadn't told her to charm the pants off the man. Hawk knew that if Lazaro could have his way, he would take Rorie to his bed tonight.

"Over my dead body," Hawk mumbled.

"What did you say?" Consuela asked.

Hawk stopped abruptly on the dance floor when he saw Lazaro lead Rorie toward the doors opening into the enormous entrance hall.

"Excuse me." Hawk released Consuela and stalked off toward the huge gilded doors.

He ran into the entrance hall, but halted when he saw Lazaro kiss Rorie's hand and order a guard to see Señorita Dean safely to her room. The general stood at the foot of the marble staircase and watched Rorie's climb. When he turned around, he threw up his hand in a greeting to Hawk.

"Your lady was tired and wanted to retire for the night," Lazaro said. "She is much woman, your Aurora Dean. If only I were the man who would share her bed tonight." The general sighed dramatically, then threw his arm around Hawk's shoulder. "Come back to the party and give your woman time to bathe and prepare herself for you."

Hawk's body tightened with arousal at the thought of sharing Rorie's bed. He would have no choice but to share her room, since Lazaro thought they were lovers. But Rorie certainly wasn't upstairs preparing herself to share a night of passionate lovemaking with him.

Rorie soaked in the gigantic marble-enclosed tub. The luxury of a warm, scented bath soothed her frazzled nerves and almost seduced her into believing that all was right with the world. But all was far from right. She was enjoying the hospitality of a man who claimed he wanted peace, who said he was tired of all the bloodshed, and yet today she had witnessed the brutality of his soldiers. The general had given her his assurance that he wouldn't harm Frankie, that indeed he would help her and Hawk get the boy out of San Miguel. And downstairs, on the dance floor, when Mateo Lazaro had looked at her with his warm, brown eyes, she had believed him. But now, an hour later, alone with her thoughts, with her mind no longer befuddled by Lazaro's charm or her own jealousy over Hawk's attentions to Consuela, Rorie questioned the general's sincerity.

So what if Lazaro hadn't been completely honest with her? All that mattered was that he keep his word about giving Hawk and her safe passage out of La Vega. Once they took Frankie away from the nuns at the Blessed Virgin Mission, they would return to Cabo Verde and wait for Hawk to arrange for a ship to pick them up and return them to the United States. After tomorrow, there would be no reason for her ever to see General Lazaro again.

Rorie dried her body with the wraparound towel and blotted her wet hair. She returned to the sumptuous bedroom suite, intending to retrieve her dirty clothes, wash them and lay them out to dry for morning. But her clothes had disappeared. A sheer, white cotton gown, adorned with heavy lace, lay across the foot of the bed. Compliments of General Lazaro? Had he instructed a servant to provide her with a gown?

But whose gown? One that Nina Hernández had not taken with her to Puerto Angelo?

Surely her clothes would be returned to her in the morning. If not, she would have to ask Hawk to find her something suitable for their journey. Hawk. Hawk!

"Humph!"

Gabriel Hawk was probably still downstairs, getting rip-roaring drunk and pawing Consuela Santiago. Or maybe he and the major had already retired for the night to one of the many bedrooms in the palace.

"I don't care if he spends the night with her," Rorie said aloud. "I don't care. I don't care."

A nagging little voice inside her head said, "Don't lie to yourself, Rorie. You do care. You care very much."

She dropped the towel to the floor, stepped over it and picked up the beautiful gown. She slipped it over her head, letting it fall loosely about her, the hem brushing the rug beneath her feet.

Turning toward the back wall, she gazed at herself in the floor-to-ceiling mirror and almost didn't recognize the alluring woman staring back at her. The sheer fabric of the gown did nothing to hide her body; it simply gave the illusion of covering. Her long mane of hair hung seductively over one shoulder, short, damp tendrils curling about her face. She looked like a woman prepared for her man. A woman ready to embrace life with passion.

But her man was with another woman—a woman who would give him exactly what he wanted.

Hawk is not your man, she told herself. He is your employee. Your guide. Your bodyguard. That's all he is. All he ever can be.

The servant who had brought the gown and taken away her dirty clothes had also turned down the satin coverlet on the bed and lit a dozen candles throughout the room. The suite reminded Rorie of something out of a fairy tale—the bedroom of a queen or a princess. But this was no more than a guest suite in the palace, one of dozens of such rooms.

Rorie heard an occasional sound from downstairs, a distant strain of music and laughter. From the streets outside the palace walls came louder celebratory noises and sporadic episodes of gunfire. The war was not over, only partially at rest. Tomorrow, Lazaro would have to make plans to move across the island to Puerto Angelo, and face the king's army once again.

And tomorrow, she and Hawk would drive to the mission high atop La Montana Grande. She couldn't wait to find Frankie, to see for herself that he was alive and well, to hold her little nephew in her arms once again. But would the child even remember her? He hadn't seen her in such a long time. He'd been a babe of three when Captain García had stolen him. Now Frankie was six years old. What if he didn't remember her? What if he didn't want to leave the mission with her?

She cautioned herself not to borrow trouble. She would face those problems if and when they occurred. What she needed now was a good night's sleep so she would be rested and ready for her journey to rescue Frankie.

Hawk stumbled into the bedroom suite. He'd had a little too much wine. But celebrating with Lazaro had given him what he needed. The general's promise of a jeep, loaded with provisions, and a pass, signed by the general himself, that gave him and Rorie free access to the areas of San Miguel that were now under Lazaro's rule.

That pass would get them out of La Vega and past several of the nearby villages, but once they were halfway up La Montana Grande, they would be out of Lazaro's jurisdiction. They would have to go through a no-man's-land, where neither King Julio nor General Mateo ruled. Parts of the mountain were patrolled by Emilio Santos and his band of renegades and the other part was the domain of nature. Only the highest crest of the mountain was sacred and civilized— the few acres held in trust by the holy sisters.

Hawk closed the door behind him, locked it and crept silently over to the bed. A dozen candles glowing around the room, burned down a third of the way, illuminated the elegant suite. When he glanced at Rorie, asleep in the bed, his breath caught in his throat. Her yellow hair was spread out over the ivory satin pillow like strands of pure gold. She had kicked back the heavy quilted coverlet, leaving only the ivory satin sheet covering her to her waist. The gown she wore was as thin as tissue paper. Her large, firm breasts were all but bare, their pink tips beckoning his fingers and mouth.

"Damn!" he mumbled.

Rorie sighed deeply and rolled over, turning her back to him. His body came to full alert, hardening and throbbing.

How the hell was he going to get through this night without taking her, when she was lying there all soft and scented and waiting? But she's not waiting for you, you stupid fool! If you needed a woman so damn bad, why didn't you have Consuela before you came up here to Rorie's bed?

Good question, he told himself. Damn good question.

Hawk went into the bathroom, stripped off his clothes and stepped into the two-person marble shower. In the past, whenever he had wanted a woman, whenever he'd needed to have sex, he'd been satisfied with almost any willing female. Consuela had been as willing tonight as she had been during their brief affair three years ago. She was his kind of woman— slender, sexy, pretty and very experienced.

But he didn't want Consuela. He wanted Rorie Dean.

When he'd watched the way Mateo Lazaro looked at her, the way he'd held her pressed intimately against his body when they danced, the way Rorie had smiled at him, Hawk had wanted to rip the general's heart out with his bare hands. He had never felt possessive about a woman. Women came and went in his life, all of them temporary conveniences. He had never loved anyone. And no one had ever loved him.

He had wanted. He had needed. He had desired. And he had taken. But he had never loved.

Scrubbing the grime and sweat from his body, Hawk reminded himself of all the reasons he couldn't have Rorie Dean. She was a virgin. She would expect love and commitment. Becoming sexually involved with an emotional woman could jeopardize the mission. If he let himself care about Rorie, he wouldn't be able to stay objective and do his best job. And if she ever found out about his involvement in her brother's and sister-in-law's deaths, she would hate him. Even though he didn't care about her, he didn't want her to hate him.

Who are you kidding? You already care about her.

Well, get over it, he told himself. She's just a woman—like any other woman. Two arms. Two legs. A pretty face. Nice breasts. And a—

Don't go there! Don't think about making love to her all night long.

Hawk dried off and walked into the bedroom. Totally naked, his long, damp hair hanging loosely down his back, he stood in the center of the room and glanced back and forth from the bed to the chaise longue. He was too big a man to sleep comfortably on the chaise. On the other hand, the bed was large enough to easily accommodate both Rorie and he.

He eased back the sheet and slipped into the bed beside her. He felt the heat emanating from her body and smelled the sweet, tempting fragrance of the scented soap and shampoo she had used.

Hesitantly, he reached out and touched her hair, then leaned over and buried his nose in the soft, damp mass. His sex grew harder and heavier, throbbing with need. He kissed her shoulder. Rorie stirred, turning toward him, slowly opening her eyes.

"Hawk! What are you doing in my bed?"

"Our bed. Mateo thinks we're lovers. Otherwise, you'd be spending the night in his bed." Hawk rose up and over her, bracing himself on one elbow as he aligned the front of his body along the side of hers. When she tried to get up, he gave her a gentle shove and covered her waist with his heavy arm, pinning her to the bed.

"Well, we aren't lovers, despite what you led General Lazaro to believe."

"General Lazaro?" Hawk questioned her. "Why so formal? Downstairs you were calling him Mateo, weren't you?"

"Downstairs, I was playing the game, remember? The game you said that I had to play if I wanted to get out of La Vega and rescue Frankie."

"And you played the game very well. Almost too well." Hawk tightened his hold on her waist. "But together we accomplished our goal. Tomorrow morning you and I can leave on our search for the prince in a jeep that's a gift from Lazaro, along with provisions for several weeks. And a pass that allows us free rein in any part of San Miguel that the general controls.''

''Oh, Hawk, that's wonderful.''

Without thinking about what she was doing, Rorie turned to Hawk enthusiastically, a smile of genuine warmth and appreciation on her face. Too late she realized that she had rolled over against his naked body and straight into his arms.

''*Bella*,'' Hawk whispered. ''*Muy bella*.''

''Don't, Hawk. Please, don't.''

Sandwiching her arms between their bodies, she shoved against his chest. He grabbed her wrists and flung her arms up, flattening them on either side of her head. She struggled against his superior strength. When he lowered his mouth to hers, she thrashed her head from side to side. But he captured her mouth with fierce pressure, taking her lips, forcing them apart. He rose up and over her. Only the satin sheet and her gown separated their lower bodies as he ground his sex against her.

Rorie wanted Hawk. Wanted him desperately. But not like this. Not with such savagery. Not when he was intent on forcing her.

She could so easily give herself to him. Her body longed for his. Her heart cried out for his love. But Gabriel Hawk did not love her. He wanted her. For tonight. Perhaps for the duration of their mission. But not forever.

She fought a battle with herself, her own desire raging against her. As Hawk deepened and softened the kiss, she whimpered her surrender to the moment of physical gratification. Straddling her hips, he eased his lips from hers and licked a moist trail down her neck and across her collarbone. He opened his mouth and covered her nipple, suckling her through the sheer cotton.

Her body tightened and released, moistening in readiness, as ripples of pleasure spiraled from her breasts to her core.

Hawk jerked the gown from her shoulders and down to her waist, exposing her large, round breasts. He cupped them in his hands, lifting them, weighing them. Rorie shuddered from head to toe.

''Tell me to stop, now.'' He scraped his palms across both nipples. She gasped. ''Tell me that you don't want me.''

"I—I can't," she said breathlessly. "Oh, Gabriel, I can't."

Gabriel. She'd called him Gabriel. Dammit! He hadn't even made love to her yet and already she was getting personal. If he'd guessed right about her, by the time he entered her body, she would be crying out how much she loved him.

Cold fingers of fear tap-danced up his spine. Was he enough of a bastard to take this woman's virginity, allow her to love him and then, when this mission was over, walk away and leave her?

Hawk nuzzled his nose between her breasts, wanting her as he'd never wanted anything in his life. Then he dismounted her body and fell flat on his back beside her.

She laid her hand on his chest. "Gabriel?"

"Don't touch me, Rorie." He flung her hand off his body. "Turn over and go to sleep. And don't touch me again. If you touch me, so help me God, I'll take you."

Without saying a word, Rorie turned over and drew up into a ball. Hawk lay still—naked and brutally, painfully aroused.

When he heard Rorie's muffled sobs, he turned over and covered his head with a pillow. Heaven help him, this woman was going to be the death of him!

Chapter 9

Murdock double-checked the supplies in the back of the jeep, then pulled the tarpaulin over the provisions and secured the strap.

"You've got a full tank of gas and about twenty extra gallons in the back with the other supplies. That should be enough." Murdock glanced around, checking to see if someone might be listening to their conversation. "If anything goes wrong, you know the villages where I have contacts."

"When you see Lazaro, thank him again for everything he's done to help us." Hawk patted his shirt pocket. "Especially the pass giving us freedom to travel throughout San Miguel."

"Yeah, I'll be sure to thank him," Murdock said. "I don't expect to see Mateo before noon. He didn't leave the banquet hall until after two this morning. And Dulcina has a way of tiring a man out."

Murdock laughed, but Hawk had to force a smile. He was worn-out this morning, but not from a night of passion. With Rorie lying so close, and yet so far out of reach, he hadn't been able to go to sleep until nearly dawn.

Hawk glanced at Rorie, who sat in the jeep, eager to begin

their journey. She looked away, avoiding eye contact with him.

Murdock pulled out a thick, folded paper from his jacket pocket and handed it to Hawk. "Here's a map that might come in handy. I'm sure y'all are going to head straight to Culebra, since it's the closest town to La Vega."

"Isn't Culebra up the seacoast?" Rorie asked. "Why would we—"

"Y'all have enough rations to last a couple of weeks," Murdock interrupted Rorie mid-sentence. "If you haven't found the kid by then, get in touch with me."

Rorie didn't complain about Murdock's rudeness or make any comments about why her question had gone unanswered. Hawk exchanged glances with her. They spoke without words—she silently saying that she understood someone might be listening to their conversation; and he replying, Good girl, you're learning.

"We'll be seeing you." Hawk stepped up into the jeep, then halted and turned back toward Murdock. "Say goodbye to Consuela for me."

Clasping Hawk's shoulder, Murdock grinned. "Don't worry about the major. I'll take good care of her." He glanced meaningfully at Rorie, then lowered his head and whispered, "You've got your hands full, taking care of that one."

Murdock slapped Hawk on the back. Hawk got in the jeep, started the engine and let it idle for a couple of minutes. He looked over at Rorie.

"Better put on your hat and sunglasses," he told her. "They'll give that lily-white skin of yours some protection, as well as disguise your blond hair and blue eyes."

Rorie did as he requested. "Anything else?" she asked.

"I'll let you know." Hawk shifted gears and headed the jeep toward the palace gates.

Rorie sat back in the seat, folded her hands in her lap and looked straight ahead. Hawk waved and spoke to the guards as he drove through the open gates.

For the most part, the streets were deserted, except for soldiers posted at intervals throughout the city. Since Hawk was wearing battle fatigues—borrowed from the general himself—and driving a jeep flying the rebel flag, none of the sentries stopped them until they reached the edge of La Vega.

Hawk whipped out the pass signed by Lazaro. He spoke rapidly in Spanish to the soldiers manning the central highway that branched into four roadways leading out of the city.

"What is your destination, Señor Hawk?" the guard asked.

"We're on our way to Culebra," Hawk said.

The young soldier pointed the direction. "This road will take you all the way into Culebra."

"Muchas gracias."

When they had traveled a half mile out of La Vega, Hawk glanced at Rorie. "Now, you can ask."

"Ask what?"

"Ask me why we're headed up the coast to Culebra instead of taking the road toward the mountains and on to Utuado." Hawk returned his attention to the long winding road, which ran parallel to the shoreline. "Nobody can overhear our conversation out here."

"I'm sorry that I didn't realize sooner why you and Murdock weren't being specific about anything in your conversation. I'm not accustomed to having people spy on me."

"So, do you still want to know why we're taking this route?"

"I think I've figured it out on my own." Crossing her arms over her chest, she cocked her head to one side and smiled at him with great self-satisfaction. "If General Lazaro had someone spying on us in La Vega, then it's possible that he might have someone following us, to check up on which direction we went."

"Smart girl. Going to Culebra first and then backtracking to Utuado will take up most of the day, especially since I intend to stop in Culebra for lunch and to make a few inquiries. By then, I should know whether it's safe for us to double back. If it is, we'll take the back roads. They're not paved and we'll have to cut through some pretty rough terrain. But if we're lucky, we won't run into any soldiers—the king's, the general's or Santos's."

"What about running into wild animals?" Rorie asked jokingly, knowing that San Miguel had no true wild animals, unless you counted a horde of exotic birds, countless insects and several species of snakes, including anacondas.

"Are you referring to the jaguars?" Hawk asked.

"Jaguars? There are no jaguars on any of the islands, unless they're in zoos."

"I take it you haven't heard the story about King Julio's grandfather."

Turning in her seat, she stared at him through the dark lenses of her sunglasses. "Is this a true story or one you're making up to pass the time and keep my mind off what might lie ahead of us?"

"True story. I promise."

She slipped her sunglasses down her nose, peered over the top rims and looked at him skeptically.

Gripping the steering wheel with one hand, he lifted his other hand and drew an invisible *X* across his chest with his finger. "Cross my heart. It's a true story. I've seen a jaguar in the mountains."

"So, tell me the story."

"I'm not sure that I want to tell you, now." He sighed forlornly, then quickly shifted his eyes to catch a glimpse of her smile. "If you ask me nicely and say please, I might tell you."

They were playing games again, she thought. Hawk was very good at games. She wasn't. But she was learning.

"Please, Hawk, tell me the story."

"If you insist. Well, it seems that about a hundred years ago, King Rodolfo had a pair of black jaguar cubs brought over from South America as a gift for his sons. The jaguars were considered pets. But one of the princes had a rather mean streak, so he enjoyed tormenting his pets."

"Oh, don't tell me!" Rorie abhorred animal cruelty. The very thought of anyone deliberately harming an animal made her sick.

"Just stay with me on this story," Hawk said, and when she nodded agreement, he continued. "One day the male jaguar, who had matured into quite a big fellow, decided he was going to fight back. When the cat nearly mauled the wicked young prince to death, the king ordered both jaguars destroyed."

"But they weren't destroyed?"

"The other young prince, who was unfortunately not the heir to the throne, bribed the soldiers who were supposed to kill the jaguars. Instead of shooting the cats, they took them into the mountains and set them free."

"What a marvelous story," Rorie said. "Too bad the kind and tenderhearted young prince didn't become king."

"Well, because of the young prince's tenderheartedness, there are jaguars roaming the mountain forests today." Hawk grinned at Rorie when she shook her head in disbelief. "Hey, I can't guarantee the complete truth of the story, but I can promise you that there are jaguars in this country. I saw one while I was on assignment here three years ago."

"Now, that's a story I'd be interested in hearing," Rorie said. "I'd like to hear about your assignment in San Miguel."

"The assignment was top secret, so the story is classified." Hawk gripped the steering wheel with white-knuckled strength. Lighten up, he told himself. Don't act like you're hiding something or she'll get suspicious. The last thing he wanted was for Rorie Dean ever to know all the gory details of his last assignment for the United States government. "Unless you've got a security clearance, I'm afraid that's one story I can't tell you."

Rorie thought he was trying too hard to make light of the assignment, but she suspected the events were so dreadful that he preferred not to discuss them with anyone.

"No security clearance, I'm afraid." She tried to make her tone as light as his, then deliberately changed the subject. "So, how long does it take to get to Culebra?"

"Less than an hour. The town should be fairly normal— that is, fairly normal for a place under military rule."

"There aren't any vehicles behind us, as far as I can see." She glanced back over her shoulder. "If anyone is following us, they're doing it at a more-than-discreet distance. Will we have to waste so much time in Culebra, if we aren't being watched?"

"You let me worry about detecting the spies and making decisions about if and when it's safe for us to leave Culebra."

"Oh, all right. Excuse me for trying to help." Crossing her arms over her chest, she slumped down in her seat and stuck out her lips in a pout. She waited for Hawk to say something, to beg her pardon for being so controlling, but when he said nothing, she tried to explain her frustration. "It's just that I hate wasting so much time running around in circles. I want to go to the mission and get Frankie as soon as possible. I want us on a ship headed back to the United States."

"Dammit, don't you think that's what I want? But I'm not going to take any chances with that boy's life by trusting Lazaro or anyone else. And if that means taking an extra day or even two to get to the mission, then so be it." He wanted to add that they couldn't be a hundred percent sure that King Julio hadn't lied to them about Frankie's whereabouts. The boy could be in Puerto Angelo with the king right now. But there was no point in worrying Rorie needlessly. If the prince wasn't with the good sisters, then he would be back to square one. And the chances of getting the child out of San Miguel alive would diminish by about ninety-nine percent.

"I'm sorry, Hawk." Rorie reached over and laid her hand on his arm. He tensed immediately. "I keep questioning your decisions after I promised I wouldn't."

He shrugged off her hand. She jerked it back as if he'd slapped it.

"I know what I'm doing," he said. "Remember that you're paying me big bucks for my expertise. I lead. You follow. Keep that in mind at all times, and I just might be able to do my job and rescue your nephew."

Rorie remembered Utuado from her one trip into the mountains—the time when she and Peter went to visit the nuns at the Blessed Virgin Mission. A large, mountainside village filled with quaint houses, some only thatch-roofed huts, and warm, friendly people, Utuado was the last of civilization before reaching the mission. Endless miles of dense forest, inhabited only by creatures of the wild, stretched up the mountainside, separating the two.

Usually a journey from Culebra to Utuado took a little over an hour. But since Hawk had chosen, for safety's sake, to take the back roads—some little more than wide dirt trails—they arrived on the outskirts of the village nearly two and half hours after leaving Culebra.

She had not questioned Hawk's decision to stay in the coastal city for most of the day. He had made half-a-dozen stops before taking her to a local restaurant for lunch, and at least as many stops after their seafood meal. She had understood, without his explaining to her, that they were putting on a performance—pretending to seek information about Prince Francisco.

The western horizon burned with hot, tropical color as the orange sun began its descent behind the mountain. Vivid crimson bled into magenta and lavender pools, splashing the blue sky with dramatic hues. Poinciana spread across the hilly slopes like giant scarlet umbrellas opened to cover the earth. Tall, evergreen breadfruits mingled with parrot pines, casting dark green shadows against the chromatic evening sky.

Dark clouds billowed upward from the village. Hawk pulled the jeep to a stop and rose from his seat, looking over the windshield.

"What's wrong?" Rorie asked.

"Something's on fire," he said. "Look closely. That's smoke and a damn lot of it."

Rorie groaned. The man couldn't seem to form a sentence without using some sort of profanity, but she had promised herself never to condemn his vulgar language again. What good would it do, anyway?

"Are you sure it's smoke and not just low-lying clouds?" Rorie lifted herself up so she could see over the windshield. "No, you're right. That is smoke."

"Too much smoke to be just one building." Hawk slid back down in his seat. "It looks as if half the village is on fire."

"Half the village. Oh, Hawk does that mean—?"

"Burning out villages is Emilio Santos's trademark."

Hawk backed up the jeep. Rorie tumbled sideways into her seat. Just as she tried to sit up straight, Hawk drove off the dirt road into a bumpy clearing.

"I'm not taking you into Utuado until I know it's safe."

"Do you think Santos's army is still there?" she asked.

"I'm going to find out."

He eased the jeep past the clearing, down a sloping embankment and into a ditch that couldn't be seen easily from the road. He jumped out, rounded the side of the jeep and opened the tailgate.

"Where are you going?" She got out and followed him.

"I'm going to see what's happening in Utuado." He unstrapped the tarp protecting their provisions and folded it back.

"You're not going to leave me here!" Putting her hands on her hips, she glared at him.

Hawk reached under the sleeping bags and drew out a heavy-barreled, bolt-action Ruger .308 rifle. He had no idea what he would find when he got to the village, but he intended to be prepared. He hated leaving Rorie alone, but he couldn't take her with him. She would be safer here, alone, than tagging along with him and walking into only-God-knew-what.

He hung the rifle strap across his back, then turned and grabbed Rorie by the shoulders. "Listen very carefully. Check your watch right now." When she stood there with a stricken look on her face, he shook her. "Do it! Now!"

Trembling from head to toe, she nodded her head, lifted her wrist and looked at her watch.

"I want you to go over there—" he pointed downward, toward a thickly wooded area "—get inside that heavy growth of vines, behind the trees. Take your pistol out of the holster, in case you need it, and wait for me."

"Hawk...?"

"If I'm not back in thirty minutes, I want you to get in the jeep and drive like hell as fast as you can down the mountain."

"No, Hawk, please..." She grabbed his wrists and squeezed tightly.

"Don't take the dirt roads," he told her. "Get on the paved road and head straight for Vieques. When you get there, find a man named Tito Álverez. He'll know how to get in touch with Murdock."

She gripped his wrists. He shook her again, a little harder. "Do you understand?"

"Yes, I understand."

He removed her sunglasses, stuck them in her shirt pocket

and ran the tip of his index finger across her cheek. "Go. Now!"

"Hawk...please, be careful."

He jerked her roughly up against him, taking her mouth in a hot, hungry kiss. Then he shoved her away, and waited until she followed his instructions and disappeared inside the heavy growth of vines and shrubs in the nearby forest.

Perspiration soaked through her clothes, trickled between her breasts and dampened her hair. Crouched close to the dark earth floor of the forest, she waited. Every squawking bird, every insect crawling over rotted leaves, every beat of her heart amplified a hundred times over, until the most natural sounds became deafening and frightening.

She clutched the automatic pistol in her hand. If necessary, would she be able to use it? Could she actually kill another human being, even to save her own life?

She checked her watch incessantly. Five minutes. Ten minutes. Fifteen minutes. After twenty minutes of waiting, she stared at the illuminated face of the timepiece. Glowing on her wrist, like a giant firefly in the darkness around her, the watch became a focal point for her. Twenty-one minutes. Twenty-two minutes. Twenty-three minutes.

Please, God, don't let anything happen to Hawk. Keep him safe. Bring him back to me.

Twenty-four minutes. Twenty-five minutes. Thunder rumbled in the distance. Or was it gunfire?

Twenty-six minutes. She couldn't leave him, could she? She couldn't just get in the jeep and run away. But what could she do if she went to the village? If Hawk had been captured...or killed. No! He wasn't dead. She knew he wasn't. She would feel it if he was. She would feel it in her heart, in her soul.

Twenty-seven minutes. Twenty-eight minutes. The underbrush rustled with movement. Footsteps?

Please, God, let it be Hawk.

But what if it wasn't? What if it was one of Santos's soldiers?

Tenaciously grasping the 9-mm handgun, Rorie rose from

her low crouch and slid upward and over, bracing her body behind a large tree. The sound of her heartbeat drummed in her ears. She didn't hear the footsteps. Had they stopped or had she simply imagined them? Maybe it was just the birds or the insects. Or maybe it was a snake!

She checked her watch one last time. Twenty-nine minutes.

Without warning, a large, salty hand covered her mouth and a big arm circled her waist. Acting purely on instinct, Rorie bit down into the fleshy palm of the hand and clawed the arm with her neatly rounded nails.

"Dammit, Rorie," Hawk said, jerking his hand away.

"Hawk!" A flood of air rushed into her lungs. She whirled around and threw her arms around his neck. "You scared me to death!"

Reaching behind his neck, he eased the gun out of her hand and returned it to her shoulder holster. "Sorry, honey, but I didn't want to call out to you, in case there were any of Santos's men still around anywhere."

Hugging him tightly, she planted a garden of tiny kisses all over his face. "Do you know what time it is?" She pulled away from him and tapped the face of her watch. "You cut it awfully close, you know." Tears welled up in her eyes. "I'd be in the jeep, headed down the mountain by now."

"I came back as soon as I could."

"One minute!" Tears spilled from her eyes and trickled down her cheeks. "You made it back one minute before time was up! One little, bitty minute. One—" She choked on her tears.

Hawk drew her into his arms. When she laid her head on his chest, he pulled the droopy, tan cotton hat off her head, stuck it into the back pocket of her pants and grasped her head.

Never in his life had anyone been so glad to see him. She was acting as if she really had been worried about him, as if it would have broken her heart if he'd gotten killed.

He petted her, stroking her head, rubbing her back. "It's all right, Rorie. I'm fine." He tugged on her braided hair. Lifting her head, she gazed up into his eyes. "Things are pretty bad in Utuado," he said. "Santos has come and gone, but he's left havoc in the village."

"What happened?" she asked. "Is it safe for us to stay the night there?"

"I'm not sure I should take you into the village."

"Why not?"

"It isn't a pretty sight," he said. "Over half the homes have been burned to the ground. Dozens of people were shot when they tried to flee. I spoke to one of the unofficial town leaders, an old guy named Berto. He said that Santos had the villagers rounded up and forced them to watch while his soldiers raped a young woman. Then they gathered up half-a-dozen women and about ten men and took them when they left."

"Oh, dear God." Rorie clung to Hawk, drawing strength from him.

"Santos's men confiscated nearly all the livestock and food the villagers had, and took every weapon they found."

"I want to go to the village," she said. "We have to do what we can to help those poor people."

"There's nothing we can do to help them." Hawk released her, then lifted her chin between his thumb and forefinger. "Our best bet is to sleep in the jeep tonight and head out at first light in the morning. I don't think it would be safe traveling tonight, when I have no idea where Santos went. He could still be fairly close. I'd have to use the headlights on the jeep if we drove any farther before morning."

"But we *can* help the villagers," Rorie said. "We have food. We have weapons. And I know first aid. I'll bet you do, too. If anyone is injured, we might be able to save their life."

"Lady, you can't save the whole damn world."

She gazed up into his eyes, her look pleading. "I know that. I'm not asking you to help me save the world. I just want you to take me into Utuado and let's see if we can't do something for the villagers."

"If you're planning on trying to comfort them by assuring them that God loves them and things will be better tomorrow and all that kind of garbage, forget it." Hawk squeezed her chin, then released her.

"Take me to Utuado, Hawk. Please."

"You're not going to like it up there, honey."

"But you'll take me, won't you?" She laced her arm
through his.

Rorie and Hawk walked the narrow dirt streets of Utuado
at twilight. Swirls of gray smoke rose from the dying embers
of the burned houses. The smell of smoke mixed with the
odor of blood and the stench of death in the tropics.

The mournful sobs of those who had lost loved ones echoed from every corner of the village. Women stood huddled
together, their dark eyes vacant as they stared sightlessly over
the destruction of their homes—of their lives. Men carried
bodies to the far end of the village, where others were digging
graves. Several small children wandered aimlessly, crying for
their mothers.

A naked woman sat in the middle of the street. Bruises
covered her body. Dried blood coated her thighs and spotted
the edges of her lips. She rocked her hips back and forth on
the hard ground, humming the same bar of an oddly familiar
tune over and over again.

"Get a blanket from the jeep," Rorie told Hawk.

Without questioning her, he turned and walked back to the
jeep. Rorie knelt down beside the woman and swept the long,
tangled strands of her hair away from her face. The woman
flinched, but didn't stop rocking and humming.

"They raped her. All of them." The quivering male voice
spoke in Spanish. "And we could do nothing but watch."

Rorie glanced up. A small, gray-haired man in a bloodstained white shirt stood over them, his eyes filled with tears.
"Are you Berto?"

"*Sí, señorita.*"

"Berto, why hasn't someone helped her?" Rorie asked.
"Why hasn't someone at least covered her?"

"Every time anyone came near her, she screamed and
fought like a tigress. Finally, we left her alone. That's when
she began humming."

Hawk returned with the blanket, but when he reached down
to cover the woman, she scooted away from him, her eyes
wild with fear. Rorie grabbed the blanket and motioned for
Hawk to step away from them. Rorie crawled over to the

woman, draped the blanket around her shoulders and pulled it together across her breasts.

"What's her name?" Rorie asked the old man.

"Josephina."

"Does she have any relatives here in Utuado?"

"Her husband was murdered today," Tito said. "And her brother and sister were taken. There is no one except her little boy."

"She has a child?"

"*Sí.* Little Pedro."

Old Berto pointed to the small child standing in the doorway of a nearby house, watching his mother silently from afar. Rorie guessed the boy to be no more than four years old. He stood as rigid as a statue, no emotion on his face and not a single tear in his big brown eyes.

Rorie very carefully slipped her arm around the woman's shoulder, then spoke to her in Spanish. "Josephina, I know you don't want to hear me. I know you want to shut out the whole world. That's all right. You go right ahead and hum your song and pretend that you're a million miles away from here. But I want you to get up and come with me."

When Rorie tried to help Josephina stand, she resisted, planting herself firmly in one spot.

"I don't think you're going to get her to move. Why don't you just leave her alone?" Hawk motioned for Rorie to get up out of the dirt and come to him.

She ignored him. "Josephina, there's someone who needs you. Your son is all alone and he needs you."

The woman stopped humming, but she continued rocking.

"Pedro is alive, but he's all alone and he wants his mother."

The woman stopped rocking and looked directly at Rorie. Rorie tried again to help her stand. With Rorie's assistance, Josephina rose from the ground onto shaky legs. Sliding her arm around the woman's waist, Rorie braced Josephina's slender body against her own more sturdy one.

"Look, Josephina." Rorie turned the woman toward her house, toward the child in the open doorway. "See, there's Pedro. He's such a tiny little thing and he's so alone and afraid. All he needs is his mother's arms around him."

Rorie all but carried the weak, battered woman toward the child. "Call to him, Josephina. Tell him that you're coming to him."

The unmoving child watched and waited. His little chest rose and fell rapidly with each breath he took.

"Say his name," Rorie urged.

"Pedro." Josephina whispered her son's name.

"Mama. Mama." The child ran to his mother, throwing his scrawny arms around her blanket-covered legs.

Josephina dropped to the ground, Pedro falling with her. Reaching out, she drew him into her arms and onto her lap. "Pedro. Pedro."

"Leave them alone for a while," Rorie told Berto. "Later, get some of the women to help her into her house. Tell them to help her bathe and put on some clothes. She will need a lot of love and support from those who care about her, but right now, she has all she needs."

Berto crossed himself and muttered a prayer of thanks. He followed along behind Rorie when she walked up the street.

"Come on, Hawk. We need to find out where these other children's mothers are. And if we can't find their mothers, we'll have to get someone to take care of them."

"I thought all we were going to do was share our supplies with these people and see if we could help save anyone who was dying." Hawk caught up with her in two giant steps. "I didn't know we were going to set up our own mission of mercy."

"Berto, where are the wounded?" Rorie asked. "Is there a doctor in the village?"

"No, *señorita*. No doctor."

"After we get these babies off the streets, I want you to take Mr. Hawk and me to where you're keeping the wounded," Rorie said. "We might be able to help. I know some basic first aid and I'm sure Mr. Hawk has removed a bullet or two in his time."

"Oh, *señorita, gracias. Muchas gracias.* We have many with burns and two with gunshot wounds who are still alive."

Rorie stopped and turned to Hawk. "I think you should bring whatever extra weapons we have to the village and set up some sort of guard system to keep watch. Don't you think that's a good idea?''

"Oh, yeah. A peachy keen idea. That way we'll know if thirty or forty armed men are approaching the village, and we can hold them off with three rifles, two handguns and a few assorted knives. Maybe a pitchfork or two and a few sling-shots.''

"You don't have to be so sarcastic. I was just trying to figure out what all we can do to—''

"To help these poor people." Hawk finished her sentence for her. Heaven save him from a softhearted, hardheaded woman with an earth-mother complex. There was no telling this woman that she couldn't do something. She was as stubborn as she was caring.

"Your woman, she is an angel, *señor*," Berto said. "An angel sent from God."

"Yeah, she's an angel, all right," Hawk mumbled. "An angel trying to cut a path straight through hell."

Chapter 10

"Hold that damn light still!" Sweat saturated Hawk's shirt, staining the armpits and circling splotches in the front and back.

Rorie held the battery-powered lantern in her hand. She steadied that trembling hand by placing the other one over it for support. She had never assisted in an operation before tonight. Had never dreamed she would ever have to. And now, this was her second time.

She and Hawk had done what they could for the burn victims. Some of the people would heal in time, with only a few ugly scars to remind them of the day Emilio Santos and his renegades had ransacked their village. But three of the victims weren't so lucky. One man would surely die before morning; his third-degree burns covered three-fourths of his body. Another man might recover, but he would be hideously scarred. The third was an elderly woman, who had died while Rorie was examining her. Her burns had not been severe enough to cause her death. Hawk said he suspected a heart attack.

Rorie had stood at Hawk's side when he'd dug two bullets from a young man's leg. Even after drinking enough whiskey to make a man twice his size drunk, the boy screamed in agony as Hawk removed the first bullet. Thankfully, he had passed out before Hawk went in for the second one.

And now she watched again as Hawk took the knife he had sterilized, first in the fire and then with the whiskey, and made the incision, delving the knife a good two inches into the man's shoulder. She glanced away, not horrified at the sight of his blood—and dear God, there was so much blood—but sympathetic to the pain he felt. Glancing down into the man's bearded face, she bit down on her bottom lip. Hector Gonzáles's big white teeth sank into the leather strap old Berto had placed in his mouth.

Tears gathered in the corners of Rorie's eyes. Don't! she cautioned herself. Don't you dare start crying. Not now! Not when Hawk needs you to help him. Not when Hector's life is at stake.

Hawk probed deeper. Hector moaned. Tears trickled down Rorie's cheeks.

"I've found it," Hawk said.

Hawk looked at Berto and nodded. The old man handed him the sterilized tweezers. Hawk maneuvered them down into the hole he'd cut in Hector's shoulder, grasped the bullet and eased it up and out. All the while, rivulets of sweat rolled down his neck.

Berto handed Hawk the threaded needle, then stepped aside so he wouldn't block the lantern light. Rorie drew in a deep breath as she watched Hawk stitch up the wound. As soon as Hawk completed the job, she handed Berto the lantern.

"I can clean the wound and cover it with gauze." She nudged Hawk aside with her hip. "Go wash up and get some coffee."

He looked directly into her eyes and saw a strength that amazed him. Trails of tears streaked her dirty face. Her voice had trembled with emotion. But here she was, worrying about him and giving him orders to take care of himself. In his whole life, had there ever been anyone who had truly tried to take care of him? Maybe the foster mothers he'd lived with, most of whom had fed him and clothed him for the money. And comrades like Murdock, who watched his back when they were on a mission. But Rorie's caring about him was a woman's care for a man—a man who meant something to her.

"Go on!" She gave him a gentle shove. "There's nothing more you can do."

Hawk nodded, then turned and walked out of Berto's house and onto the porch. Hector's wife and two children waited, their eyes beseeching Hawk for an affirmation that the man they loved was still alive.

He spoke to them in Spanish. "I removed the bullet. Señorita Dean is cleaning him up now. I think he has a chance." Hawk would not give this family any false hopes. Hector had lost a great deal of blood, but he was strong and tough. With a little luck, he would live. "You can go on in and see him."

Hawk made his way through the village to the mountain stream not far from where he'd parked the jeep. He removed his holster and laid it on the bank. Then he tugged his shirt out of his pants and walked into the stream. The cool water came to his knees. He lay down on the stream bed, immersing himself fully. He shivered as the cleansing flow rippled over his body, washing away the blood from his skin, as well as from his shirt and pants. Lifting his head enough so that he could breathe, he lay there and wished that the water could wash away the sins of his soul; the invisible bloodstains from the countless missions that marred his life. If only the soul's guilt could be removed as easily as Hector Gonzáles's fresh blood.

Rorie stood on the bank in the moonlight and watched Hawk rise from the stream, like a god springing from a watery bed. Big and tall and gloriously male, he came up out of the water, droplets falling from his hair, his clothes stuck to his muscular body.

Hawk stepped up onto the bank. Rorie held out a mug of coffee. He glanced from her tired face to the earthenware mug.

"I suppose this is some of our coffee," he said.

"You know it is." She didn't take her eyes off him while he sipped the weak brew.

"You watered it down some, didn't you?"

"It will go a lot farther that way. Coffee for more people."

"Did you save us any?" he asked.

"A little."

"What about our other supplies?"

"I left one rifle, one sleeping bag, the machete, enough food for a couple of days, one of the lanterns and—"

"I get the picture." Sliding his hand down the length of his ponytail, he squeezed the excess water from his hair. "These people are going to need a lot more than what we had to give them."

"Do you suppose Murdock could arrange to have some supplies brought to Utuado?"

"Hell, what do you think Murdock is, a damned missionary?" When she glared at him, he shook his head. "Don't look at me that way."

"When we contact Murdock about our boat back to the United States, couldn't we ask him to send some supplies to these villagers?"

"Maybe."

Satisfied with his reply, Rorie sat down on the bank, removed her shoes and socks and stepped into the stream. Hawk strapped on his holster and sat down, watching her while she bathed. He would have preferred for her to strip down to her skin, but even fully clothed, she put on quite a show as she washed the blood and dirt from her face and arms and legs. When he became aroused to the point of being tempted to drag her out of the stream and take her hard and fast, Hawk glanced up at the night sky. He couldn't go on this way much longer, wanting this woman so desperately.

When Rorie finished cleaning herself and her clothes the best she could without any soap, she dragged herself up onto the bank and sat down beside Hawk. She shivered when the cool night breeze touched her wet flesh.

Taking her by the shoulders, Hawk turned her so that her back faced him. Then he grabbed her long, wet braid and unplaited it, as he'd done the night before last in the Cabo Verde hotel basement.

She had beautiful hair. Hair the color of sunshine. Warm and golden. He threaded his fingers through the long, wet strands.

"You're a natural blonde, aren't you?" Hawk had voiced

a statement more than a question. "Your brother was blond, too. He and his wife were exact opposites."

Rorie whirled around excitedly and looked at Hawk. "You knew Peter and Cipriana? Why didn't you tell me that you—"

"I didn't know them." Damn his big mouth! Why had he mentioned her brother and sister-in-law? Where was his mind?

Obviously his mind had shifted below his belt and was concentrating on one thing—how much he wanted to make love to Rorie. Beautiful Rorie, with a heart as beautiful as her lovely face and voluptuous body.

"But you said—"

"I saw them once, when I was here in San Miguel," Hawk explained. "Someone told me who they were." He wasn't going to out and out lie to Rorie, but he couldn't—he wouldn't—tell her the truth. Not now. Not ever. "The gorgeous young princess, the apple of her father's eye, had rejected her father and given up her religion for the love of a poor, young missionary from America."

"They were deeply in love," Rorie said. "After Frankie was born, my parents begged them to come to the United States. But Peter was determined to stay on and finish the five years of mission work he had pledged to the church."

"Keeping his pledge to the church cost him and his wife their lives."

"You're wrong." Rorie jumped up from the ground. "Emilio Santos and his renegades took Peter's and Cipriana's lives, not Peter's devotion to his calling."

Hawk stood, walked over to her and grasped her shoulders, drawing her damp body back against his. She shivered. Lowering his head, he nuzzled her neck.

"You're right, honey." Hawk eased his arms around her, crossing them over her belly. "Your brother did what he thought was right. It wasn't his fault that he couldn't save himself and his wife. Sometimes life has no rhyme or reason and a man has to accept the fact that he's powerless to stop the actions of a madman."

She turned in his arms, her eyes questioning him. "Hawk?"

He grasped her hand and tugged her along with him as he walked toward the jeep. "Come on. We need to get a little rest, if we're going to head out to the mission in the morning."

"I could sleep for a week," Rorie said.

He glanced at his watch. "I can give you about four hours. We should leave at daybreak, but if you're too tired, we—"

"Wake me when you're ready to leave."

He nodded. "I imagine there's room enough for you to sleep in the back of the jeep since you cleaned out most of our provisions."

"Where will you sleep?" she asked, glancing away quickly so that he wouldn't get a glimpse of her expressive face.

"I'll sleep beside the jeep, out under the stars."

"Won't you be chilly?"

"Didn't you leave us at least one blanket?"

"I didn't think about it," she admitted. "I thought that with the sleeping bag, we could open it up and it would be big enough to use as cover for both of us, if we needed it."

"Then it looks like I'll just have to share the sleeping bag with you."

"Now, Hawk, we aren't going to—"

He placed his finger over her mouth. "I'm too tired to jump you tonight, honey. I promise."

The declaration was a lie. He knew it. And she knew it. But Rorie found a level grassy spot on the left side of the jeep and spread out the open sleeping bag. She removed her holster, lay down and placed the gun beside her. She pulled the sleeping bag up to her waist. Hawk followed, repeating her actions and placing his holster to the right of his head. He looked up at the stars. Within a couple of minutes, he realized that Rorie was staring at him.

"Yeah? What is it?" he asked.

"You were really wonderful tonight. You know that, don't you?"

"What the hel— What are you talking about?" He rolled over onto his side and glared at her in the semidarkness.

"I'm talking about the way you helped me with the children and the burn victims. The way you treated Berto with the respect due a village elder. And you probably saved two men's lives by removing the bullets from their bodies.''

"I just did what had to be done.'' Hawk cleared his throat as he rolled over onto his back.

"You didn't even yell at me for giving away nearly all our provisions.'' She snuggled up to Hawk's side.

"I should have,'' he grumbled. "Something could happen and we might need those supplies. You won't like it if we wind up eating bugs.''

"You know what? You're a good man, Gabriel Hawk.'' She laid her hand on his chest. "You're a very good man.''

He stilled instantly; even his heart stopped beating for a split second. Rorie thought he was a good man. If she knew the truth—if she knew that he had been considered a member of Emilio Santos's renegade army when they executed Peter and Cipriana Dean—she wouldn't think he was a good man. She'd know him for what he was.

He flung her hand off his chest and turned his back to her. "I'm not a good man. I'm a bad man. One of the baddest of the bad.''

A denial lodged in her throat. *No, you aren't a bad man*, she wanted to tell him. *You just pretend you are.* But she remained silent.

She heard Elizabeth Landry's voice inside her head. *He is a man tormented by demons. He is plagued by a past he cannot undo. I sense a true goodness in you. A goodness that can cleanse Gabriel's soul.*

What demons tormented him? Rorie wondered. What was so terrible about his past that it plagued him?

And was Elizabeth right about her? Did she truly possess the power to cleanse Gabriel Hawk's soul?

Hawk removed the rebel flag from the jeep before they left Utuado shortly after dawn. Berto and several of the villagers waved a sad, silent farewell as Hawk drove out onto the paved roadway leading up and into the deep forests of La Montana Grande. With tears lodged in her throat, Rorie turned to look back at the devastated little town.

The road ahead followed the path of the mountain stream

in which Rorie and Hawk had bathed the night before. Winding around and around, but forever upward toward the cloud-covered peaks, the narrow one-lane highway cut a path through the pristine beauty of the verdant forest.

Rorie had never forgotten how enchanted she had been with the glorious sights on her trip up to the Blessed Virgin Mission with Peter four years ago. Despite the circumstances and the impending danger, she was no less enchanted on this return trip.

Occasionally she caught a glimpse of a waterfall spilling into a lush, green glade. Yellow-flowering nightshade combined with the other heavy foliage to create the dense underbrush. The woody vines of the lianas grew from their deep ground roots and wrapped themselves around the giant bamboos and other towering trees.

"It looks like paradise, doesn't it?" Hawk said. "But that forest can be deadly for anyone who doesn't know it."

"Did your assignment here in San Miguel take you into the forest?" Rorie asked.

"My assignment took me all over San Miguel, even into the forest."

"Then if we had to go off the road and into the forest, you'd be able to take care of us and still get us to the mission, wouldn't you?"

"Let's hope that won't be necessary."

For the first thirty minutes, their journey up the mountain seemed like a pleasure trip. They limited their conversation to shared observations of the surrounding terrain, refraining from discussing more serious subjects and ruining the sense of being lost in Eden.

Hawk rounded a bend in the road. To the left lay the steep mountainside, lush with life. To the right a deep chasm dropped two hundred feet, promising certain death.

Voices—at least a dozen—talking and laughing, blended together with the rumble of vehicles. The sounds echoed from high above them, on an upper terrace of the roadway. Hawk stopped the jeep and listened. Snapping around in her seat, Rorie stared at him, questioning him silently. He placed his index finger over his lips. She nodded.

The noise grew louder. Whoever they were, they were

coming down the mountain, heading straight for Hawk and Rorie.

Hawk searched the roadside, seeking an escape route. There was nowhere to run. Nowhere to hide. Suddenly he remembered a trail that led into the forest. He'd seen it about a mile back down the mountain. But there was no place to turn the jeep. He shifted the gears into reverse, looked over his shoulder and guided the jeep backward, down the winding mountain road.

Glancing behind, Rorie uttered a silent prayer for their safety, then looked forward, up the road, keeping watch for whoever was marching toward them. Who were they, she wondered, with those loud voices and roaring vehicles? Were they members of Santos's renegades? Or were they Lazaros's rebel soldiers? Or could they be the king's men—a troop he'd sent to the Blessed Virgin Mission to get Frankie?

When Hawk reached a section of roadway with a wider shoulder that didn't immediately reach straight up the mountain or plunge a hundred feet on the other side, he whipped the jeep around and sped down the highway.

"Hold on, honey," he said. "We're going off the road and onto that trail over there." He nodded toward a narrow dirt path leading straight into the forest. "And say a prayer that those guys are making too much noise to have heard our jeep."

Hawk drove off the road and onto the bumpy trail. They jostled up and down as the tires rolled over deep ruts and large rocks. The farther they went into the forest, the narrower the uphill dirt path became and the thicker the vegetation. Low tree branches and shrubbery limbs beat against the jeep's sides, several ripping across Hawk's and Rorie's shoulders.

Abruptly, the path ended at the edge of a stream. Hawk eased his foot down on the brake pedal as the jeep dived headlong into the shallow creek bed. Rorie toppled forward. Throwing up her hands against the windshield to brace herself, she avoided being tossed out.

Hawk glanced at her. "Are you all right?"

She gulped in huge swallows of air. "I think so."

He threw the gears into reverse and backed up several feet, out of the stream and onto dry land. "Just sit still and be quiet," he told Rorie. "All we can do is wait and listen. And hope our noisy mountain climbers don't come in our direction."

The minutes dragged by slowly. Rorie tried not to look at her watch, but when she heard the sound of vehicles and trampling feet out on the highway, she checked the time. Eight minutes since Hawk had hidden them away.

Her heartbeat roared in her ears like a jet engine. Rubbing her sweaty palms together, she glanced at Hawk. He seemed oblivious to her, his attention focused totally on listening to the sounds of their enemy. She knew that whoever they were, the men on the highway were definitely not their friends.

"Stay here." Hawk eased out of the jeep.

"Where are you going?" She reached across the driver's seat, grabbing for Hawk.

"Listen," he said. "Can you hear? They've stopped and gotten out of their trucks and jeeps. They aren't going any farther down the mountain."

"So? What can you do?"

"I'm going to check out the situation and find out whether or not they heard our jeep and are looking for us." He removed the rifle from under the seat, where he'd placed it this morning. "Keep your pistol ready, just in case."

"Hawk, don't leave me."

"You'll be all right. I won't be long."

Not again! she wanted to scream. But she remained silent as Hawk strapped the rifle across his back and headed down the narrow path that led to the road. She refused to look at her watch. No matter if two minutes or twenty passed, each second would seem like an hour.

She prayed for Hawk's safety. Prayed for the success of their mission. Prayed that she would find the strength and courage to save Hawk and Frankie, if that time ever came. And prayed that she did possess the kind of goodness that could cleanse Gabriel Hawk's soul.

Rorie's eyelids flew open as her mouth gasped in a silent cry, as Hawk jumped back into the jeep.

"It's all right," he said. "They've only made a pit stop to eat. They're not venturing far off the road."

"Who are they?" Rorie asked.

"Rebels. Their jeeps are flying Lazaro's flag."

"I thought you said that this was Santos's territory."

"Lazaro's troops are everywhere, fighting both King Julio's army and Santos's renegades."

"If those are Lazaro's men, why are we still hiding?" Rorie grabbed Hawk's arm. "We have a pass signed by the general that gives us permission to go anywhere on San Miguel."

"If we show ourselves now and word gets back to Lazaro, then he'll know where we're headed. The only civilization farther up La Montana Grande is the Catholic mission."

"You're right." Rorie sank into her seat. "I wasn't thinking."

"Besides, there's always a chance that those are Santos's men. They've been known to fly Lazaro's rebel flag whenever it suits their purposes."

The rebel troops headed out after a leisurely hour's break. By the time Hawk backed the jeep out of the forest and onto the highway, Rorie's patience was near the breaking point. She was beginning to wonder what else could possibly happen to delay their journey to the mission.

"Sit back and relax," Hawk told her. "We should be at the mission by noon."

An hour later, Hawk had to eat his words. He cursed a blue streak when he saw that the bridge crossing the mountain gorge had been destroyed. The handiwork of Lazaro's troops? Or Santos's renegades?

"Now we know what those rebel troops were doing up here," Hawk said. "They were blowing up this bridge."

"Oh, dear Lord." Rorie stood straight and stared at the open chasm between the two halves of the highway.

Hawk slammed his fist down on the top of the dashboard. "Dammit! Another hour and we would have been at the mission."

"Isn't there any other way to reach the mission?" Rorie looked at him, a glimmer of hope in her eyes.

"There's always another way," he said. "But no other direct route." He reached under the seat.

"What's that?"

"A map. The one Murdock gave me before we left La

Vega.'' He opened it and spread it out across the steering wheel.

Leaning over toward Hawk, she glanced at the map. ''It's hand drawn,'' she said.

''Yes, it is,'' was his only reply to her comment. He pointed to a spot on the map. ''This is where we are.'' He studied the markings. ''Looks like there's only two ways to get to the mission from here, now that crossing this bridge isn't an option.''

''What are the two ways?'' Rorie clasped his shoulder.

He turned and faced her. ''On foot, through the forest.''

''Or?''

''Or we take the old road up to the mission.''

''What old road?''

Hawk pointed to the line on the map. ''The old road that was cut out of the jungle over two hundred years ago when the mission was first built.''

Tears misted Rorie's eyes. She folded her hands in a prayerful gesture and placed them over her mouth. ''Thank you, God.''

''Don't be too thankful,'' Hawk told her. ''That old road hasn't been used much in the past twenty years, since this paved roadway was put in. It may not even be passable anymore. We could get halfway to the mission and find ourselves in the middle of a jungle.''

''What other choice do we have if we want to go on?''

''None, really,'' he said.

''Then let's find that road.''

Hawk traced the line of the winding roadway with his finger. ''This looks like a damn drunk built the old road. See how it snakes around the mountain, joins another road and then comes up on the back side of the mission? There's no way, even if the road is partly clear, that we'll make the mission before night.''

''Are you saying that a trip, that would take us an hour on the highway, is going to take all day on the old road?''

''Probably. My guess is we'll have to travel at a snail's pace and get out from time to time to clear the way.''

''You're trying to tell me that it could be another day before we reach Frankie, aren't you?''

"I'm trying to tell you—" He hesitated, realizing there was no point in telling her what he suspected.

He was only guessing. He couldn't be sure. But his gut instincts told him that someone else knew Prince Francisco was at the Blessed Virgin Mission and also knew that Rorie Dean was en route to get him and take him with her back to America. Someone had told either Lazaro or Santos where the boy was being hidden. Had that someone wanted to slow down his and Rorie's rescue mission until they could reach the mission themselves? Or did they already have Frankie and simply wanted to delay being found out?

But who could have revealed Frankie's location? No one knew, except King Julio, Nina, Captain García and Murdock.

"What are you trying to tell me?" Rorie jerked on Hawk's shirtsleeve.

"I'm trying to tell you that you might have to spend another night out under the stars sharing a sleeping bag with me."

Chapter 11

Hawk heard a waterfall in the distance. From the sound, he deducted that it wasn't very far away—perhaps no more than thirty-five or forty feet off the road.

Evening shadows fell across the overgrown dirt trail, which had become little more than a wide path through the forest. When night fell, it would become more and more difficult to detect the obstacles blocking their trail up the mountain.

As he had suspected, the old road to the mission was nearly impassable in places where the jungle had reclaimed the land. The low-growing vegetation had been easy enough to drive over. But where bushes and saplings had sprung up, he had used the machete to cut through the heavy growth, while Rorie eased the jeep along behind him at a snail's pace. The biggest obstacle they'd encountered, up to this point, had been a huge downed tree, obviously severed by a long-ago lightning strike. Finding it useless to try to move the heavy, rotting pine, he had cleared enough brush along the roadside to drive around the tree. Hours had slipped by as they made their way, mile by mile, sometimes foot by foot, upward into the cloud-covered forest.

"We're going to stop for the night," Hawk said.

"No! Please, let's go on. I can make it a little farther."
Grasping his shirtsleeve, Rorie looked at him pleadingly.
"We can't be that far from the mission. We've been traveling
all day."

"The mission could be a mile away or it could be ten,"
he told her. "It doesn't matter. You can't go on. You're exhausted."

She opened her mouth to protest. Hawk pulled the jeep to
a halt, snapped his head around and glared at her. His hard
look silenced her immediately.

"You're hot and dirty and hungry and thirsty and probably
dying to...to relieve yourself." He cleared his throat. "We've
stopped only once all day since we detoured off on this old
road, and that was for less than fifteen minutes."

"We could stop for a few minutes and then go on. Really,
Hawk, I can make it."

"Well, I can't. In another hour it'll be too dark to see a
foot in front of us and there's no telling what we could run
into in the darkness. Even with the headlights to guide us,
too many dangers would be easy to miss." He backed the
jeep off the road and over some heavy underbrush.

"Go do whatever you need to do." He nodded behind him
at the thicket of greenery. "Don't go very far. Stay as close
as possible and hurry back." Hawk jumped out of the jeep
and rounded the hood.

Not protesting in any way, Rorie nodded agreement. When
she started to step down, Hawk caught her around the waist
and lifted her out of the jeep, then set her on her feet and
released her quickly. She scurried away from him and into
the thicket. He slung the rifle over his shoulder and lifted the
machete in his hand. Pushing through as much of the vines
and branches as would give way to the invasion of his big
body, Hawk headed toward the sound of a waterfall. Several
yards off the road, the sound grew louder and the vegetation
denser. He hacked his way toward the sound and within
minutes came upon a breathtaking sight.

A watery deluge flowed down the mountain, dropping off
in a pure white shower as it cascaded into a secluded glade
draped with lianas and ferns. Rippling over moss-coated rocks
and rounded boulders, the teeming flow spilled over into a

pond. The excess water continued its journey, splashing over the rocky streambed that spiraled ever downward toward the Rio Azul, on the windward side of San Miguel.

Flame-orange flowers of the lobster-claw heliconia plant arched above the pond. Hawk wondered if this spot had changed any since the first Spanish conquerors had set foot on the island nearly five hundred years ago. Paradise untouched. Eden revisited.

The dying sunlight filtered through the trees and dense forest growth, dappling the greenery with white gold and the crystal-clear pool with a soft shimmer.

Hawk met Rorie back at the jeep and together they unloaded their meager food supply and carried the sack to the waterfall. She stood perfectly still and gazed at the incredible scene.

"It's as if we've gone back in time," she said. "As if we've walked straight into the middle of another century, maybe even a different millenium."

"I agree it's a beautiful sight."

Hawk looked directly at Rorie, scanning her from head to toe as she stood at the edge of the pond. Filtered sunlight touched her hair with tiny white-gold fingers and slid down her body, caressing it with wavering glimmers. *La dama dorado.* Golden lady. As awe-inspiring as the secluded waterfall, the enticing pool and the emerald canopy of life that surrounded them, Aurora Dean was woman in all her glory.

Hawk's body responded as it always did when he allowed his mind to dwell on thoughts of Rorie.

"We don't have much time to waste on sight-seeing." His voice was harsher than he'd intended. "We don't have a lot of daylight left, so we need to eat and bathe before it gets pitch-black."

"Can't we use the lanterns or the flashlights?" she asked. "Or you could build a fire." Realization dawned on her before Hawk could reply. "No, of course not. What was I thinking? Any kind of light could be seen and give us away."

"Come on." He motioned for her to follow him. "We need to cover the jeep and then take advantage of the remaining light."

Using limbs from nearby trees and shrubs, Rorie helped

Hawk camouflage the front of the jeep, which was partially visible from the road. He wished he could gather wood and build a fire for Rorie. But he didn't dare take any chances—not where Emilio Santos was concerned. The renegade leader and most of his troops might be far away, but a roaming band of cutthroats could be heading for the mission. Or they might already be there. Hawk wanted to believe that Santos would honor the sanctity of the mission, the way Lazaro and King Julio did, but he figured the odds were against it.

"I'll spread out the sleeping bag in the back of the jeep," he said. "You get us some fresh water and open a couple of those delicious dinners Murdock packed for us."

"Did anyone ever tell you that you have a warped sense of humor?" Placing her hands on her hips, she glowered at Hawk. "You can eat those army rations, if you want to. I think I'll make a meal of the fruit we have left."

They ate hurriedly, aware that daylight was fading fast. Rorie shared the papaya and bananas with Hawk, but refused to even taste the brown lump he held out on his fork for her to sample.

"You want to bathe first?" he asked. "Or do you want to stand guard and let me go first?"

"'Stand guard'? Do you think that's necessary?"

"We're in the middle of a jungle filled with snakes. And you never know when the descendants of old King Rodolfo's jaguars might be prowling around." Hawk grasped her wrist. "I don't think we have to worry about any of Santos's troops, but there's always a chance that a small band of them could be close by."

"I understand. I'll bathe as quickly as I can."

"Feel free to undress and take a real bath," he said. "I promise to keep my back to you and not peek."

"Can I trust you?" she asked, half seriously, half jokingly.

"If you can't trust me, who can you trust?" He unstrapped her shoulder holster and removed it. When she stared at him with her blue, blue eyes, he held his breath for a split second, then swatted her on the behind and laughed. "Get a move on. I don't want to bathe in the dark."

Hawk found himself a large, smooth rock to sit on. With

his back to the pond, he crossed his arms over his chest and looked straight up, through the towering trees dripping with heavy vines. An hour, perhaps less, of daylight remained.

The water splashed when Rorie entered the pond. Hawk envisioned her naked body.

He listened to sounds of the evening in the jungle, a mixed chorus of birds and insects and the distinct song of the tiny coqui, an island frog only an inch long.

After hurriedly unbraiding her hair, Rorie plunged deeper into the pond and swam across its narrow width. Finding a shallow spot near the opposite bank, she dipped into the cool, refreshing water and scrubbed her face and body with her hands. As the grime and perspiration washed away, her skin tingled from the brisk rubbing.

Swimming back toward the bank, she looked up and saw Hawk's broad back. True to his word, he didn't turn around when she rose from the pond and stepped onto the grass. She slipped into her slacks and shirt, then picked up her bra, panties and socks and dunked them at the water's edge.

"You can turn around now," she called out over her shoulder as she wrung out her underwear.

Hawk walked over to her and hung Rorie's holster over her shoulder. "Now it's your turn to guard the camp, while I take my bath."

"All right." She gazed up into his dark eyes—such a deep, pure brown that they appeared almost black. He was close—close enough for her to feel his breath.

He wrapped his arm around her waist and hauled her up against him. Her lips parted. He lowered his head, covered her mouth and slid his tongue inside. She melted in his arms, her limbs softening. She dropped her underwear to the ground.

While he ravaged her mouth, he speared his fingers through her long, wet hair and grasped her head. Holding it firmly, he urged her into the kiss, seeking a response. Rising on tiptoe, she twined her arms around his neck and pressed her breasts into his chest. Hawk groaned. She moved her tongue from side to side, encountering his tongue with her movements. He retreated, then flicked her lips with the tip of his tongue, encouraging her to respond. Timidly, she entered his mouth and slowly explored the interior. He sucked tenderly. Rorie shivered. Involuntarily, she rubbed her lower body against his.

Breaking the kiss, Hawk grabbed her shoulders and pushed her away from him. They both breathed raggedly, as if they'd been running.

"I'd better take my bath now," he said.

"Yes, you'd better." Her cheeks flushed with warmth and her body quivered with arousal.

"Keep your back turned." He grinned. "And don't let me catch you peeking."

"It'll be difficult not to watch you strip, but I'll try to control myself." She laughed, wanting desperately to imitate his lighthearted banter.

But if she was honest with herself, she would have to admit that she was curious about Hawk's body. Although she'd seen him in nothing more than brief swim trunks and felt his naked body hovering near her in the darkness, she could only imagine how magnificent he was, completely unclothed.

She reached down, picked up her wet undergarments and bundled them together. Forcing a smile to her lips, she nodded to Hawk and walked past him.

He sat down on the bank, removed his shoes and socks and then looked across the clearing to where Rorie had taken her perch on the same rock where he'd kept watch. More than anything, he wanted to tear her damp clothes off her body and drag her into the pond with him. Would it be so wrong to make love to Rorie? To take his pleasure in her soft, sweet body?

After placing his rifle and holster on the bank, he removed his clothes and walked into the pond. He swam to the deepest part of the lagoon and dived beneath the water. The moment he sprang from the depths, he heard Rorie calling his name.

"Hawk. Hawk!"

Shaking nervously, her eyes round with fear, Rorie backed toward the pool. Hawk trod water for a couple of seconds. Then he heard it—the loud, deep roar of a marauding cat. A big cat. And the only big cats on San Miguel were the descendants of old King Rodolfo's black jaguars.

"Don't panic, Rorie," he called out to her. "He's close by, but he's probably in a tree."

Hawk rose from the pond, totally naked, water falling from his body in rivulets. He reached down to the ground and lifted his rifle, then slid his arm around Rorie and drew her back up against his hard, wet body. She gasped.

"I want you to get behind me," he said.

She obeyed his command instantly, allowing him to shove her behind him. The dark shadows of twilight waved around them like eerie gray phantoms. The animal cried out again. Rorie trembled. Hawk focused on the direction of the sound. To the right. On higher ground. But close. Very close.

"Is it a jaguar?" Rorie whispered.

"Yeah, that would be my guess."

The leaves rustled. Rorie gasped. Hawk lowered the rifle and pointed the bolt-action Ruger. Less than twenty feet from them, a large black cat stalked out of the jungle and into the clearing. With gleaming golden eyes, the beast glared at them. Hawk aimed the rifle directly at the jaguar. The moment his finger touched the trigger, Rorie knocked the weapon sideways.

"What the hell are you doing?" he whispered in a growling hiss.

"You aren't going to kill it, are you?"

"That was my plan."

"Please, don't kill it unless you have to." Rorie laid her hand on Hawk's back.

"What do you want me to do, give him a chance to attack us?"

"Maybe he won't attack us. Maybe he's just curious. Or maybe he came to the pond for a drink."

Hawk shrugged her hand off his back and aimed the rifle. Why should he listen to Rorie?

"Please, give him a chance." She held her breath.

As if considering his options, the big cat moved forward, looked around tentatively, then turned and ambled back into the jungle from which he'd come.

Rorie let out the breath she'd been holding. Hawk lowered the rifle. Why did I hesitate? he wondered.

Momentarily oblivious to his nakedness, Rorie whirled

around Hawk, grabbed his face and kissed him squarely on the mouth. "Thank you for not shooting him. See? I was right. He was just curious."

"Dammit, woman, I won't be able to sleep soundly tonight knowing that animal is out there. Just because he went away peacefully, doesn't mean he won't come back."

"He won't be back. I think that mean look you gave him scared him away."

"You're crazy, honey. One of these days, that soft heart of yours is going to be the death of me."

Rorie suddenly realized that Hawk was stark naked. She glanced upward, trying to avoid taking an inventory of his physical assets.

He slung the rifle strap over his shoulder, reached down and picked up his clothes, boots and shoulder holster and shoved them into Rorie's arms.

"What—"

Before she could finish her sentence, he swooped her up in his arms and silenced her with a kiss.

When he ended the kiss, she looked straight into his eyes. Dark, smoldering eyes. "Hawk, what—what are you doing?"

"I'm taking you back to the jeep." He carried her away from the pond and through the clearing he'd cut in the thicket.

"Couldn't you put on your clothes first?"

"I can do that later," he said.

When they reached the jeep, he eased the rifle down on the open sleeping bag, then lifted Rorie onto the tailgate.

"I feel very uncomfortable with you being undressed." She held out his clothes, boots and holster.

"I'll remedy that problem right now."

He accepted the items she offered him, then tossed his clothes into the jeep and laid the holster on the edge of the sleeping bag.

Grasping her shirt, he undid the top button. She stared down at his hands, brown and rough against the smooth whiteness of her skin.

"What—what are you—"

"I'm going to make you more comfortable."

"But I didn't mean for you to... I wanted you to put on your clothes, not take mine off."

"Since I'm going to have to stay half-awake all night just in case our visitor returns, don't you think you owe me something for my trouble?"

He undid another button. She slapped at his hand. He undid a third and then a fourth button. Rorie tensed. He jerked the shirt loose from her khaki pants and spread it open to expose her naked breasts. Her breathing quickened. She made tiny gasping noises as she sucked in quick gulps of air.

Hawk let out a long, low sigh. "You don't know how much I've wanted to look at your breasts." He lifted them in his hands, weighing their fullness. "And how much I've wanted to touch them."

His big hands encompassed her, kneading gently. His touch was hot, his palms sandpaper-coarse against her tender skin. She wanted to tell him to stop, that he shouldn't be touching her like this. But here in the forest, in an Eden unspoiled by civilization, Rorie felt the primitive urges of desire spring to life inside her.

She sat perfectly still, except for the undulating movements of her chest as she struggled to breathe. She allowed Hawk to remove her shirt and toss it into the jeep. He spread his hands across the tops of her shoulders and shoved her backward. When her heels raked over the edge of the tailgate, he reached up and unfastened her pants.

"Hawk, please..." Please what? Please, don't do this to me. Or please, don't stop. She was uncertain why she was pleading with him.

"I'm going to please you. I promise."

He unzipped her pants and tugged them down around her hips. Sliding his hand beneath her buttocks, he lifted her enough to free her pants and then pulled them down her legs and over her ankles. He tossed her pants on top of her shirt.

When he crawled up in the jeep beside her, she backed away from him as far as she could. Fear of the unknown, no matter how tempting that unknown might be, claimed her completely.

Sensing her fear, Hawk knew he had to soothe her before he could pleasure her. Before he could teach her to pleasure him. God knew, he had tried to keep his hands off her. He'd fought a valiant fight to preserve her innocence. But he couldn't fight both himself and the desire he saw in her eyes. She needed him just as much as he needed her, whether or not she realized what that need was.

If he buried himself deep in her body, the way he longed to do, she would be his forever. But he couldn't offer her the "forever" she would expect. All he could give her was this one night. He could and would make love to her, but he wouldn't make her his completely. He would take what he needed and give her what she needed, but he would leave her her most prized possession.

"I'm not going to hurt you," he promised. "I want to kiss you and touch you. That's all I'm asking. Just let me show you what it can be like to have a man worship every inch of your body."

"Hawk, I—"

He ran the tip of his finger from her chin to her navel. She shuddered. He ran his finger upward, then over her breast and flicked one beaded nipple. She drew in a raspy breath.

"You like that, don't you? You like the way my touch sends quivers through your body."

She reached out and circled his tiny male nipple with her index finger. Smiling, Hawk sighed.

When he pulled her into his arms, she resisted momentarily, then succumbed to the seduction of desire the instant her aching breasts encountered his muscular chest.

His mouth devoured hers as he pressed her down into the jeep's bed and straddled her hips. She tried to protest when she felt the heavy weight of his body, but he relieved some of the pressure by lifting his chest and placing his hands on either side of her shoulders. He lowered his sex until it nestled in the thatch of golden hair at the apex of her thighs. Instinct guided her movements as she lifted her hips to meet him.

For a couple of seconds he felt as if he was going to explode. *I can do this. I can do this.* He silently repeated the phrase again and again, until the words became a litany.

Easing his body alongside hers, he broke the kiss, then lowered his head to one breast and lifted his hand to the other. With gentle, repetitive strokes of his tongue, he laved one nipple, while he pinched the other between his thumb and forefinger. He alternated attentions from one breast to the other, until Rorie writhed beneath him, her body begging for release.

"My breasts ache," she told him. "And I'm throbbing. I'm..."

He grabbed her hand and dragged it down her body, pushing it against her mound. "Is this where you're throbbing, Rorie? Is this where you're hurting the most?"

On a timid, hushed little breath, she mumbled, "Yes."

"Then let me take away the hurt."

Darkness surrounded them. The last glimmering glow of twilight silhouetted their faces as they gazed at each other.

"Please," she whimpered. "Please."

Hawk kissed and licked a hot, damp trail from her breasts to her navel. He spread her thighs apart, lifted her legs over his shoulders and kissed her inner thighs. When he nuzzled her intimately, she moaned. When his mouth covered her, she thrust her fist into her mouth to muffle her cry. She squirmed, trying to free herself, afraid of the way he made her feel. But he held her hips in his big hands and made love to her with his lips and tongue. Stroking. Sucking. Pressing.

Rorie writhed under his masterful attentions, lost to reality; no longer thinking, only feeling. Ever so slowly, her body coiled tighter and tighter. Hawk increased the tempo and the pressure of his caresses as she dripped with passion. When he sensed she was on the brink, he added just the right amount of quick, hard pressure, pushing her over the precipice and headlong into an earth-shattering release.

When he pulled her trembling body into his arms, she clung to him, weeping as the last echoes of her fulfillment rippled over her nerve endings.

"Gabriel." She whispered his name against his chest.

He wanted to take her, thrust into her with powerful force and ease his agony.

"It's all right, Rorie. It's all right." He petted her, rubbing her back, stroking her hair. "I wanted to be the first man to give you pleasure."

"I never dreamed something like that could be so...so very wonderful." She wrapped her arm across his chest.

"I'm glad I made it wonderful for you." He kissed the top of her head.

She lifted her head from his chest and searched his face in the darkness. "But you didn't... I mean you must need—"

He grabbed her hand and urged it down his body. She followed his lead as he guided her hand toward his arousal and began a slow, steady movement. When she picked up the rhythm, he removed his hand and allowed her to take over the task completely.

"Am I doing it right?" she asked, knowing that if they hadn't been shrouded in darkness, she might not have been able to touch him so intimately.

The growl started deep in his chest, rose up to his throat and then erupted from his mouth. "Yes!" His body jerked once, twice. He groaned louder, his cry the muted roar of a male animal in the throes of release.

Hawk drew Rorie into his arms and kissed her, while the aftershocks of fulfillment spiraled through his body. He eased her onto the tailgate, then lifted the rifle and slipped the strap over his shoulder. He picked her up and took her back to the pond.

Leaving the rifle within reach on the bank, he carried her into the water. He bathed her and then himself.

She clung to him, feeling as if she were almost a part of him. "Oh, Gabriel. Gabriel!" She surrendered completely, giving herself over to him.

And when he brought her back to the jeep, she cuddled in his arms, too happy and content to worry about what the morning would bring.

Chapter 12

Rorie awoke alone in the jeep. She rubbed her eyes and stretched. Suddenly realizing she was naked, she crossed her arms over her breasts and clasped her elbows. Memories of last night flooded her mind. Gabriel's lips on hers. His hands and mouth on her body, giving her the ultimate pleasure. And her hand circling him.

Sighing as she remembered the way his tender, intimate loving had made her feel, Rorie sat up quickly and looked for him. A hundred jumbled thoughts rioted in her mind. Emotions of various kinds warred within her. She had allowed Gabriel intimacies that should have been reserved for her husband. She had given herself over completely to his desires, letting him do with her as he wanted. If he had asked for more, she would have given it to him. She would have given him everything.

She should feel remorse and shame. But she didn't. There had been nothing ugly or dirty or evil about what she and Gabriel had shared. The experience had been the most beautiful and profound moment of her life.

But how did Gabriel Hawk feel about what had happened?

Somehow she doubted that their lovemaking held the same significance for him as it did for her.

Glancing around, Rorie noticed her boots sitting on the tailgate beside her folded clothes. Morning sunlight filtered through the forest's jade canopy. She checked her watch. Seven-thirty. Why had he let her sleep so late? They should have resumed their trek up the mountain at dawn.

She dressed hurriedly, groaning when she discovered her bra and panties were still slightly damp. Just as she stuffed her shirt into her pants and pulled up the zipper, Hawk approached the jeep. He held two metal cups in his hands. Rorie slid off the open tailgate and met him.

He offered her one of the cups. "Sorry it's not hot coffee. Fresh water will have to do."

"Thanks. Fresh water sounds great." She took the cup from him, deliberately letting her fingers brush across his.

When he looked at her, she smiled. He returned her smile. She had slept in his arms all night, her naked body nestled against his. He had rested in a semiawake-semiasleep state. His instincts had warned him to be on guard for the jaguar, for unexpected human intruders—and for a resurgence of passion. Realizing that she was his for the taking had made it all the more difficult not to make love to her again—fully and completely.

No woman had ever held any power over him. No woman had ever been a fever in his blood. He sure as hell wasn't going to let some Goody-Two-Shoes virgin wrap him around her little finger and make him vulnerable.

"Sleep well?" he asked.

"Like a log." She took a sip of the cool water. "Why did you let me sleep so long? We should have gotten an earlier start."

"We both needed the rest." He finished his cup of water. "There's one melon left. Want to split it for breakfast?"

"Sure."

Walking past her, he leaned over into the jeep, pulled out their ration bag and rummaged in it. He retrieved the lone melon and held it up as if it were a trophy.

Rorie sensed the strain between them. She wondered if Gabriel felt as awkward as she did. Probably not. After all, what had happened last night was hardly a new experience for him, even if it had been for her. She didn't like to think about how many other women he had given the same shattering ecstasy. Or about how many women had given him far more than she had.

Rorie heard the melon split open and turned to see Gabriel holding the machete in his hand and the ripe fruit lying on the ground. She stared at Hawk. He looked so big and powerful and almost savage in his wrinkled fatigues, with his long, black ponytail and his four days' growth of dark stubble.

He cocked his head slightly, as if listening for the sound of predators. Dappled sunlight hit the gold ring in his left ear. When he lifted his ponytail and flung it over his shoulder, Rorie stared at the coiled-cobra tattoo on his left hand. Her stomach tightened into knots. Dear Lord, this savage-looking man was the real predator. Dangerous and deadly. And yet every instinct within her cried out that she could trust him. That he would never harm her. That to others he might be a predator, but to her he was a protector.

Gabriel stuck the machete into a melon half, lifted it and held it out to her. She slid the fruit off the big knife and brought it to her mouth. While nibbling on the juicy flesh, she watched Gabriel as he speared the other melon half, lifted it to his mouth and bit into it hungrily. He threw the machete into the ground with the expert ease of a man accustomed to handling knives.

Rorie shivered, remembering the vivid sensations of Gabriel feasting on her body. The moist sounds. The musky smells. Her own taste on his lips when he'd kissed her. And the hot, unbearable pleasure.

Heat rose up her neck and flushed her face. She glanced away, not wanting him to realize what she was thinking. She nibbled on the melon, each bite lodging in her throat.

Gabriel tossed the melon rind aside, wiped his hands on his pants and pulled the machete out of the ground. He slid the knife under his seat in the jeep, then turned and looked at Rorie.

"As soon as you...uh...freshen up, we can leave," he said. She nodded her understanding, took a couple more bites out of the melon and then tossed it on the ground. Relieving herself in the seclusion of the nearby thicket and washing her hands and face in the pond took a quick five minutes. When she returned to the jeep, she found that Gabriel had cleared away the camouflage of limbs and was already behind the wheel. The minute she climbed into her seat, he started the engine, but didn't shift the gears.

He glanced at her. She felt his heated gaze. Turn around and face him, she told herself. You can't pretend that what happened between the two of you last night didn't really happen. But she didn't want to face the truth, didn't want to accept the fact that, for him, last night had been nothing special. Instinctively, she knew he was going to say something that would break her heart.

Taking a deep breath, she glanced at him. He reached out and clasped her chin, cradling it in the hollow between his thumb and forefinger.

"There's no need to be embarrassed, honey."

"I can't help the way I feel," she said. "I've never done anything like that before and…and I've never allowed anyone to…to do those things to me."

He squeezed her chin. "Don't make a big deal out of this, okay? It all boils down to one simple thing—I'm a man and you're a woman. We both needed a little relief. So, I gave you pleasure, and you gave me pleasure. That's what happened. That's all that happened."

"That's all that happened." She repeated his words like a trained parrot.

"I admit that you might have lost a little of your innocence, but you didn't lose your virginity. You still have that to give to the lucky guy you marry."

He released her chin, turned around and shifted the gears. When he pulled the jeep onto road, Rorie leaned back against the seat and closed her eyes, covering her tears.

He was right; she hadn't lost her precious virginity. What he didn't know—what he must never find out—was that she had lost something far more valuable. She had lost her heart.

Thirty minutes and only-God-knew-how-few miles later, they came to a crossroads—one path leading upward to the

Blessed Virgin Mission, the other a wide, clear, dirt trail apparently running parallel to the old road, only farther east down the mountainside.

Hawk pulled the jeep to a halt, removed Murdock's map and scanned the area where the two roads met. The cleared pathway led down the mountain to the heart of Santos's main camp, one of the first villages the renegade had conquered—the village where Peter and Cipriana Dean had been executed.

"Where does that road lead?" Rorie asked. "It looks like someone has cleared it recently, doesn't it?"

"It leads to a village about two miles from the limestone cliffs overlooking the southeastern shore of San Miguel. A little place called Mayari."

"Why would anyone have cleared the road from Mayari to the mission?"

"Look, Rorie, you might as well know that Mayari is Emilio Santos's stronghold. It's a remote little village that he secured years ago and has held on to. Besides this road up the mountain, which not too many people know about, there's only one other road into the village and it's guarded day and night."

Glaring at the mountain route to Emilio Santos's camp, Rorie shivered as thoughts of her brother filled her mind. Had Peter and Cipriana died in Mayari? She'd never known the details, had never been told the specifics of their executions. Had Santos buried their bodies in the village? Had he thrown them over the cliffs and into the ocean? Or had he disposed of them in the jungle?

Grasping her forearm, Hawk squeezed gently. She glanced at him and saw the compassion and understanding in his eyes.

"I'm sorry about what happened to your brother and his wife." Hawk tightened his hold on her arm. He wanted to draw her closer, to bare his soul, to tell her the truth and ask her to forgive him. If Rorie could forgive him, then maybe he could finally forgive himself. But would seeking absolution from Peter Dean's sister be asking for the impossible?

Rorie laid her hand over Hawk's. "I wish you had known Peter. He was such a good man. Kind. Caring. Loving." She gazed into Hawk's eyes. "I think you two would have liked each other. Despite Peter's gentle nature, he was a strong, brave man. Like you. And despite your gruff, crude exterior, you possess a good soul, as he did.''

Hawk flung off her hand, hurriedly shifted gears and looked straight ahead—up the recently cleared path to the mission.

"You've got me confused with some imaginary man you've conjured up," he said. "I have nothing in common with Peter Dean. Don't kid yourself, lady. I barely have a soul anymore, and what's left of it sure as hell isn't good.''

Rorie bit down on her bottom lip, as tears lodged in her throat. Poor Hawk. Elizabeth had been right. He was tormented by demons. And those demons had convinced him that they were destroying his soul. Closing her eyes, Rorie said a silent prayer. *Dear Lord, give me the power to cleanse Gabriel Hawk's soul.*

They rode up the mountain in silence. The closer they came to the mission, the more uneasy Hawk felt in his gut. The remainder of the old road had been recently cleared, too, just as the trail down to Mayari had been. Hawk didn't like the looks of this. Not one damn bit. What reason would anyone have had to clear the old road other than to secure a back entrance to the mission?

Not King Julio. Not General Lazaro.

Had Santos sent someone to the mission to search for Frankie Dean? If so, who had tipped him off about the boy's hiding place?

Damn, don't let us arrive too late! Don't let Santos already have the young prince!

Hawk parked the jeep in a clearing within walking distance of the weather-beaten, two-hundred-year old mission. Moss coated the northern walls of the stone structure. Vines spiraled from the ground, clinging to the gray rock, enclosing several of the arched windows.

Hawk double-checked his pistol, then draped the rifle over his back and stepped out of the jeep. Rorie jumped out and met him.

"The doors to the Blessed Virgin Mission are never locked," she said. "We can walk right in."

"That's convenient for us." Should he tell Rorie to prepare

herself for bad news? Or should he wait and hope for a miracle? Maybe Frankie was still in the good sisters' custody.

"I remember exactly where the reverend mother's office is," Rorie told him. "We had tea there, when Peter and I came to visit the mission, shortly after my arrival on San Miguel. Peter believed that despite being of different faiths, we should work with the sisters to provide spiritual guidance to the citizens of San Miguel. During the years Peter lived here, he came to the mission several times."

Hawk kept alert to every sound and movement as they made their way down the rock pathway leading to the huge, wooden entrance doors. Rorie opened the doors with little effort, despite their size and weight. They entered a wide, stone-floored foyer, flanked by two dark, narrow hallways.

Rorie veered to the right. "This way. Reverend mother's office is the first door."

Hawk scanned the dim, damp interior. Silence. Absolute silence. He'd never spent time around churches or convents or holy people of any religion. But he couldn't help wondering if the unnatural silence inside the mission was normal.

When Rorie lifted her hand to knock on the door, Hawk removed his gun from its holster. She glanced over her shoulder and frowned.

"I hardly think you'll need your gun. I can assure you that the reverend mother isn't dangerous."

"I didn't figure she was, but we don't know whether or not she has other visitors," Hawk said. Rorie opened her mouth to speak, but he cut her off short. "Go ahead and knock."

Rorie knocked softly. No response. She knocked harder.

A strong feminine voice responded. "Yes, who's there?"

"Reverend Mother, I'm Rorie Dean. Peter Dean's sister. I'd like to speak to you, please."

Footsteps crossed the wooden floor. The door squeaked as it opened. A small, wrinkled woman with pale, faded hazel eyes stared at Rorie, then glanced behind her and surveyed Hawk.

"Do you remember me, Reverend Mother?" Rorie asked.

"Yes, of course, my dear. Won't you and...and—"

"This is Gabriel Hawk. A friend of mine," Rorie said.

The elderly nun nodded. "Won't you come inside and sit down?"

When they entered the small, cool room, with a large open window overlooking a garden area, Rorie followed the reverend mother and sat down in a chair across from her desk. Hawk stood to the left of Rorie, his back to the wall, as he examined the room. From his vantage point, he had a clear view of the door and the window.

Placing her clasped hands atop her desk, the reverend mother leaned forward. "What can I do for you, Miss Dean?"

Rorie scooted to the edge of her chair. "King Julio told us that he'd sent Prince Francisco to you for safekeeping."

The elderly nun tightened her clasped hands. "Yes, Captain García brought the young prince to us some time ago, and we took great delight in caring for him."

"Reverend Mother, I am Francisco's legal guardian. Peter and Cipriana stated their wishes in their wills." Rorie paused to give the woman a chance to comment. She didn't. "King Julio has agreed for me to take my nephew to the United States." Rorie looked the reverend mother squarely in the eye. The woman didn't bat an eyelash. "I've come to take Francisco with me."

"I see." The reverend mother unfolded her hands, eased back her chair and stood. She walked over to the window and looked out into the garden. "I'm afraid there has been some sort of mix-up, Miss Dean. You see…King Julio sent for the prince several days ago."

"Are you saying that Francisco Dean is no longer at the mission?" Hawk asked.

"I am saying that the boy is no longer under my care."

The nun's gaze met Hawk's and held for a split second. Long enough to convey a message. *Something was wrong.*

"The king sent someone for Frankie several days ago?" Rorie rose from her chair. "But why would he do that? He knows the danger of having Frankie with him. I can't believe he's so selfish that he would put his own grandson's life at risk."

The reverend mother turned and glanced down at the open Bible on her desk. She looked at Rorie. "I'm afraid I do not know the motivation for the king's actions." Absently, she flipped through the pages of the Bible. ''Perhaps, if you consult God's word, you will find the answers you seek, my child.''

The old nun turned the Bible and slid it across her desk in front of Rorie. Grasping the edge of the leather-bound book in her hand, the reverend mother curled all her fingers, except her index finger, which pointed directly at a verse. With her heart beating like a jackhammer, Rorie willed herself to stay calm. She looked down at the holy book and read hurriedly. Opening her mouth in a silent gasp, she exchanged a knowing look with the reverend mother.

''I'm disappointed that King Julio lied to us,'' Rorie said. ''He's made a terrible mistake taking Frankie away. But Hawk and I are going to get my nephew, no matter what we have to do.''

''You have my blessings, Miss Dean.'' The reverend mother held out her hand. ''I will pray for Prince Francisco's safety.''

Rorie grasped the old woman's hand. ''Thank you.''

''Now, what?'' Hawk asked. ''Do we head back for La Vega or do we go to Puerto Angelo and see King Julio?''

Rorie realized that Hawk was playing games again. Otherwise, he would never have asked her opinion on what to do next. He understood that the reverend mother had given her a secret message, one that required them to leave the mission and regroup if they wanted to save Frankie.

They left the mission, walked to the clearing and got into the jeep. Hawk started the engine.

''Just sit tight,'' he said. ''I'm going back down the road, so if anyone is watching, they'll see us leave. But as soon as we're out of sight of the mission, I'll park the jeep and then circle around to the back on foot.''

''I'm coming with you.''

Hawk shrugged. ''I never doubted that for a minute.'' He shifted gears, backed up and headed down the road.

''You think Frankie is still at the mission, don't you?'' Rorie asked.

''I think the reverend mother is afraid of someone and that someone is at the mission. Whoever it is, he could very well be holding Frankie hostage in order to force the nuns to do what he tells them.''

"Would Lazaro instruct his men to sell Frankie to the highest bidder?'' Rorie grabbed the dashboard when the jeep hit a large rut.

Hawk pulled the jeep off the road, through a flimsy wall of vines and shrubs, and parked it between two towering trees festooned with orchids.

He turned to face her. "No. Lazaro would take the boy himself.''

"What about Santos?''

"Santos would use Frankie in any way he thought it would benefit him. He would use him as a bargaining tool. He wouldn't sell the boy. Only someone working independently would be stupid enough to offer the prince to the highest bidder.''

"Then we're probably dealing with someone like that.''

Grabbing Rorie's shoulders, Hawk peered into her eyes. "Don't you think it's about time you tell me exactly what information the reverend mother gave you?''

"She opened the Bible to Genesis, chapter 37, and pointed directly to verses 26 and 27.''

Hawk gave Rorie a blank stare. "I'm not familiar with the Good Book, so just cut to the chase and fill me in.''

"The verses concern Joseph being sold into slavery by his brothers,'' Rorie said. "I think the Reverend Mother was trying to tell me that whoever has Frankie intends to sell him.''

"Damn!'' Hawk inadvertently looked at Rorie for a reaction to his cursing, but there wasn't a hint of censure on her face. "If you're right, then my guess is that somebody's double-crossing their boss, be it Santos or Lazaro, and they're going to try to sell Frankie to whomever forks over the most *dinero.*''

"We have to stop them.''

"We can try.'' Hawk jumped out of the jeep, checked his weapons and then motioned for Rorie to follow. He would have preferred her to stay with the jeep, just in case things got nasty. But he knew the only way to keep her there would have been to hog-tie her.

She followed where he led, through some thick underbrush

and up a steep, rocky incline. When they reached the back
side of the mission, Hawk jerked her down onto her belly and
signaled her to be silent. They crawled through the high grass
and weeds leading up to the six-foot wall separating the old
building from the forest. Shooting straight up, Hawk pulled
her with him. He flattened himself against the wall; she did
the same. Easing open the unlocked wooden gate, he slid
inside, checked the perimeter and when he found it clear,
reached outside and yanked Rorie into the courtyard.

"What are you—" Rorie whispered.

Hawk slammed his hand over her mouth. She glared in-
dignantly at him and he removed his hand very slowly.

Hawk pulled his 9-mm out of its holster. With Rorie directly behind him, he searched the hallways and rooms, seeking an intruder. The nuns were conspicuously absent, as if
they had exited en masse. When Hawk and Rorie passed by
the chapel, they found it filled with black-attired sisters on
their knees, praying. Hawk motioned for Rorie to be quiet
and continue following him.

When they rounded the corner a few yards from the reverend mother's office, they heard the front doors slam shut.
Hawk shoved Rorie up against the wall and motioned for her
to stay put. With gun in hand, he ran around the corner and
toward the front door.

"Mr. Hawk," the reverend mother called to him as she
rushed out of her office. "They have Prince Francisco. They
came only a little while before you and Miss Dean. They
threatened to kill the child if we let on that they were here."

Hawk nodded quickly to the elderly nun, then swung open
the front doors and raced outside. He caught a glimpse of a
man, with a bundle over his shoulder, running toward an on-
coming truck. Hawk holstered his pistol, slid the rifle off his
back and aimed it. The bundle was in the way of a clean head
or body shot. When Hawk fired the first shot, he hit the man
in the leg. The bullet slowed the kidnapper, but didn't stop
him. When the rusty, battered vehicle pulled up beside him,
the man tossed the bundle into the truck bed, then jumped in.

Rorie ran out of the mission and up beside Hawk.

"The reverend mother said that they have Frankie."

"We've got to get to the jeep."

Rorie raced behind Hawk, wishing her legs were longer, but thankful for every lap around Le Bijou Bleu that Hawk had forced her to make. He reached the jeep long before she did.

"Go without me!" she yelled.

He backed the jeep up to her. "Get your butt in here!"

She jumped in. He sped away, in hot pursuit of the kidnappers. Within minutes, they spotted the truck. Guiding the jeep with one hand, Hawk braced the rifle on his other shoulder, aimed the weapon and fired. The man in the back of the truck returned fire.

"Get down!" Hawk told Rorie.

She ducked down in the seat. Hawk fired again and again. The kidnapper's bullets missed them. Except for one that pierced the back of Rorie's seat. She swallowed hard and said a silent prayer of thanks.

Hawk's next shot hit its target. The man in the truck bed fell to his knees, then rolled out and onto the road. Rorie caught a quick glimpse of the dead man's bloody body as the jeep roared past him.

The truck picked up speed on its descent down the mountain. Hawk kept pace, but couldn't seem to catch up. The bundle lying on the truck bed rolled back and forth, several times coming precariously close to tumbling out.

Hawk got off another couple of shots, one hitting the cab of the old vehicle, the other grazing the front fender. The woman driving stuck her hand out the open window and fired her gun. The bullet hit the jeep's windshield, directly between the two front seats.

When the truck came to the fork in the road, the woman took the trail that led to Mayari. Making a quick turn, Hawk followed her. If she was unafraid to travel into Santos's territory, then there was a good chance she was one of his followers—a greedy follower who actually thought she could double-cross the renegade leader. The woman was a fool!

The chase continued, with Hawk and the woman exchanging occasional gunfire whenever the jeep caught up with the fast-moving truck. Rough and rocky, but cleared of the jungle's overgrowth, the road led downward, often swirling around steep embankments. The woman slowed the truck as they neared a dangerously narrow section of road, with a deep fifty-foot hollow on one side and the mountain on the other. Hawk didn't slow the jeep's speed. When the two vehicles cleared the deadly hollow, the jeep raced along, less than six feet behind the truck bumper.

Hawk's next shot shattered the truck cab's back window. The driver aimed and fired. Her bullet hit the jeep's front left tire. The tire blew instantly. Hawk struggled to control the jeep's rapid lunge off the road.

Try as he might, he couldn't prevent the four-wheel drive's headlong dive off the shallow embankment and straight into a row of slender pine trees.

The sudden, hard impact threw Rorie out of the jeep. The steering wheel momentarily trapped Hawk. He shoved the seat backward, jumped out and rushed to Rorie. She lay, unmoving, on the ground. The moment he reached her, he knelt at her side and gently rolled her over from her stomach to her back.

"Rorie? Honey? Dammit, lady, don't you be dead!" He checked the pulse in her neck. Thank God, she was alive. He stroked her face. "Rorie? Wake up!"

No response. She was unconscious. Checking her for broken bones, he found no obvious signs of any. No shards puncturing the skin. No swelling. He figured she probably had a concussion, but how bad a one he didn't know. And there was no way he could tell if she had any other internal injuries.

Hawk lifted Rorie in his arms and held her up as if she were a sacrifice. He screamed out to the heavens.

"Don't let her die! Do you hear me? Whatever you want from me, God, you've got it. I promise.

"Just don't let Rorie die!"

Chapter 13

Rorie regained consciousness gradually. Her eyelids fluttered several times before she managed to fully open her eyes. Hawk's worried face filled her line of vision. She tried to lift her hand to caress his cheek, to soothe him, but her arm wouldn't cooperate. Pain sliced through her skull. She shut her eyes, hoping to block out the pain. *Dear Lord, what happened to me?*

Lifting her head, she groaned when the pain intensified. Strong arms held her tightly, securely. Even through the fuzzy cloud encompassing her brain, Rorie knew that she was going to be all right. Gabriel was with her. He would take care of her.

"Rorie, honey?" He brushed a strand of hair away from her face and tenderly patted her right cheek. "Open your eyes again. Please, try. For me."

She focused on the task for several minutes before she was able to accomplish the simple action. When she opened her eyes, she was rewarded by Hawk's beautiful smile.

"That's my girl." He kissed her forehead.

She opened her dry mouth and licked her lips. "Hurts," she said. "Head hurts."

"You took a bad spill," he told her. "You've been unconscious for nearly an hour."

Looking up into his concerned eyes, she asked, "What happened?"

"Don't you remember?"

"We were chasing the truck. They had Frankie." She licked her lips again. "Shooting. A lot of shooting. You—you killed one of them."

Hawk brought the canteen to her mouth and lifted her head just a fraction. She moaned, but opened her mouth and drank the water greedily.

"The woman driving the truck shot out our right front tire and I wrecked the jeep." Hawk removed the canteen from her lips, recapped the lid and set it on the ground beside them. "You were thrown out of the jeep on impact."

"Are you all right?" With a great deal of effort, she lifted her hand slowly toward his face.

He grabbed her hand, brought it to his lips, then held it against his cheek.

"I'm fine, now that I know you're okay."

"You've been worried about me?"

"Yeah, I've been worried about you," he admitted. But she would never know just how worried. She would never know that he had bargained with God for her life. Nothing had ever been as important to him. Caring about a woman enough to offer to pay any price necessary to save her life made Hawk uncomfortable with his own emotions. If you didn't care about anyone, you couldn't get hurt. You would never be abandoned. You would never be vulnerable.

"Please, help me sit up."

She struggled with the effort. Hawk lifted her into his lap. She nestled her head on his shoulder.

"Do you hurt anywhere else, other than your head?" he asked.

She stretched a little, then groaned. "I'm sore all over, but no excruciating pain." She rubbed her right temple. "But I've got a doozy of a headache."

"You're damn lucky you didn't break your neck."

"What *am* I going to do about your foul mouth, Gabriel Hawk?"

He looked at her and grinned when she smiled at him. She was so beautiful the sight of her took his breath away. "I guess you're just going to have to put up with my cursing."

Glancing around the spot where they sat on the grass, Rorie realized that the forest canopy surrounded them on three sides. Through the clearing, she saw the wrecked jeep, its hood smashed against a row of pine trees.

"I'd like to try to stand," she said. "I can't just lie here. We have to catch up with that truck. Why didn't you put me in the back of the jeep and go on?"

"The jeep isn't going anywhere."

"What do you mean? You can change the flat tire and—"

"I can't repair the busted radiator. Without a new radiator, that jeep is staying where it is."

"We can walk back to the mission and borrow a... No, we can't do that. The nuns don't have a vehicle of any kind." She clasped Hawk's shoulder. "What are we going to do?"

"We aren't going to do anything until I know you're all right."

"I'm all right, except for a bad headache." She tried to lift herself from his lap, but he held her firmly around the waist. She glared at him. "We came so close to getting Frankie, and now he's with some woman who probably intends to sell him. Oh, Hawk, what if Emilio Santos buys Frankie? He'll kill him, won't he?"

"If King Julio is in the bidding war, then he'll buy his grandson. He has more gold than Lazaro and Santos combined."

"But what if—"

Hawk scooted her off his lap, then swept her into his arms as he stood. "Let's concentrate on the here and now and what our next move is going to be." He slid her down the front of his body and onto her feet.

Automatically, she draped her arms around his neck. "And what is our next move?"

"We pack up our supplies and head out on foot. Do you think you can make it?"

"I can make it." Removing her hands from around his

neck, she stepped backward and circled around him. "See, I'm not even dizzy anymore. So, where are we going?"

"We'll follow the road until it starts getting dark," he said. "Then we'll find a safe little nook to spend the night. It could take us two or three days to reach Vieques."

"Vieques? How are we going to get to Vieques if this road leads straight to Mayari?" Rorie stretched her sore muscles, groaning softly as she forced her body to cooperate.

"We can follow the road about half-way down the mountain, then we'll have to cut off and head into the forest. If necessary, we'll hack our way through the jungle to Vieques."

"And while we're hacking our way to Vieques, what's going to happen to Frankie?"

Reaching down, Hawk grasped her hand and squeezed tightly. "I don't know. But you believe in the power of prayer, don't you, honey?"

She nodded.

"Then pray. Pray hard and pray often."

She understood what Hawk meant. Only God's intervention could save Frankie now. "Let's pack up our supplies and get started."

Ten minutes later, they headed down the dirt trail. Heavy clouds overshadowed the late-morning sun. Rorie carried two canteens of water over one shoulder and her holster across the other. Hawk had wrapped the machete in the sleeping bag and stuffed it into their food sack, then strapped the sack to his back.

A descending walk was far easier than a climb, so they traipsed along at a comfortable speed. Hawk monitored Rorie's movements, her facial expressions and the sound of her breathing. She appeared to be all right. But he still worried that the concussion she'd suffered might have caused damage that had no external symptoms.

"I've been wanting to ask you about something since that first night at my apartment," Rorie said as she walked along at Hawk's side. She knew he had slowed his gait to match hers, allowing her to set their pace.

"And just what would that be?" he asked. "Why I wear a gold earring?"

"Well, I did wonder about that, but what I'm really curious about is that snake tattoo on your hand."

Laughing, Hawk lifted his left hand and looked down at the emblem. "When I was a teenager, I belonged to a Hispanic gang in El Paso. We were the Cobras."

"Why did you belong to a Hispanic gang?"

"Are you asking why I belonged to a gang or why the gang was Hispanic?"

"Both, I guess."

Hawk slowed momentarily, readjusted his backpack and straightened the rifle strap. "I was in a gang because, in my neighborhood, all the boys who weren't wimps belonged to a gang. I was a real tough guy when I was a kid."

"Didn't your parents try to stop you from—"

"I didn't have any parents." When he realized how sharply he'd spoken to Rorie, he glanced at her, checking her reaction. She looked at him with her blue, blue eyes, eyes filled with tender compassion, and he wanted to pull her into his arms and find the comfort she silently offered. He cleared his throat. "I told you. I'm a bastard. I grew up in a succession of foster homes. Even my name isn't my own. The cops who found me were Jim Hawk and Tomás Gabriel."

"What happened to your parents?"

"Who knows?" He shrugged, trying to pretend to himself and to Rorie that he didn't care. Hell, he didn't. He'd stopped caring a long time ago. "The police picked me up in a rest room in an El Paso bus station, where I'd been left. I was two years old, wearing nothing but a soiled diaper. And I couldn't speak a word of English. I'm told I could jabber a few words in Spanish."

Rorie wondered if he realized that the pain and anger he felt vibrated in his voice as he spoke. Probably not. No doubt, he believed he had conquered all his emotions; that his childhood anguish held no power over the man he was today.

"So, they assumed your parents were Hispanic because you didn't speak English and could say a few words in Spanish," Rorie said.

"Yeah, that and—" He stopped in the middle of the road and held open his arms. "Take a good look at me, lady. You can't say I've got a pure Anglo bloodline, can you? The cops turned me over to social services in El Paso instead of sending me to Mexico because they assumed one of my parents was Anglo, and nobody could prove otherwise.''

Crossing her arms over her chest, she stepped back and surveyed him from head to toe. ''Mmm. Jet black hair. Dark brown eyes. Light copper skin. Wide, full mouth. Broad shoulders. Narrow hips. I see a handsome man. An incredibly handsome man.''

''You see a mixed-breed mongrel who doesn't know who his parents were and doesn't give a damn.''

A faint rumble of thunder echoed in the distance. Rorie grinned at Hawk. ''See, the Good Lord objects to your bad language.''

The low-lying clouds swirled with gray fury. A barely discernible breeze fluttered through the towering trees in the nearby forest.

Hawk grabbed Rorie's hand. ''Let's get off the road and under some trees before the bottom falls out.''

He led her into the wooded area near the roadside, carrying her farther and farther into the thicket. When he reached a spot where an umbrella of tree limbs covered the sky, he slowed his pace. The heavens opened up, drenching the mountain with its daily noontime shower. Rain spilled from the clouds, seeping its way through the jade canopy and onto Hawk and Rorie.

Leaning back against a tree, Hawk pulled Rorie into his arms, pressing her close, as the rain soaked into their clothes. She lifted her face to his. He lowered his head. She parted her lips in unspoken invitation. His mouth covered hers with savage possession.

She clung to him, returning the passion of his kiss, ravenously taking from him and then giving back in full measure. He broke the kiss, gasping for air.

Rising up on tiptoe, she kissed his pierced left earlobe. ''Tell me about the gold earring.''

He chuckled, the deep sound resonating up from his chest. ''Are you sure you want to hear this?''

''Now you have to tell me, and you know it.'' Lifting her arms from his waist, she draped them around his neck.

"I was fifteen the first time I got la— Er...uh...the first time I had sex."

Rorie's eyes rounded. Her mouth dropped open. "Fifteen?"

"Yeah, I was a late bloomer."

"You!" Laughing, she poked him in the ribs.

He grabbed her jabbing hand and laid it over his heart. "Her name was Rita and she was my buddy Domingo's big sister. Rita was nineteen and a very experienced woman by the time she— Well, Rita had this ritual. Whenever she made a man out of a boy, so to speak, she pierced his ear afterward and marked him with one of her many ruby-red glass studs. Being seen wearing Rita's mark of manhood was quite a coup in my neighborhood. You were the envy of every other guy."

Flushed with naive embarrassment, Rorie lowered her head, unable to look Hawk in the eye. Tucking his fist under her chin, he lifted her face.

"Are you sorry you asked?" He grinned wickedly.

"That's only half the story." Rorie glared at him, her cheeks stained pink and her blue eyes flashing.

"What more do you want to know? Are you asking for details?"

She shook her head vehemently. "No. I'm just wondering when you traded Rita's ruby stud for a gold hoop? I assume that involves another woman, doesn't it?"

"Well, as a matter of fact..."

Hawk kissed her quickly. She gasped. He laughed. She frowned.

"I wore Rita's fake-ruby stud for about six weeks, then I traded it in for a rhinestone stud another girl gave me. But for my sixteenth birthday, I bought myself this gold hoop, with money I'd earned washing cars at a garage."

Rorie laid her head on Hawk's chest and listened to the steady beat of his heart. He held her, wanting her as he had never wanted another woman. That desperate need scared him. And he wasn't a man who scared easily.

How had this happened? he wondered. How was it possible that his desire to have sex with Rorie had become interwoven with a gut-wrenching need to possess her completely—body and soul?

While they stood under the protective trees, wrapped in each other's arms, the rain slacked off and gradually stopped altogether. By the time Hawk eased Rorie from his arms and turned her toward the road, he was painfully aroused.

They talked very little for the next couple of hours as they trekked down the primitive road. The distant rumble of thunder followed them as did dark, heavy clouds.

Hawk felt certain it would rain again tonight.

Not hearing or seeing signs of any other humans was a lucky break for them. As long as they remained in Santos's territory, they ran the risk of running into one of his marauding bands.

"We'll stop soon," he said.

"I'm okay," she told him. "Don't stop on my account."

Damn stubborn woman! Her face was flushed, but a pale ring circled her mouth. Occasionally he caught a glimpse of her frowning. He knew the signs. She was in pain, but didn't want him to know. Didn't she realize by now that she didn't have to keep proving herself to him? He already knew how brave and strong she was.

"Well, I'm thirsty," he told her. "And I need to take a—"

She cleared her throat loudly. "All right. I need to, too. And to be honest, I'm dying of thirst."

They made two brief pit stops during the afternoon. Each time, he questioned her about her head and she assured him that the headache was almost gone. He didn't believe her.

"We need to find some shelter for the night. A cave or the base of a dead tree," Hawk said. "We're going to get a lot of heavy rain before long, so if we don't find some type of cover, we'll get soaked."

"My mother always says that the Lord will provide." Rorie sighed as warm and happy thoughts of her parents filled her mind. They had given her a secure life, a home filled with love and devotion. How different Hawk's life had been. Abandoned as a toddler. Unloved and unwanted through his entire childhood. No wonder he tried so hard not to care about anyone or anything.

"Well, I hope your mother's right. We could use a little divine assistance about now."

The swirling clouds obscured the late-afternoon sun.

Knowing that night would come early because of the impending rainstorm, Hawk led Rorie off the road and into the forest, in search of shelter. The mountain was littered with enormous tree-trunk buttresses rising out of the rich forest earth. Surely there was a still-standing copse of one of those trees somewhere close by. Or a cave. A honeycomb of underground caverns spiraled beneath the surface in many areas. All they needed tonight was one small hole in the mountainside.

They trudged deeper and deeper into the forest and farther and farther from the road. Hawk retrieved the machete from his makeshift backpack and hacked a path in front of them. Not one hollow tree anywhere. And not a sign of a cave or even an overhanging boulder. If they didn't find some sort of shelter soon, he would have to cut down some saplings and build them a temporary lee.

"Look!" Rorie cried out, pointing to the right, through a curtain of spiraling vines. "That's some sort of stone building, isn't it?"

Thunder echoed through the damp, verdant forest. A raindrop hit Hawk's hand, then another splashed down on his head. Cutting through the heavy vegetation he led Rorie forward toward the towering stack of rocks. He stopped dead still. Running into his back, Rorie steadied herself by grabbing him around the waist.

"My God, take a look at this," he said.

Rorie eased around beside him. "Oh, my." She stared in awe at the sight before her.

The jungle had reclaimed the once-magnificent structure. Part of the building lay in ruins. Grass and weeds grew up between the individual rocks comprising the floor. Vines curved and curled upward and over the closely fitted stonework. The back section of the ancient structure, which had been carved into the mountain, remained intact. A series of etched birds and snakes and human figures graced the stone archway leading into the building.

Thunder rolled overhead. The rain increased in intensity. Hawk grabbed Rorie's hand and together they ran up the stone steps and into the inner sanctum.

Drenched and breathless, Rorie and Hawk clung to each

other as the rains came down outside in a heavy deluge. He dropped the machete to the stone floor. Lightning shot out of the sky and struck a nearby tree. Fire sparked between the severed limbs, but the rain doused the flames. Rorie snuggled closer to Hawk, grasping the back of his damp shirt.

"What is this place?" Her voice quivered.

"I'd say it was some sort of temple." He rubbed his hands up and down her arms. "You're shivering, honey. Are you cold?"

"I'm just chilled, that's all. The rain is cold."

"I can't build a fire, but…" He hesitated making the suggestion. "I can pull out the sleeping bag and we can take off our wet clothes and—"

She laid two fingers over his lips. Her hand trembled. He kissed her fingers and eased her hand away.

"I'll spread out the sleeping bag and we can sit down and have a picnic. I'm sure I can find something edible in our sack." Dropping his hands from around her, he stepped back a few inches.

Smiling weakly, she nodded. "You do that and I'll fill our canteens and cups with rainwater."

She set the canteens out in the rain, then held the two cups under the downpour until they overflowed. She placed the cups on a carved niche in the stone wall and watched Hawk draw the sleeping bag out of the sack and lay it on the floor.

Did he know how very tempted she had been to agree to his suggestion? The moment he mentioned taking off their clothes, her body recalled last night's pleasures. But if she gave herself over to her desires tonight, things would be different. And she was sure Hawk knew that, too. The loving they had shared last night would never be enough again. If he touched her tonight, he would ask her for more. And she would give it to him.

She was already in love with Gabriel Hawk. She hadn't intended for it to happen. She had fought her feelings with all her strength. But she had come to realize that there was no point in fighting the inevitable. Gabriel was her destiny. And she was his. He might not realize it yet, but eventually he would. He could no more fight the powerful magnetism between them than she could. He probably thought that it was nothing more than lust. But he was wrong.

"Dinner is served, m'lady." He bowed quite gallantly.

She picked up their cups and carried them across the shadowy gray room. Nighttime would soon encompass the old temple and seal Hawk and her into a dark, safe hideaway. She handed him a cup, then sat down on the outspread sleeping bag. He sat down beside her and handed her one of Murdock's "gourmet" meals. Hawk finished off the unknown foodstuff hurriedly, washing it down with the water. Rorie ate more of the concoction than she'd thought she would, taking sips of water after every bite.

The moment she finished her meal, Hawk shoved aside the empty containers and metal cups. Instinctively, Rorie scooted away from him.

"I'm not sleeping in my wet clothes, so if you don't want to see me naked, you'd better turn around," he said.

She turned quickly, facing the opposite direction. Her heart beat wildly as images of Gabriel's magnificent naked body flashed through her mind. Shivering from head to toe, she clasped her hands in her lap and prayed for the strength to resist temptation.

She tried not to listen to the noises he made while he undressed. The thump of one boot and then another as they hit the floor. The swirl of air when he stripped off his shirt. The metallic swish when he unzipped his pants.

Hawk knelt behind her. Rorie scooted to the edge of the sleeping bag. He touched her hair. She jumped. Soothing her, he stroked his hand across her shoulder. She didn't move, barely breathed while he unbraided her hair. Keeping her back to him, she sat stiffly when he spread out the long, damp strands.

"I love your hair," he said, his voice deep and dark and incredibly soft. "Even in this dim light it shimmers like pure gold."

She swallowed hard. Cupping her shoulders with his open palms, he closed his hands over her wet sleeves in a tight grasp. She tensed momentarily, but when he lowered his head and nuzzled her neck, she gasped and let her body lean backward into his. Nuzzling aside her hair, he kissed her neck.

"You know how much I want you, don't you?" he whispered in her ear.

He eased his hands down and then back up her arms. She sighed. His fingertips trailed across her collarbone. His palms covered her straining breasts. Tossing back her head, she melted against him and knew that now there would be no resisting temptation, no turning back from the inevitability of what lay ahead for them.

With fingers that had suddenly lost their dexterity, Hawk fumbled with the buttons on her wet shirt. She lay back against him, neither helping nor hindering his efforts. He stripped the shirt from her body, then unhooked her bra and tossed both shirt and bra toward the foot of the sleeping bag.

Encompassing her breasts, he squeezed gently, then lifted them and raked their peaks with his thumbs. Rorie moaned from the painful pleasure as he flicked her nipples into tight pink nubs. He placed a row of slow, damp kisses across one shoulder and then the other, all the while tormenting her breasts with his hands.

"I've never wanted anyone or anything in my whole life the way I want you." He slipped one hand down between her thighs and clutched her intimately. She moaned as tremors rippled through her. "I won't take your virginity. You've saved that for the man you'll love someday. But we can give each other the same pleasure we shared last night."

"I want you, too." Her voice quivered ever so slightly.

"Ah, Rorie, honey." What was it about her that drove him insane? What did this sweet, stubborn little do-gooder have that made her so irresistible?

He turned her to face him, grasped each side of her waist and drew her up on her knees. He hoped the light would last long enough for him to see her while he made love to her. He wanted to watch her fall apart.

He lifted her to her feet, unzipped and removed her slacks, along with her panties, then kicked them aside.

A sudden weakness claimed her limbs. Her knees buckled. Hawk wrapped her hair around his hand and drew her closer. Inserting his foot between her ankles, he gently kicked her legs apart. She gasped at the instant sensation of being exposed. Lowering his head, he kissed her. A slow, languid kiss.

Nibbles on her lower lip. Licks circling her whole mouth. Tentative jabs into the warm interior.

Circling his waist with her arms, she inched her fingers up his naked back. He walked her backward on top of the sleeping bag until her buttocks encountered the wall. He pressed his hard body against her, allowing her to feel the heaviness of his throbbing arousal. She didn't flinch when he lifted his head and looked deeply into her eyes as he eased his fingers up her thigh, parting her farther. He slipped inside her, testing her. Instinctively, she closed her thighs around his intruding hand.

She twisted and turned, inflaming her own desire as well as his. He probed and retreated, then probed again. He raked his thumb across her core. Pressing her head back against the wall, she groaned as he played the intimate game. Color washed up her neck and over her face.

Hawk petted her with knowledgeable strokes while he lowered his mouth to her breast. He ached with need.

"Please, oh, please..." she whimpered.

"Let it happen, honey. Just let go."

Hot, wild sensation consumed her. Pressing, pressing, pressing. With one final stroke, he broke the tightly coiled spring inside her, unraveling the pleasure. Her body jerked repeatedly as fulfillment claimed her.

While the aftershocks of release still tingled along her nerve endings, Hawk drew her hand down to circle his erection. She held him, caressing him tenderly.

She kissed the center of his chest, then slid her tongue up to his throat. "You said you wouldn't take my virginity—"

"And I won't." *No matter how desperately I want to make you mine completely.*

"What if I want to give it to you? What if—"

"Don't do this to me. Don't—"

Releasing her intimate hold on him, she stood on tiptoe and wrapped herself around him. "I love you, Gabriel. I realize you probably don't want my love, but you have it. And because I love you, I want you to be my first lover." *My only lover. Now and forever.*

"You shouldn't love me. I'm no good, honey. I'm no good

for you.'' All the while he tried to reject her, his arousal pulsed against her belly.

"It doesn't matter," she said, her voice echoing in the shadowy twilight, as the heavy rain created a cocoon around them inside the ancient temple. "Don't you understand? I'm good for you, Gabriel, and that's what's important.''

"God, forgive me.'' He was no saint. He was only a man. He didn't possess the strength to reject her precious gift.

Lifting her in his arms, he carried her away from the wall and lowered her to the sleeping bag, then gently straddled her hips.

Take it easy. Go slow. Don't hurt her. He probed her with his fingers, parting her, petting her, preparing her. Then he lowered himself over her, easing slowly into her. She tensed. He murmured soothing, almost-incoherent words to her.

Lifting her head, she captured his mouth. When he thrust his tongue inside, she lifted her hips, bringing him deeper inside her. Unable to resist her invitation, he drove into her. Slipping his hands beneath her hips he lifted her, sealing them together. He filled her completely, making their bodies one.

Hawk held Rorie, unmoving, waiting for the pain from his invasion to ease. She gasped as the pain sliced through her, but she swallowed her cries. Tears gathered in the corners of her eyes and trickled into her hair.

"I'm sorry. I didn't want to hurt you.'' He mouthed the words against her cheek.

She rubbed his buttocks, then pressed down on his spine, urging him to continue. "There's more to making love, isn't there? I want it all," she said.

He worked her back and forth, thrusting and retreating, plunging, pleasuring, giving her all of him and taking back everything from her. He couldn't make it last, couldn't take the time to bring her to a fulfillment again. When he felt the tingling warnings of his imminent release, he rammed his tongue into her mouth.

Rorie urged him to the edge with every breath she took, acting purely on instinct. Wanting to give him pleasure, she lost herself in the pursuit of his release.

He groaned into her mouth. He froze for an instant, then hammered into her with quick, sharp, frantic jabs.

She felt his release, warm and moist inside her. And she listened, with happiness, to his triumphant, deep-throated growl of completion.

Hawk eased his body alongside hers, then lifted the sleeping bag over them and zippered them inside the padded warmth. She cuddled in his arms.

He kissed her. "Rest now, honey."

Rorie fell asleep almost instantly, sated and secure. Hawk held her close. She was his now—in every way a woman could belong to a man. His feelings of possessiveness about Rorie surprised him. But he could no more control those feelings than he could stop the sun from rising tomorrow.

He claimed her again during the long night, taking her with wild abandon in the darkness. They shared the pleasure the second time—Rorie shattering into ecstasy as he exploded inside her.

At first light of dawn, she awoke when Hawk drew her on top of him and urged her to ride him. She was sore, her body aching from the two previous lovings and the aftereffects of their wreck. But her desire for him made her more than willing to give and find pleasure once again.

Afterward, they slept for a brief time, then washed and dressed quickly. Rorie braided her hair, while Hawk prepared their breakfast. They shared another of Murdock's meals, then packed up and left the ancient temple.

Halting before they entered the forest again, Rorie took one last look at the ruins. She would never forget the night she'd shared with Gabriel, within the sheltering arms of a building once held sacred by a people who long ago had vanished from the earth.

Hawk pulled Rorie close and kissed her. "No regrets?" he asked.

"None," she told him.

The sun was high in the sky when Hawk told her they would soon have to leave the road again and return to the forest. The road would have led them straight to Mayari. Only by making their way through the jungle could they reach Vieques, find Tito Álverez and send word to Murdock.

They stopped for a midmorning rest and to relieve themselves. While hidden within the green walls of the forest, Hawk heard voices and booted footsteps. The men were on the road, less than thirty feet away. Rorie! Did she hear the soldiers?

Hawk crept through the underbrush, looking for Rorie. He found her crouched behind a tree. He slipped his arm around her and drew her up on her feet. He motioned for her to keep quiet. She nodded.

Hawk peered around the tree and through the thicket. Six men with beards and scraggly black hair had stopped on the side of the road—armed soldiers wearing fatigues. When one of them glanced into the forest, Hawk got a good look at his face and recognized him. He couldn't remember the man's name, but knew he was one of Santos's gorillas.

Hawk could make out bits and pieces of their conversation. Unimportant jabber. The soldiers would be on their way soon, and he and Rorie could head in the opposite direction.

Rorie tugged on Hawk's sleeve. He shrugged off her hand. She tugged again, more insistent the second time. When he glanced at her, she pointed down at the ground directly in front of them. A giant anaconda slithered through the underbrush.

Several minutes later, while Hawk's attention was diverted by trying to silently reassure Rorie that the huge snake wouldn't hurt her, he heard the rustle of tree limbs. Shoving Rorie behind him, he drew the 9 mm from his holster. Then he saw a flash of something move through the thicket.

One of the soldiers, who had apparently sought privacy off the road, was running through the forest, calling out to his comrades.

"Damn!" Hawk grabbed Rorie's arm.

"He saw us, didn't he?" she asked.

"They're going to come after us," he said. "And I don't think we can outrun them, but we can try to outsmart them. If that fails, then we'll have to take cover and fight."

"Do you mean we're going to have to shoot at them?"

"That's exactly what I mean." He looked her square in the eye. "Can you do that, Rorie? Can you shoot to kill?"

Chapter 14

In less than five minutes, Hawk realized that they were surrounded by the renegades. He pulled Rorie into the thicket, behind a huge, moss-covered rock. There was nowhere to run and nowhere to hide. All Hawk could figure out was that there had been more than one group of Santos's soldiers—the ones on the road and another searching the forest. But searching for what? For Rorie and him?

If he were alone, he might have a chance of eliminating enough of the enemy to facilitate his escape. But with Rorie's safety to worry about, his hands were tied. A gun battle with two dozen men could end only one way—in his and Rorie's deaths.

But the alternative didn't appeal to Hawk in the least. The thought of being handed over to Santos galled him. There was a fifty-fifty chance that Santos wouldn't kill them. He didn't like the odds, but they were better than the ones they faced here in the jungle with twenty-four guns pointed in their direction.

"Señorita Dean?" one of the soldiers called out from several yards away, only the heavy forest vegetation blocking him from their view. "I am Paz Santos, the brother of Emilio

Santos," the man said in Spanish. "Emilio has sent me to find you and escort you and Hawk to Mayari."

Clutching Hawk's arm, Rorie looked into his eyes, questioning him silently. Hawk shook his head in a negative response.

"*Señorita*, we know you came to San Miguel seeking your nephew," Paz Santos said. "Rosa, the woman who stole little Francisco from the Blessed Virgin Mission is one of my brother's loyal followers. She brought the boy straight to Mayari. Your nephew is now under Emilio Santos's protection."

Rorie bit down on her bottom lip in an effort not to scream. Dear Lord, her worst nightmare had become a reality. Emilio Santos had Frankie. She looked at Hawk, hoping he would tell her that what the man had said wasn't true.

"It makes sense," Hawk whispered. "Paz knows too much to be lying. Somehow we figured it wrong. This Rosa wasn't planning on selling Frankie to the highest bidder. She was taking him straight to Santos."

"What are we going to do?"

"We have two choices," he told her. "We can fight and die or we can give ourselves up and hope Santos doesn't kill us."

"I don't like either choice."

"*Señorita*, if you wish to save your nephew, you and Hawk must come with us," Paz Santos said. "Emilio would like for you to be his guests. He will tell you how King Julio's grandson can bring about an end to the war."

"If we accept your invitation—" placing his hand over Rorie's mouth, Hawk called out from their hiding place "—I'd like your word that Señorita Dean will come to no harm while we're under Emilio's 'protection'."

Paz Santos's deep laughter rumbled through the eerie hush of the forest. "Only you, Hawk, would make demands, as if you were in charge, when you are surrounded by my men."

"I can kill you where you stand, Paz, and you know it." Removing his hand from Rorie's mouth, Hawk gave her a warning look, then rose from behind the rock and aimed his rifle. "And after you're dead, I can take out several of your men before they kill me."

"Let us not speak of killing each other, my old comrade,"
Paz said. "Come with me to Mayari and I give you my word
that Señorita Dean will be safe."

Tugging on Hawk's pant leg, Rorie glared up at him. "That
man is a renegade, a killer, Peter's murderer. How can you
possibly trust him?"

"Paz Santos is all that you say he is, but he is a man of
his word, unlike his brother."

"You didn't tell me that you knew Emilio Santos personally. Why did his brother call you his old comrade?" Rorie
asked.

Hawk grabbed Rorie's arm and pulled her to her feet to
stand at his side. "I met the Santos brothers while I was on
my last government assignment. Paz is his brother's right-
hand man, but unlike Emilio, if Paz gives his word, he keeps
it."

"We're going to surrender, aren't we?" Rorie slid her pistol into the shoulder holster.

"Tell your men to hold their fire," Hawk said. "Señorita
Dean and I have decided to accept Emilio's invitation."

"A wise decision," Paz said. "Put your hands over your
heads and come out where I can see you."

Hawk draped the rifle strap over his shoulder, grabbed Rorie's arm and led her forward, toward their captor. With her
heart hammering loud and fast, she glued herself to Hawk's
side as they revealed themselves to the enemy. Within a minute, they were surrounded by armed men, a few little more
than boys. Half-a-dozen pairs of black eyes glowered at them.

A short, slender man in his late twenties emerged from the
thicket. "I'm sorry, but we'll have to take your weapons."
Paz smiled, his teeth bright white against his dark bronze skin.
"Just a precaution. I know what a marksman you are,
Hawk."

"Take off your holster and give it to him." Hawk pointed
to the soldier at Rorie's side. She did as Hawk commanded.
Hawk allowed the soldier on his left to take his holster and
rifle.

"Come. We have trucks and jeeps waiting for us several
miles from here," Paz said. "We should be in Mayari in a
few hours." Paz placed his arm around Hawk's shoulder.

"Emilio is eager to see you again, and to meet Señorita Dean."

Paz Santos looked appreciatively at Rorie, leisurely inspecting the way her shirt molded her full breasts.

Hawk flung Paz's arm from his shoulder. "I expect you to keep your promise that Señorita Dean will be safe."

"I keep my promises." Paz nodded his head to Rorie. "You are a beautiful woman. I meant no offense in looking at you. None of my men will touch you. I have given Hawk my word to keep you safe."

Rorie swallowed hard. She stared at Paz Santos, not knowing how to respond to his comments.

"Doesn't she speak Spanish?" Paz asked Hawk.

Rorie looked Paz straight in the eye and spoke to him in Spanish. "I understood what you said. Hawk might trust your word, but I do not. I could never trust anyone who was a member of the renegade army that murdered my brother and sister-in-law."

The smile on Paz's face vanished. He returned Rorie's hard stare, then glanced at Hawk. The two men exchanged an unspoken question and response. Hawk knew that Paz would not betray him, but he also knew that he could not count on Emilio to be as discreet. It was only a matter of time now before Rorie learned the truth—the whole truth. And when she did, she would hate him.

He did not want to go to his death knowing that Rorie hated him.

"You tell Emilio that she is your woman." Paz spoke to Hawk in English.

"She *is* my woman," Hawk replied.

Paz nodded. "I thought as much."

Turning abruptly, Paz ordered his men to escort Hawk and Rorie to the road. When they began their march down the mountain, two dozen soldiers surrounded them.

A few miles along the trail, several vehicles waited, and another half-dozen men. Paz Santos stepped up into a battered jeep and issued orders to his driver. Some of the soldiers crowded into a Hummer. Hawk lifted Rorie into the cab of a truck driven by a boy she doubted was even eighteen, then Hawk jumped up and into the seat beside her.

The vehicles roared down the bumpy mountain path, jostling Rorie from side to side. Hawk draped his arm around her shoulders and drew her close. She reached out and grasped his hand. He squeezed hers, reassuringly. She glanced at him and found comfort in his look of concern.

Signs of recent clearing littered the old trail down the mountain. Hawk had no doubts now that Emilio Santos had somehow known not only Frankie's whereabouts, but that he and Rorie were headed to the mission for the boy. Santos's men, not Lazaro's, had destroyed the bridge that crossed the main roadway leading to the mission. Only a handful of people possessed the secret information about Frankie and about Rorie, and one of those people had betrayed them. But who?

Mayari lay high atop the limestone cliffs, a secluded little village accessible by one main road leading to Vieques. Hawk remembered how well guarded that one entrance was—indeed, how completely secure the entire village was. Sentries were posted around the clock.

Hawk would never forget the day Peter Dean and his young wife had been paraded through the village and beheaded in front of a cheering crowd. Santos's renegades and their families hated Americans almost as much as they hated King Julio.

The truck stopped. A soldier opened the door and ordered Hawk and Rorie to step outside. Paz Santos waited for them at the entrance to the building Hawk recognized as Emilio's headquarters.

"Follow me," Paz said. "Emilio will want to see you immediately."

"Is Frankie here?" Rorie asked.

"My brother can answer all your questions, *señorita*."

Hawk clasped Rorie's hand in his. She took a deep breath and followed him up the wooden steps and into the square, stucco building. They walked down a dark, narrow hallway. Paz knocked on a door at the end of the corridor.

The door opened and a young soldier saluted Paz, then stepped aside to allow him entrance. Paz motioned to Hawk and Rorie.

Late-afternoon sunshine flooded the room through the two windows facing west. Despite the fresh evening breeze wafting in through the open windows, an overpowering odor of human sweat permeated the office. Except for the one armed guard at the door, the only other occupant was a small, wiry man in his early thirties, who sat behind a large desk. Rorie halted as she took a good look at Emilio Santos—her brother's murderer.

Dark, almond-shaped eyes stared at her. Not moving a muscle, not batting an eyelash, Rorie stared back at him. Curly black hair snaked about his ears, meeting his sideburns that grew into his neatly trimmed beard. He stood and walked around the desk. When he smiled, Rorie's first thought was that this renegade killer was not as handsome or charming as General Lazaro.

"Hawk, my friend." Emilio grabbed Hawk's shoulders, then glanced back and forth from Rorie to Hawk. "I never expected to see you in San Miguel again. Not after what happened."

Rorie was surprised by how well the man spoke English. She watched with curiosity the friendly attitude Emilio displayed toward Hawk—even friendlier than Paz's.

"I came on business." Hawk eased out of Emilio's grasp, but kept his gaze riveted to his face. "Personal business. I've brought Peter Dean's sister to San Miguel to get her nephew and take him to the United States."

"Is Frankie here?" Rorie asked.

Emilio turned his full attention to Rorie. "Your nephew is safe, *señorita*. Believe me, Prince Francisco is worth far more to me alive than dead. For now."

Rorie wanted to strangle the man. She'd never felt such hatred for another human being, but then she had never met a monster like Emilio Santos.

"Where is Frankie?" Rorie took a tentative step toward Emilio. Hawk moved quickly to stand at her side, his stance threatening.

Emilio looked at Hawk, then smiled and nodded. "You are her bodyguard, *sí*. And more. She is your woman."

Emilio laughed. Every muscle in Hawk's body tensed. A chilling sense of foreboding tingled up Rorie's spine.

"She's my woman." Hawk slipped his arm around Rorie's waist. When he drew her to his side, she went without protest.

"Since you are my old friend—" Emilio's wide smile revealed two chipped teeth "—and she is your woman, I will show you my hospitality. I will feed you and give you a place to rest for the night."

"Where's Frankie?" Rorie tried to pull away from Hawk, but he held her firmly in place. "I want to see my nephew!"

"Prince Francisco is not here in Mayari," Emilio said. "I have sent the boy into safekeeping with Rosa, until General Lazaro meets my demands."

"What demands?" Rorie's stomach fluttered with nausea.

"I have sent word to Lazaro that I have the boy," Emilio said. "And if the general will agree to join forces with me, to combine our armies, together we can defeat King Julio."

"What part does Prince Francisco play in your scheme?" Hawk asked.

"Lazaro will offer King Julio an exchange." Emilio slowly circled Rorie and Hawk, his gaze surveying Rorie from head to toe. "In Puerto Angelo, the king is safe. With his large army, he could hold the city and continue the war for a very long time. But if he brings his army out of Puerto Angelo for a meeting with Lazaro—a meeting to exchange the prince for a large amount of gold—well..." Emilio reached out and touched a loose tendril of Rorie's hair.

Rorie drew back, unnerved by the man's bold move. Hawk stepped in front of Rorie. Emilio laughed.

"I gave Hawk my word that his woman would be safe here," Paz Santos said.

"She is safe." Emilio clasped Hawk's shoulder. "Both Hawk and his woman are safe...for now. But we must detain them for a while." He looked directly into Hawk's eyes. "I am giving you a secluded little love nest, in one of the caves on the other side of the village. You'll be alone for several days, perhaps a week or more. That will give you time to explain to her why you have kept the truth from her."

Hawk knew Emilio would take great delight in telling Rorie all the details of Peter Dean's death, especially Hawk's part in her brother's execution. "You're going to *detain* us until King Julio meets with General Lazaro to exchange the prince for a fortune in gold. You're selling the boy to his grandfather." Hawk brushed Emilio's hand from his shoulder. "But what King Julio won't know is that you and Lazaro have joined forces. The king knows his army is an even match for Lazaro's, so he will feel safe in meeting with him away from Puerto Angelo."

"You were always too smart for your own good. I knew you would figure out my plan." Emilio sized Rorie up, his gaze lingering on her breasts, just as Paz's had. "Perhaps when your woman knows the truth, she will prefer me to you?"

"The king won't be expecting an attack from both rebel factions, will he?" Hawk knew that Emilio was toying with him, playing a deadly game, a game as sick and perverted as Emilio himself. The renegade killer was going to tell Rorie about Hawk's part in the deaths of Peter and Cipriana Dean, and there was nothing Hawk could do to stop him.

"Once Lazaro and I join our armies in a common goal, the war will end quickly," Emilio said.

He circled Hawk and Rorie again, edging closer and closer to Rorie. Hawk turned her quickly, keeping her out of Emilio's reach.

Planting his hands on his slender hips, Emilio puffed out his chest and threw back his head. "I give you a choice, *señorita*. You may go into a dark, damp cave with Hawk or you can stay in my house with me, where you will be treated like a queen. Which do you prefer?"

"You must be insane to think I would choose to stay with you." Rorie leaned into the protection of Hawk's big body.

"Emilio, do not do this." Paz looked pleadingly at his brother. "It is not honorable."

"I'm not an honorable man," Emilio said. "You know this about me. I am a man of action. A man who takes what he wants and does as he pleases. And it will please me to see the look in Señorita Dean's eyes when I tell her that her man is not who she thinks he is."

"You can't tell me anything about Gabriel that would change the way I feel about him." Rorie winced when Hawk's tenacious hold on her waist tightened painfully.

"And how do you feel about Hawk?" Emilio's grin spread across his face. "You love him, *sí*? Would you love him if you knew he played a part in the deaths of your brother and sister-in-law?''

A tingling numbness began in Rorie's face and slowly spread down her neck and through her entire body. A deadly shiver of cold pulsated along her nerves. She tilted her chin defiantly. "I don't believe you. You're a liar as well as a murderer."

"*Señorita*, it is not the way Emilio would have you believe." Paz glared at his brother. "Hawk was on a mission for his government. Like any other man fighting for his country, he did what he had to do, just as you and I do what we must for the good of all San Miguel."

Ignoring Paz completely, Emilio concentrated his attention on Rorie. "Your man was once a member of my army. He fought at my side. He was like a brother to me. He was one of the men I sent to kidnap Princess Cipriana and her husband on their journey to Puerto Angelo."

Rorie turned to Hawk, her eyes questioning him. He returned her stare, the truth revealed in his dark eyes.

"You—you helped kidnap Peter and Cipriana?"

Hawk said nothing, only continued staring at Rorie. What could he say? Yes, I helped kidnap your brother and his wife. Yes, I did everything I could to save them. I sent word to Murdock to bring General Lazaro to stop Emilio's madness. I even tried bribing the guards. But in the end, I was powerless to stop their executions.

"Paz, see that Hawk and his woman are taken to the caves," Emilio said. "Give them food and water and blankets—a last night of comfort. Then seal the entrance to the cave and post a guard. If Señorita Dean decides she prefers my company to Hawk's, she can tell the guard. Otherwise, she can live and die with her man."

"I gave Hawk my word that she would be safe," Paz said. "Hawk understood that you might send him to his death, but he asked me to spare his woman's life."

"His woman has a choice. If she chooses me, she lives."

Rorie heard Emilio Santos's evil laughter. She understood every word of the Santos brothers' conversation. But a whirling sound and a queasy dizziness inside her head grew stronger and stronger. A rigid numbness claimed her body.

When Hawk grasped her arm and pulled her along beside him as he followed Paz out of the room and into the hallway, she walked with him, her steps slow and awkward. Her legs felt heavy, her feet weighted down. She tried to think coherently, to reason, but her mind refused to cooperate. It was as if her brain had shut down temporarily.

Once outside in the late-evening light, Rorie glanced around at the hive of activity in Mayari, but nothing held any meaning for her. As if in a trance, she allowed Hawk to lift her into Paz's jeep.

Hawk squeezed her hand. "Rorie, honey, say something to me." When she stared at him with sightless eyes, he patted her cheeks. "Don't shut down like this. Don't let what Emilio told you weaken you. You're strong and brave and you can survive this."

Rorie made no response by word or action. She knew she should say something, should ask Hawk a hundred questions, should cry and shout and rant and rave. But she felt only a deep, painful emptiness inside her.

Following his brother's orders, Paz deposited Hawk and Rorie in a huge underground cave. He gave them a canteen of water, a small sack of fruit, two blankets and a couple of flashlights.

They were being sent to their deaths. Hawk knew only too well what fate lay ahead of them if Emilio had his way.

Standing outside the cave entrance, two soldiers at his side, Paz spoke to Hawk in English. "My brother does not know these caves as I know them. They run deep into the earth. When morning comes, find the river and follow it to the sea."

Hawk nodded his understanding, thankful for Paz Santos's sense of honor, then he pulled Rorie away from the cave entrance. The soldiers and Paz rolled a large stone over the entrance, leaving only a few inches at the top exposed.

Immediately, Hawk turned on one of the flashlights and set it on the ground, beaming it straight up at the foot-long stalactites hanging from the cave ceiling, their shapes reminiscent of large plant leaves. He spread out a blanket, clutched Rorie's arms and eased her down on it. Kneeling in front of her, he grabbed her shoulders and shook her soundly.

"Snap out of it! Dammit, woman, we're not going to die

in this cave. But I've got to have your cooperation to save us.''

"Is it true?" Crossing her arms over her chest, Rorie rocked back and forth.

Hawk released his hold on her shoulders, then slumped down beside her. "Yes, it's true. I was on a mission in San Miguel. I was supposed to infiltrate Santos's renegade army and discover the whereabouts of a U.S. missile that had been stolen." He took a deep breath. "To make a long story short, I became an active member of the renegade army and took part in some things I'd prefer to forget."

"Like kidnapping Peter and Cipriana?" The numbness in Rorie's body began to subside, leaving behind a tingling ache.

"Murdock was my contact," Hawk said. "I got word to him as soon as I could that Santos planned to execute the princess and her husband. I knew that only Lazaro could stop Santos."

"*You* didn't try to stop him?" she asked, her big blue eyes filled with tears.

"Dammit, Rorie, I wanted to, but I knew that if I tried, all I'd wind up doing was blowing my cover and getting myself killed in the process."

"So you did nothing? You let them kill Peter and Cipriana?"

"I sent word to Murdock. I tried bribing the guards. I talked to Paz and together we tried to persuade Emilio to use Peter and Cipriana as a bargaining tool, the way he plans to do with Frankie now. But he wouldn't listen to anything we had to say. He was obsessed with beheading the princess and her husband and sending their heads to King Julio. Emilio's hatred for the king made him blind to reason."

"The—the day they executed Peter and Cipriana, where were you? What were you doing?"

The flashlight's glow filled the cave with wavy shadows. When Hawk looked at Rorie, his dark eyes begging for her understanding, the ghostly illumination revealed his shaded face. "I was bound and gagged."

"Bound and gagged?"

"Paz actually saved my life," Hawk said. "He suspected I'd do something foolish and get myself killed, so he had me bound and gagged and kept inside his house while the executions took place. He had no idea, at the time, that I was working for the U.S. government. He just thought I was a man with a conscience, who didn't want to see two young innocent people executed.''

"Why should I believe you?" Rorie asked. "You've lied to me all along—by omission. You should have told me the truth before you took the job as my bodyguard."

The man she had trusted not only with her life, but with her heart, had been a part of the renegade army that had kidnapped and executed Peter and Cipriana. Hawk had allowed her to give herself to him, body and soul. He had taken her innocence and accepted her love. And all the while he had kept his horrible secret.

"When I first agreed to this assignment, I didn't think it was important for you to know." He caressed her cheek with the back of his hand. She drew away from his touch. "I thought I owed you and your family something for not being able to save Peter and Cipriana. I thought that if I helped you save Frankie—"

"You could ease your conscience."

"I knew that sooner or later you'd find out. And I thought that if you could forgive me, I might finally be able to forgive myself."

"You want my forgiveness?"

"Yes. I want you to tell me that you understand why I did what I did. And I want you to tell me that you forgive me for not being able to save your brother and his wife."

Elizabeth Landry's words echoed in Rorie's mind. *I sense a true goodness in you. A goodness that can cleanse Gabriel's soul.*

Can my forgiveness cleanse his soul? Rorie wondered. No, forgiveness alone did not possess the power to wash away the darkness hiding Gabriel's soul from him. Only love possessed that kind of power.

"Can you ever forgive me, Rorie?" Hawk asked.

Looking directly at him, she wiped the tears from her eyes. "You need more than my forgiveness. And I'm not even sure I can give you that much."

Chapter 15

Another person's opinion had never meant so much to Hawk. He hated the weakness in him that made him need Rorie's forgiveness and yearn for her love. He'd never given a damn what others thought of him. Had never given a second thought to how his actions might affect another—not until he'd been unable to prevent Peter and Cipriana Dean's deaths.

And he hadn't wanted love. Hadn't needed love. He'd learned as a child never to depend on anyone except himself. Women came and went in his life. Disposable. Expendable. But Rorie was different. He needed her in a way he'd never needed anyone or anything.

Why was it that when he'd finally found someone who mattered to him, she had to be the sister of a man he had helped Santos kill? Was this his punishment for a ruthless, destructive life? Was forgiveness as unobtainable for him as happiness?

"Rorie?" Hawk reached down and lifted her hand in his.

She jerked away from him, her eyes widening with anger. "Don't touch me. Please, don't touch me."

The numbness in her body disappeared entirely, replaced by an unbearable emotional pain that consumed her. She was in love with a man who had been part of the renegade army that had executed Peter. Mentally, she could weigh every side of Hawk's situation when he had helped kidnap Peter, and she could understand that he'd done what he had to do. But emotionally, she could not accept his part in her brother's death.

Rorie jumped up from the blanket and paced around in a wide circle. Wringing her hands together, she stopped and glared at Hawk. "How could you have made love to me? How could you let me fall in love with you? I hate you for not telling me the truth!"

Her words were a knife in his heart, piercing deep and cutting him wide open. *I don't want you to hate me. I want you to love me.* "I'm sorry," he said. "You'll never know how sorry I am."

"How could you have let them kill Peter and Cipriana? How could you have—" Tears choked off her words.

Hawk stood and reached for her. "Oh, God, Rorie. Don't, honey. Please, don't."

She slapped his hands away and screamed, "You let me fall in love with you!" Tears streamed down her face. "I hate you! I hate you!" She pelted his chest with her tight fists. "I hate you!"

He stood straight and unmoving, letting her vent her fury. She pummeled his chest repeatedly until she'd spent her energy. Hawk drew her into his arms, his embrace extremely tender. She fell against him, laying her head on his chest. Weeping so strongly that her body shook with spasmodic sobs, she clung to Hawk.

He was her tormentor and her savior. Contemptible stranger and treasured lover. He personified both danger and survival. Both hatred and love.

When her sobs subsided, Hawk led her back to the blanket and drew her down to the cave floor. With one arm draped around her, he reached over and wiped her face with his fingertips.

"If I could have saved Peter and Cipriana, I would have," he told her. "But I couldn't."

She sniffed several times. "I thought I knew what kind of

man you were. I thought I understood about the life you'd lived. But I never... I never—''

"It's all right, Rorie. Hate me if you must. But trust me." He cupped her face in his hands. "Believe me when I tell you that we have a chance of escaping. It will be dangerous, but if you'll trust me and come with me, I'll give my life, if necessary, to get you to safety."

"What are you talking about?" She looked deep into his dark eyes and wanted desperately to believe him.

"Didn't you hear what Paz told me?" Hawk ran the tip of his thumb across her bottom lip.

"Not really," she said. "Something about following a river to the sea. It didn't make any sense to me."

"These caves are part of an underground structure that water seeping through the pores in the rocks has sculpted. There is a labyrinth of deep sinkholes, huge caves and long underground passages all over San Miguel, especially in this area near the limestone cliffs."

Rorie drew Hawk's hands from her face, but held them securely. "I'm afraid I don't understand."

Turning his hands over, Hawk captured her hands between his. "I think Paz was trying to tell me that somewhere back there—" he nodded toward the black hole of the cave behind them "—in that cavern is a subterranean river that is a passageway straight to the ocean."

"Are you saying that if we can find this river, we could swim our way to freedom?"

"I think it's our only chance to survive." He brought her hands to his lips and kissed the top of each one. "Paz said when morning comes, find the river and follow it to the sea. The only reason to wait until morning is for the sunlight. So that must mean that somewhere inside this cave—possibly near the river—the sunlight can get through.

"We can use the flashlights to guide us deeper into the cavern, but once we have to enter the river and start swimming, the flashlights will be of no use to us."

Pulling her hands out of his, Rorie clutched the front of Hawk's shirt. "If we escape, you can get word to Murdock, can't you? He has to help us find a way to get Frankie away from Santos. You know that once Santos gets what he wants from Lazaro and King Julio, he'll kill Frankie."

Hawk looked her square in the eye. "Do you trust me enough to follow me into the belly of this cave and find the river? Will you put your life in my hands once again?"

"Yes." She released her tenacious hold on his shirt. "I'll follow wherever you lead and I'll do whatever you tell me to do. I will put my life in your hands." She turned away from him.

He grasped her shoulders. "You'll trust your life to me because I'm your only hope for survival and maybe Frankie's only hope. But you won't trust your heart to me again, will you, Rorie?"

She closed her eyes, wishing she could block out the pain as easily as she shut out the dim light inside the cave. But the pain wound its way around inside her like an insidious parasite, feeding on her emotions, growing stronger with her every doubt and fear.

"Why should you care about my heart?" she asked. "You never wanted my love. All you wanted was my body."

She clasped her hands together and held them in her lap, afraid if she didn't control herself, she would turn and throw her arms around Hawk's neck. Her body yearned for his. She could no more deny her desire to belong to him than she could deny that she still loved him.

Loving Gabriel Hawk seemed like a betrayal of Peter, a betrayal of everything she believed in, everything she held dear. Gabriel was indeed a man chased by the demons of his past. He had lived a life of sin, associating with true evil when he became ensnared with Santos's band of renegades.

Did she truly possess the goodness to save Gabriel, to cleanse his soul and bring him out of the darkness and into the light? Did she love him enough to forgive him? To offer him the redemption she alone could give?

Hawk tightened his hold on Rorie's shoulders for one brief moment, then he released her. If she could never forgive him, never bring herself to love him again, she would be better off not knowing how he really felt about her. It would be better for her to think that all he'd ever wanted was her body.

"We need to eat, then get some rest," he said. "Once we

reach the river, if we can find it, I have no idea how long the swim will be from inside the caverns to the ocean. We'll need all our strength."

Rorie glanced over her shoulder. "If I don't make it...if I don't have the strength to swim all the way, I want you to promise me that you'll do everything you can to save Frankie."

The very thought that Rorie might die in their escape attempt was more than Hawk could bear. Didn't she realize that he would never leave her and swim away to freedom? Didn't she know that he would die himself before he would let anything happen to her? "We'll make it to the ocean together," he said. "And I promise you that we'll find a way to save Frankie."

She nodded her head, then turned away from him again. Rummaging in the sack, she grasped a banana. Hawk was right; they needed to eat and rest. "Here," she said as she tossed the banana to him.

He caught the fruit in midair. While Hawk peeled and ate the banana, Rorie retrieved another from the bag. They ate in silence. When they finished, she dipped into the sack again.

"Ouch!" Rorie jerked her hand out of the sack and stuck her finger in her mouth.

"What's wrong?"

"I cut my finger on something in the bag." She sucked on her finger, licking the blood off the tip.

Hawk emptied the sack. A melon and two papayas dropped onto the blanket, then a knife fell out, clinking against the limestone floor.

"Well, I'll be damned!" Hawk picked up the small, carved-handled knife.

"Paz Santos truly is a man of his word, isn't he?" Rorie asked. "He promised you my safety. So when his brother didn't honor his word, Paz tried to help us."

"Few people are all good or evil," Hawk said. "And there is often honor in men who have committed crimes against the laws of their land, even against the laws of God."

"I've always seen the world in black-and-white," Rorie admitted. "I suppose it was the way I was raised—to believe that there is a great distinction between good and evil, between right and wrong. But I'm beginning to understand, more and more, that real life is painted in various shades of gray.''

"Don't get too philosophical on me, honey." Hawk took the knife and split open the melon. ''I want you to concentrate on getting out of this cave and making our way to Vieques. Eat and rest. And save all your strength for tomorrow.''

Despite the knots in her stomach and the sour taste in her mouth, Rorie consumed as much of the melon as she could. After finishing the meal, she lay down and curled into a fetal position. Hawk lifted the edge of her blanket and wrapped it around her.

He wanted to spread his blanket beside hers, slip his arms around her and hold her all night long. But he knew she wouldn't welcome his touch tonight. She would not accept him with open arms as she had done last night and the night before.

He spread out his blanket a couple of feet away from hers. Then he reached out, picked up the flashlight and extinguished their only source of light.

When he heard Rorie's indrawn breath, it took every ounce of his willpower not to pull her into his arms. ''Do you want me to turn the flashlight back on?''

"No," she said. "We don't know how far away the river is. We might need both flashlights. There's no need to waste the energy.''

Hawk cleaned the knife on his sleeve, then slipped it into the side of his boot. He lay down, covered himself with half the blanket and closed his eyes. He'd never been a man who prayed. Bargaining with God for Rorie's life after the jeep wreck had been the first time he'd prayed since he was a kid. Back then he'd prayed that his real parents would appear out of nowhere and take him home with them. They would love him and promise to keep him with them forever. When he'd finally realized the foolishness of that prayer, he had asked God for good people to adopt him. And when that dream had proved as impossible as the first, he had stopped praying.

Until he met Rorie Dean.

He knew that only a power outside himself, a supernatural

power, could help him and Rorie escape and find a way to save her nephew's life.

In the dark, silent tomb of the cave, Hawk prayed once again. *I don't care what happens to me. Just keep Rorie safe. And keep little Frankie safe. Punish me, if You have to, but if You're the God of love she believes in, take care of her. Please.*

"Wake up, Rorie." Hawk shook her gently until she opened her eyes. "Time to head out. It's morning."

Pulling herself into a sitting position, she looked at Hawk and nodded. He handed her a flashlight, then helped her to her feet.

"Stay right behind me," he said. "And do whatever I tell you to do without question."

"I will."

Hawk held out his hand to her. She hesitated, then placed her hand in his. "We're going to make it."

"Yes, we're going to make it," she repeated.

Dark and damp, the cavern's stone walls surrounded them. They walked deeper and deeper into the interior of the mountainside, constantly aware that they faced the unknown. After a long trek, they came to a narrow passageway not high enough to walk through, so Rorie followed Hawk's lead when he got down on all fours. They crawled into the small opening, which eventually led them into an enormous cave.

Hawk drew Rorie to her feet. The cavern floor was encrusted with pearl-like, limestone-coated snail shells. Overhead, huge stalactites hung from the ceiling like giant icicles.

"Look!" Hawk pointed to the tiny hole in the dome of the cave. A thin shaft of sunlight shone straight down, like the beam from a miniature spotlight. "We're not that far from the surface."

He grabbed her hand and led her slowly across the length of the central cave. The cavern soon narrowed again, but remained high enough for them to continue walking.

Hawk stopped abruptly. "Listen."

Rorie halted, her body only inches from his. "It sounds like running water."

"We're getting close to the river."

Within minutes they reached the source of the sound. The river flowed from along its subterranean course, bursting to life directly in front of them. Pouring through the opening where the gigantic cavern had collapsed, sunlight sparkled across the waterway, reflecting the green of shrubbery above. The river disappeared underground several yards away.

"Are you ready?" Hawk asked. He wished he could spare her this treacherous swim, one that could easily end in death for both of them.

"I'm ready."

Hawk tested the depth of the river and found it quickly dropped from a couple of feet to well over his head. He swam back to the edge and motioned for Rorie to join him.

"It's the only way out for us," he said.

"I know." She followed him into the river, all the while praying repeatedly that they would make it to the sea.

They swam to the end of the cavern and then plunged beneath the water's surface. Holding her breath, Rorie swam forward, wondering how long it would be before she could resurface and thankful for the two weeks of training Hawk had put her through.

Just when she reached the point where she thought her lungs would burst, she saw daylight ahead. Hawk jerked her to the surface inside a small cavern near the entrance to the ocean. She gulped in huge swallows of air.

"We're close, honey," he told her. "Listen carefully and you can hear the ocean."

Breathless and weak, Rorie only nodded. She allowed Hawk to support her weight while he trod water.

"I don't think it's much farther," he said. "You can make it, can't you, Rorie?"

"I can make it."

With aching arms and legs, Rorie swam underwater toward the sound of the sea. Telling herself over and over again that she had to survive, she had to rescue Frankie, she had to succeed, Rorie followed Hawk to freedom. The brief minutes underwater had seemed endless. When Hawk pulled her head above the water again, she looked straight up at the sky as she gasped for air. Ocean waves washed over them.

Once she had caught her breath, Rorie took in her surroundings. Twelve-hundred-foot high limestone cliffs towered above them. Huge limestone boulders littered the coastline.

"How—how are we going to get up there?" she asked. "We can't climb those bluffs."

Circling her waist, Hawk drew Rorie along with him as he swam toward the rocky shore. Stopping short of the jagged stones guarding the rain-gouged gullies that sliced through the cliffs, he stood and lifted Rorie upright. The ocean swirled around her waist when her feet touched the bottom.

"We can rest for a while." Hawk brushed the damp strands of her hair away from her face. "Then we'll have to swim about a half mile before we can go ashore. It's too dangerous here. There's a narrow beach several miles away from the cliffs."

Half an hour later, drenched to the skin, badly bruised and covered with scratches, Hawk and Rorie crawled ashore on the sandy beach. After a short rest, they followed the shoreline for several miles until the cliffs disappeared and were replaced by softer hills. They climbed a grassy embankment. Atop the knoll, Hawk pulled Rorie into his arms and they looked down over the road that led from Mayari to Vieques.

"We can't take the road," Hawk said. "It would be too dangerous. But we can follow the road, if we stay well hidden in the thicket."

"How long will it take us to get to Vieques?" She rested her head on Hawk's chest, thankful for his strength.

"On foot, I'd say a good four, maybe five hours."

With every muscle in her body already screaming with pain, Rorie wondered how she could endure four or five more hours trudging through the underbrush, without totally collapsing.

"Oh, dear Lord," she moaned quietly.

Hawk grabbed her shoulders. When he shook her, she rolled her head from side to side, then flung it back and blew out a deep breath.

"Come on, honey, show me how tough you are. What's a four-hour walk to a lady like you? The strongest, bravest lady I've ever known."

* * *

They arrived in the village of Vieques that afternoon. And although they received numerous curious stares, no one stopped them or questioned them. The first three people to whom Hawk spoke, asking if they knew Tito Álverez, shook their heads and scurried away. The fourth person, an elderly woman in a fish market, gave them directions to Tito's house.

When they reached the small wooden shack at the edge of town, a tall, slender man with a thick black mustache motioned them inside, then quickly shut the door behind them.

Rorie's weak knees gave way. Hawk lifted her into his arms, carried her into the interior of the one-room house and placed her on the bed.

He turned to Tito. "I need to get a message through to Murdock as quickly as possible."

"And who are you, *señor?*" Tito asked.

"I'm Hawk. And that is—" he nodded toward Rorie "—Señorita Aurora Dean. She is the sister of Peter Dean, the missionary who was married to Princess Cipriana."

"*Sí, sí.* I have been expecting you and the *señorita*. Murdock, he say to bring you and the lady to La Vega."

"Then Murdock knows we don't have Prince Francisco with us," Hawk said.

"Murdock say if you come to see Tito, I tell you—" Tito scratched his head "—I tell you Lazaro make the deal and the prince is in La Vega."

"Oh, dear God!" Rorie rose from the bed. "It's happening, isn't it? Santos is getting what he wants."

Ignoring Rorie's outburst, Hawk grabbed Tito's arm. "How can we get to La Vega?"

"I drive you in my car," Tito said. "We be there before sunset."

Hawk patted Tito on the back. "Do you have some coffee and maybe a bite of something to eat for Señorita Dean and me?"

"Plenty of coffee." Tito pointed to the wood-burning stove in the center of the room. "And bread and fish."

Late that evening, the guards at the entrance to La Vega detained them until they checked with the general. But once

Lazaro issued orders that the threesome was to be allowed to come directly to the palace, the guards' attitude changed immediately.

Murdock waited for them outside the palace, and rushed to meet them the minute Tito parked his battered old Chevy.

Hawk swung open the door and stepped out, then turned to help Rorie. She slid across the seat and out of the car. After taking a couple of steps, her knees gave way to the weakness claiming her whole body. Catching her before she fell, Hawk lifted her into his arms.

"Good God, you two look like hell," Murdock said. "What happened to y'all?"

With one arm draped around Hawk's neck and her head resting on his shoulder, Rorie reached out to Murdock. "Where is Frankie? Is he here in La Vega?"

"Come on inside and we'll talk." Turning to Tito Álverez, Murdock handed the man a packet. "Thanks for getting them here safely."

Accepting the packet filled with gold pieces, Tito nodded several times as he thanked Murdock profusely.

Following Murdock, Hawk carried Rorie into the palace and straight to Murdock's room. He eased her down in the middle of the big four-poster bed. She clung to him.

"Where's Frankie?" she asked.

"Take it easy, honey," Hawk said. "Rest, for now. I'll talk to Murdock and find out what's going on and if he knows where Frankie is."

She didn't want to fall asleep. She wanted to stay awake and question Murdock herself. If Frankie was in La Vega, she wanted to go to him. But she was tired—so very, very tired.

Hawk watched Rorie close her eyes and drift off to sleep. She had been relentless, struggling to be as strong as he was. Several times in their odyssey from the caves, to the ocean, and along the trail to Vieques, he'd seen her come close to giving up. But she had fought the physical weakness and the mental fatigue. She had endured.

Looking at her now, he wondered how he ever could have thought she was soft and weak and incapable of surviving a mission into San Miguel.

"She's quite a woman, isn't she?" Murdock clasped Hawk's shoulder.

Hawk nodded. "I've never known anyone like her."

"If she'd been with anyone other than you, I'd have given her up for dead," Murdock said. "You want to tell me what happened?" He pulled out a silver flask and handed it to Hawk.

Hawk lifted the flask to his mouth and took a swallow of whiskey. The liquor burned a trail down his throat and ignited a fire in his belly. He quickly recounted their ordeal.

"So what's happened?" Hawk asked when he was finished. "The message Tito gave us was that Lazaro made a deal with Santos, and Prince Francisco is here in La Vega."

"Just as soon as Santos got hold of the prince, he didn't waste any time offering Lazaro the deal of a lifetime." Murdock gripped the edge of the table. "Lazaro doesn't trust Santos and he hates the very thought of their joining forces, but he has agreed to the deal because he wants this war ended."

"Then Frankie Dean is here in La Vega?"

"He's here at the palace," Murdock replied. "He's under the very watchful eye of Rosa Martinez."

"Any way we can get to the boy?"

"I can make arrangements with Mateo for Miss Dean to see her nephew, but there's no way she can take him with her. Not yet. Not until King Julio meets with Lazaro."

"Not until King Julio walks into the trap set for him," Hawk said. "With Santos's and Lazaro's combined forces, the war should be over in a few days, a week at most. Right? So what happens when the war ends? What are our chances of getting Frankie?"

"Mateo has promised to give the boy to Miss Dean." Murdock took a deep breath and shook his head. "But Mateo won't be the only one giving orders then. And my bet is that Emilio Santos has no intention of letting the young prince live."

Chapter 16

Rorie awoke suddenly, gasping for air. She felt the watery weight of the river bearing down on her, pushing her farther and farther below the surface. Disoriented and afraid, she thrashed about in the bed. A pair of strong arms encompassed her body and drew her into a warm embrace.

Soothing her with his touch and his words, Hawk comforted Rorie. "You're safe," he whispered. "You're safe."

Reassured by his nearness, Rorie relaxed in his arms. Hawk wanted to protect her from the evil world around them. He wanted to take away her every pain and fill her life with peace and joy and happiness. And he knew that someday, another man would give her all that he longed to give her. Someday another man would love her. He couldn't bear to think about someone else possessing Rorie, claiming her for his own. No matter how selfish his desires, Hawk wanted Rorie to belong to him forever—body and soul.

Lifting her head, she gazed into Hawk's eyes. "How long have I been asleep?"

"About four hours." He caressed her cheek and died a little inside when she flinched. "Murdock brought us some clean clothes. I've already showered and changed. Do you want me to help you to the bathroom?''

"No." Rorie pulled out of Hawk's arms and scooted to the edge of the bed. Her muscles ached. The scratches and scrapes on her body itched and burned. "Did you find out anything about Frankie?''

"He's here in the palace, but he's under guard. Rosa is with him.''

"The woman who kidnapped him?''

"Murdock is trying to arrange something with Lazaro right now, so you can see Frankie.''

Rorie stood on wobbly legs. When Hawk reached for her, she knocked his hands away. "I'll be all right. I want to... Where are those clean clothes? I should take a bath and change. I feel so dirty.''

Hawk clamped his teeth together, tightening his jaw. The vein in his neck throbbed. Did her words hold a double meaning? Did she feel dirty because she'd allowed her brother's kidnapper to make love to her?

He sat on the side of the bed and watched Rorie walk slowly and unsteadily across the room. When she closed the bathroom door, he slammed his fists down on the bed. Cursing silently, he stood and paced back and forth, all the while damning himself for hurting Rorie. He'd known that the truth about his association with Santos would come out sooner or later, and he'd known she would never be able to forgive him for his part in Peter's death. Regardless of her feelings, he had taken her innocence, and he'd let her fall in love with him. She had every right to hate him. Hell, he hated himself!

When Rorie emerged from the bathroom, clean and fresh and neatly dressed in the green army trousers and matching, too-large shirt, she found Hawk and Murdock deep in conversation.

"Is General Lazaro going to let me see Frankie?'' she asked.

At the sound of her voice, Hawk and Murdock turned toward her. They exchanged a look that told Rorie something was wrong.

"Has something happened to Frankie?" She rushed over to Hawk, but stopped abruptly before she actually touched him. Her instinct had been to attack him, to beat her fists against his chest as she'd done in the cave. The anger she felt for him continually boiled inside her, threatening to overflow. She hated him. And she loved him. And she had never been so confused in her life. "What's wrong? Tell me!"

"Nothing's wrong," Hawk said. "Not exactly."

"What does that mean?" she asked.

"It means that plans have changed." Murdock glanced questioningly at Hawk, who nodded an affirmative response. "Lazaro has taken the prince with him to meet King Julio."

Rorie gasped. "Frankie is going to be right in the middle of the fighting, isn't he?" She reached deep within her, garnering all the emotional strength she possessed. She would not fall apart. She would not allow fear to rule her actions.

"The boy will be in some danger," Murdock said. "But left here at the palace with Rosa and Santos's guards, the prince would have been in more danger. This way, Prince Francisco will be under the general's protection. Lazaro has given me his word that, once the prince has served his purpose and drawn the king out of Puerto Angelo, he will send the boy back to La Vega—to you, Miss Dean."

"Lazaro is going to send Frankie back here to me?" She desperately wanted to trust the general's word. "Do you believe him?"

"We have no choice," Hawk said. "There's no way we can get to Frankie. We're pretty much under house arrest here at the palace. Only Lazaro can set both us and Frankie free."

"What about Emilio Santos?" Rorie asked.

"Santos's main objective right now is helping Lazaro defeat King Julio," Hawk told her. "Once the war ends, then Santos will try to find a way to eliminate Frankie."

"Lazaro understands Santos," Murdock said. "He knows Santos wants to see the heir to the throne dead. Although Lazaro is joining forces with Santos to end the war, he doesn't trust him. Lazaro knows our best chance of saving the prince's life is to get him out of San Miguel while the war is raging."

"We're pretty much at General Lazaro's mercy, where Frankie is concerned," Hawk said. "All we can do is wait."

"Wait and pray." Clasping her hands in a prayerful gesture, Rorie closed her eyes and pleaded with God for his help.

"I'll have a ship standing by off the coast of Cabo Verde," Murdock told them. "As soon as Lazaro sends Frankie to us, we'll move quickly." He walked to the door, clasped the handle and looked back over his shoulder. "Let's hope this plan falls together without any glitches. If it does, y'all will be back in the U.S., along with the prince, very soon."

"Mr. Murdock?" Rorie called out to him just as he opened the door.

He closed the door and turned to face her. "What is it?"

"How did Emilio Santos find out that Frankie was at the Blessed Virgin Mission and that Hawk and I were going there to get him?"

"A very good question, Miss Dean."

"Only four people, other than Hawk and me, knew where Frankie was and that Hawk and I were going to the mission."

"Do you think I betrayed you?" Murdock asked.

"I don't know. Did you?"

"I'd trust Murdock with my life," Hawk said. "I can promise you that he didn't betray us."

"Then who did?" Rorie asked. "We know King Julio didn't. Despite who and what that man is, he loves Frankie more than anything. So that leaves Captain García, who is completely loyal to the king, and Nina Hernández, who told me how fond she is of Frankie."

"Nina and Rosa are cousins, Miss Dean," Murdock said, shifting his feet restlessly. "Does that narrow your list of suspects?"

"Nina Hernández and Rosa, the woman who kidnapped Frankie from the mission, are cousins? How do you know?"

"I had a little talk with Rosa," Murdock said. "After I praised her for her part in Santos's and Lazaro's upcoming victory, she was more than glad to fill me in on a few details."

"And what are those details?" Rorie's stomach knotted painfully.

Hawk came up behind Rorie, close enough so that she felt the heat from his big body. But he didn't touch her.

"Nina was quite fond of the prince, but..." Murdock paused briefly. "Nina is pregnant with King Julio's child. She expected the king to marry her and proclaim her child the heir to the throne. Old Julio refused to do either. He told Nina that Prince Francisco would remain the heir to the throne."

"So, Nina betrayed the king," Hawk said, as he considered Nina's motive for putting the prince's life at risk. "She used you to get the information about where the prince was hidden. Apparently, King Julio wouldn't tell her where he'd sent Frankie."

"Nina knew that if Santos got his hands on the prince, he would eventually eliminate the boy," Murdock explained. "What Nina didn't know was that Santos would use the prince to bring about the king's defeat."

Rorie's shoulders slumped. Her hands trembled. She despised this world, this country filled with hate and betrayal and lust for power. She loathed Santos and Lazaro and King Julio. She even hated Murdock, who was a part of all this evil. But most of all she hated Hawk because he had kept the truth from her.

Murdock opened the door, "Try to get some rest. And be ready to leave at a moment's notice," he said, closing the door behind him.

"Why don't you go back to bed?" Hawk said. "It could be hours, maybe even tomorrow, before Lazaro sends Frankie back to the palace."

Rorie walked away from Hawk and sat down on the side of the bed. "Do you really believe that Lazaro will send Frankie back to us?"

Hawk wanted to wrap Rorie in his arms, to comfort her and promise her that everything was going to be all right. But he knew she didn't want him to touch her. And he couldn't honestly promise her Frankie's safe return.

"I believe there's a good chance Lazaro will keep his word."

"Unless?"

"Think positive thoughts, Rorie. Otherwise you'll go crazy while we're waiting."

Fully clothed, Rorie lay down across the bed and closed her eyes. Memories of Hawk filled her mind. His wicked smile. His deep, sensuous laughter. His strong arms holding her. His soft lips taking hers in a ravenous kiss. His body covering hers.

Suddenly her eyes flew open. She willed her breathing to slow from its frantic pace. Taking several deep breaths, she sat up in the middle of the bed and crossed her legs at the ankle.

"Why is Murdock in San Miguel working for our government?" she demanded.

Hawk snapped his head around to face her. "What?"

"What is Murdock doing here in the middle of this civil war?"

"Unofficially, the United States has backed Lazaro since the beginning of the war," Hawk told her.

"Yes, I know that. But what does Murdock do, exactly?"

There was no point in lying to her, Hawk reminded himself. She was a smart woman. She'd probably already figured out most of it, anyway.

"Murdock is a facilitator. He makes things happen with as little fuss and bother as possible. He does whatever is necessary to bring about the desired results."

"Then you were a 'facilitator,' too, weren't you?"

Hawk saw the fear and rage in her eyes. *Let her be angry. Let her hate me. But don't let her be afraid of me.*

He walked toward the bed. She sat perfectly still and watched his approach. He sat down, reached out and grasped her hands. Her bottom lip quivered. Her chin trembled.

"Please, don't be afraid of me, Rorie." He lifted her hands to his lips. "I would never hurt you. Don't you know that I'd die to protect you?" He kissed her hands.

She jerked her hands out of his. Looking at his bowed head, the defeated slump of his shoulders, Rorie's heart ached for him. Reaching out, she cupped his face in her hands.

He looked up into her gentle, caring blue eyes and thought he would die from the need to hold her. "I'm sorry. I never should have—"

She covered his mouth with her hand. "Shh. Hush. Don't

say anything else. We can't change the past. We can't go back and undo what was done.''

Rorie eased Hawk's head against her breasts and encompassed his big body in her embrace. He slipped his arms around her waist and lay against her, listening to the sound of her heartbeat.

This woman—this rare and beautiful woman—could have been his for the rest of his life. She had loved him enough to give him her innocence; and greedily, he had taken all she had offered. But because of his past, there could be no future for them. He had committed unpardonable sins. If Rorie could not offer him absolution, then he would live and die unforgiven.

Shortly after dawn, Hawk awoke. Rorie lay beside him, snuggled close, her arm draped across his waist. The soft, repetitive knock on the door alerted Hawk to what had awakened him. He shook Rorie. She mumbled something incoherent and cuddled closer.

The door eased open. Murdock slipped inside. Hawk sat up, turned and flung his legs off the bed. With the straps of two shoulder holsters crisscrossing his broad chest, Murdock crept across the room.

''Lazaro sent the boy, with four guards, back to the palace,'' Murdock whispered. ''They're waiting for us. Get her up and come with me. Now!''

''Rorie.'' Hawk shook her again.

She opened her eyes and jumped straight up. ''What?''

''Frankie's here,'' Hawk said. ''Lazaro sent him back to us. We've got to leave now.''

Hawk and Rorie followed Murdock up the dark hallways and down the back stairs. Three armed men and one woman surrounded the young prince, near the back entrance to the palace. The moment Rorie saw her nephew, she wanted to run to him and pull him into her arms. But she wondered if Frankie would even recognize her.

When they approached the guards, Murdock spoke rapidly in Spanish, issuing orders. Then, turning to Hawk, he drew his old friend aside.

"Two of the guards are Lazaro's men and two are San-tos's," Murdock whispered. "Santos wouldn't let the boy go unless Lazaro agreed to splitting the guards. The woman and the man with the beard are the renegades."

"Damn!" Hawk cursed quietly, hissing the words between clenched teeth.

"The plan is for me and one of Lazaro's men to go on ahead and make sure all is safe." Murdock grabbed Hawk's arm. "Unless I send word otherwise, I'll be waiting with a rowboat to take y'all straight out to the cruiser sitting about a mile off the Cabo Verde coast."

Murdock removed the two shoulder holsters and handed one to Hawk and the other to Rorie. "Be careful. And good luck."

Murdock motioned for one of the guards to come with him, and the two of them left together. Hawk strapped on the holster and then turned to help Rorie put on hers.

"We're going to follow Murdock in a second car after he makes sure it's safe," Hawk told her. "He'll have everything ready for us." He drew Rorie into his arms and whispered in her ear, "The woman and the bearded man are Santos's soldiers."

She gasped silently, then pulled out of Hawk's arms and turned to the three remaining guards. "May I see my nephew?" she asked in Spanish.

The guards separated. Standing there in his pajamas, his big brown eyes so like Peter's, Frankie stared up at Rorie. He looked so small and helpless. And so frightened. But he put on a brave front, with his little chin held high and his shoulders squared.

Rorie walked over and knelt down in front of him. Speak-ing in Spanish, she said, "Hello, Frankie. Do you remember me? I'm your Aunt Rorie. Your father's sister. When you were a very little boy, we spent a great deal of time together."

The child gazed at her, confusion in his eyes. He glanced around at the three armed, uniformed guards.

"Your Grandfather Julio is going to let you go to the United States and visit me and your Grandmother and Grand-father Dean."

Prince Francisco remained silent, his dark eyes expressing

his uncertainty. Rorie wanted to finger his black curls, caress his chubby cheek, draw him into the safety of her arms. But she knew better than to touch him. The last thing she wanted to do was scare him.

"When you were little we used to sing a song together. Maybe you'll remember." Rorie sang an entire verse of "Jesus Loves Me."

Frankie nodded his head and began to sing along with her. Tears gathered in Rorie's eyes and trickled down her cheeks. She continued singing. Frankie smiled as he sang along with her.

"You do remember me, don't you, Frankie? I'm your Aunt Rorie."

"*Tía* Rorie?" A glimmer of recognition flickered in the child's eyes.

"Yes, darling, *Tía* Rorie." She opened her arms and waited, praying that Frankie would remember enough to trust her.

Staying where he was, making no attempt to go into her arms, the child held out his little hand. Rorie clasped it in hers and uttered a silent prayer of thanks. She led him away from the guards and across the room to Hawk.

"Frankie, this is Hawk. He's my... He's my friend, and he's going to take us to the ocean where we'll board a big boat and go all the way to the United States."

The female soldier stepped forward, halting behind Rorie. "It is time for us to leave. We will go to the car now. We are to follow Señor Murdock, after waiting ten minutes."

Daylight spread across the horizon, the sky pale blue and clear. The guards hustled Rorie and Frankie into the back seat, Santos's female soldier joining them. Hawk was sandwiched between the two male soldiers in the front.

As the miles passed, taking them farther and farther from La Vega and the war raging in the distance, Rorie grew more and more uneasy. They were only a few miles from Cabo Verde—their destination. Murdock would be waiting and within an hour, she and Hawk and Frankie would be safely aboard the cruiser and headed for home.

She held Frankie's hand securely in hers and tried to push aside all her doubts and fears.

The car gave a sudden lurch. After coughing and spluttering several times, the motor died. Cursing loudly, the driver slammed his hands down on the steering wheel.

"What's wrong?" Rorie asked. "Why are we stopping?"

"Something is wrong with the engine," the female soldier said. "We will get out and walk about while Diego checks under the hood."

Hawk glanced over his shoulder, giving Rorie an unspoken warning. Her heartbeat accelerated. Dear God, what was going on? What did Hawk think would happen once they got out of the car?

The female guard opened the door and stepped outside, then motioned for Rorie and Frankie to follow. The driver got out, walked over and lifted the hood. The guard to Hawk's right, opened the passenger door and stepped out. Hesitantly, Hawk slid across the seat and eased out of the car.

From the thicket near the road came the rat-a-tat-tat of gunfire. Four men suddenly appeared.

"Take cover, Rorie!" Hawk yelled as he drew out the 9-mm pistol Murdock had strapped on him. He hit the ground and rolled over and over, firing repeatedly at their attackers.

Rorie grabbed Frankie and shoved him under the car, then crawled in beside him. Santos's female guard clasped her hand around Frankie's leg and dragged him from beneath the car. Rorie screamed at the woman, but she didn't pay any attention.

As Rorie slid out from beneath the car, she drew her pistol from the shoulder holster. Gunfire erupted all around her. The four attackers lay dead on the ground as did the male guard Santos had sent with Frankie. Lazaro's guard, his gun in his hand, knelt over Hawk, who lay crumpled against the right rear fender. Hawk held the 9-mm against his belly.

Salty bile rose in Rorie's throat. Blood stained the front of Hawk's shirt. His face was chalk white. Sweat dotted his brow and upper lip.

Rorie glanced back quickly at the female, who had one arm draped beneath Frankie's throat. In her other hand she held a gun that was pointed directly at Rorie.

Rorie tightened her hold on the pistol in her trembling

hand. "Let Prince Francisco go," she said. "Let him come to me, right now."

"The boy is going nowhere, *señorita*," the woman said. "General Lazaro is weak, but Emilio Santos is strong. He does not let his enemies live to attack him again." She tightened her hold on Frankie's neck. The boy cried out in fear. "Prince Francisco dies! You all die!"

The woman's eyes held a wild, insane look, like a mad dog, crazed and ready to kill.

Elizabeth Landry's prediction reverberated inside Rorie's head. *In the end it will be you who must save both Frankie and Gabriel. If you have the courage. If your love is strong enough.*

Without thinking, without planning, acting purely on instinct, Rorie aimed the semiautomatic and fired. The gun in the female soldier's hand went off once, twice, the bullets piercing the earth, then fell from her fingers to the road. Blood gushed from the wound in her head. She slumped slowly to the ground. Frankie pulled free and ran toward Rorie.

Gripping the gun tightly, Rorie stared at the weapon she had used to kill another human being. For one split second she froze, the reality of what she'd done hitting her full force. And then she felt Frankie clinging to her, burying his little face against her stomach. She dropped to her knees, flung her arms around him and lifted him onto her hip.

"*Señorita*, your man is badly hurt," Lazaro's guard said.

Carrying Frankie, Rorie rushed around the car. She stopped dead still. "Hawk!"

"It's only a couple of miles to the beach where Murdock is waiting," Hawk told her. "Take Lazaro's man here with you and get Frankie to the boat."

"What about you?" Rorie set Frankie on his feet. He clung to her. She knelt beside Hawk. "We can't leave you here like this."

"I'll be all right. Murdock can send someone back for me." Lifting his bloody hand, Hawk let it hover near Rorie's cheek. "Get the hell out of here. Now!"

"Dammit, Gabriel Hawk, don't you curse at me! And don't you give me orders."

Rorie stood, picked up Frankie and handed him to Lazaro's

guard. "Take him to Murdock. And tell Murdock that Hawk and I will expect him to come for us as soon as he can."

"No! Dammit, Rorie, you're not staying here with me. I want you to go with Frankie."

She turned to the guard, who looked back and forth from Hawk to Rorie, obviously uncertain what he should do.

"You must get Prince Francisco to Murdock as soon as possible." Rorie clutched the soldier's arm. "I will stay with my man."

Frankie cried out for Rorie. She kissed his cheek and tried to reassure him, then waved goodbye as Lazaro's guard headed off down the road to Cabo Verde.

Rorie knelt down beside Hawk. "Do you think you can stand? We can't stay out here in the open like this. It isn't safe."

"It isn't safe for you here with me," Hawk told her. "Why the hell did you stay?"

"Because I couldn't leave you."

She lifted his arm and draped it around her neck, then slid her arm around his waist and urged him to stand. Using every ounce of her strength, she helped him to his feet. When he swayed, she tightened her hold and led him off the road and into a nearby thicket.

When the burden of his weight became too much for her, Rorie and Hawk dropped to the ground. With quick, quivering fingers, she unbuttoned his shirt and examined his wounds.

"I've got to stop the bleeding," she told him, knowing if she didn't do something, Hawk would bleed to death. Hurriedly she removed her shirt, ripped it apart and used it for makeshift bandages.

"I think one of the bullets went all the way through," Hawk told her. "But the other one is still in me."

"How—how long do you think it will take Murdock to get Frankie aboard the ship and get back here to help us?"

Hawk's eyelids flickered. Rorie grabbed his face between her hands. "Gabriel! Gabriel!"

"What's the matter?" He slurred his words.

"You nearly passed out."

"Need to get the bullet out," he mumbled.

"Me?" her voice squeaked. "You want me to remove the bullet? But how?"

Hawk reached toward his boot, then promptly passed out cold. Rorie unlaced his boot and discovered the knife Paz Santos had hidden in the sack of fruit he'd given them.

She held up the knife, staring at it as if it were an unknown object. How did Hawk expect her to remove the bullet? She had some first-aid training, but she'd never operated on anyone in her life.

Hawk's eyelids fluttered again. He opened his eyes. "Did I faint?" he asked.

"Yes, you fainted."

He looked at the knife she held in her hand. "You know what you have to do."

"I can't do it," Rorie said. "I'll kill you if I try to remove the bullet. I don't know how."

"I'm a dead man if you don't," he said.

"But how——"

"You assisted me in two surgeries that night in Utuado. You saw what I did. Just stick the knife in the wound and dig for the bullet."

"But we don't have any way to sterilize the knife and nothing to use as anesthesia, not even whiskey."

"It won't matter." He gripped Rorie's hand. "I'll probably pass out from the pain and won't feel a thing."

Rorie leaned over, kissed Hawk on the lips, then removed her belt and slid the leather between his teeth. He grinned at her. A silly, cockeyed grin. Tears spilled from her eyes. He reached up and wiped her face, mingling the blood on his fingers with her tears.

Using her ripped shirt, she smeared the blood away from the open wound in Hawk's shoulder, then glanced at his other wound. The bandage on his side was soaked with fresh red blood.

Lifting the knife, she prayed for divine assistance. *Please, dear Lord, give me the strength and courage to do this. I don't want Gabriel to die. I love him. I love him so very, very much.*

Rorie embedded the blade a couple of inches into Hawk's shoulder. He roared with pain. Her hand trembled. A thick stream of blood poured from the gunshot wound. Rorie probed deeper. Hawk cried out, then bit down on the leather belt in his mouth. She glanced at his pale, clammy face. Perspiration covered his forehead. Rivulets of sweat poured down his neck.

Slowly, carefully, she continued delving into Hawk's flesh, seeking the bullet. When he groaned again, she took a quick look at his agonized face. His eyes closed. His mouth gaped open. The belt slid out and down over his chin.

Rorie thanked God that Gabriel had finally passed out. She eased the knife deeper and encountered the bullet. She had no tweezers, no means of removing the bullet. She had no choice; she would have to dig it out with the knife.

Gabriel Hawk's blood covered her hands as she worked diligently to remove the bullet. With her tears almost blinding her, she continued relentlessly.

"I love you," she told an unconscious Hawk. "I love you and I forgive you. Do you hear me, Gabriel? No matter what you did in the past, I forgive you. You can't die." She lifted the bullet higher and higher, praying she could bring it to the surface without losing it. "I won't let you die!"

Chapter 17

Six hours later, Murdock found them in the thicket, less than thirty feet off the road from where the stalled car sat with the hood still open. Rorie held Hawk's head in her lap, her bloody hand pressed gently over the ripped-shirt bandage covering the bullet wound in his side.

"Is he still alive?" Murdock asked.

Rorie nodded. "Yes, he's alive. He's unconscious. He passed out while I was removing the bullet from his shoulder."

"Well, I'll be damned."

"How is Frankie?" Rorie asked.

"Last I saw of the young prince, he was crying his eyes out, but he was on our cruiser headed for the States."

Rorie let out a deep breath. Fresh tears misted her eyes. "Thank you." She mouthed the words as her emotions lodged in her throat.

Murdock removed his shirt, leaned over and draped it around Rorie's shoulders. "I'm sorry it took us so long to get back, but we ran into a little trouble. It seems the war is spreading quickly all over the island."

"Gabriel needs a doctor." Rorie caressed his pale cheek. "He should be in a hospital."

"There's another ship on its way to pick us up. It should be waiting for us by the time we get to the beach. We'll go straight to Miami. I'll radio ahead and have a medical helicopter waiting for us the minute we dock."

"He thought I'd leave him." Lowering her head, Rorie lifted Gabriel in her arms and laid her cheek against the top of his head. "He actually thought I'd leave him."

Murdock grasped Rorie's shoulder. "Arturo and I can carry him to the truck."

Murdock called for the guard's help, then eased Rorie away from Hawk. The two men lifted him and carried him toward the back of the truck. Rorie slipped on Murdock's shirt, then stumbled along behind them, her body weak and her mind fuzzy from exhaustion. She rushed over and lowered the tailgate, then crawled up and onto the truck bed. Arturo and Murdock lifted Hawk into the truck, placing him back in Rorie's arms.

"He's tough," Murdock said. "He'll make it."

"Yes, I know. He's a big, strong man." Tears cascaded down Rorie's cheeks.

Within an hour they were on the ship, headed for Miami. Rorie stayed with Hawk, cradling him in her arms. Their adventure to hell and back would soon come to an end. They had accomplished their goal. They had rescued Frankie. Her parents would be overjoyed to know that both she and their grandson were safe.

When they reached Miami and she knew for sure that Hawk was going to be all right, she would catch the first plane to Chattanooga. As much as she wanted to stay with Gabriel, she realized that the longer she stayed with him, the harder it would be to leave him.

If she'd thought that he loved her, that he wanted a lifetime commitment, no power on earth could have torn her from his side. But although Gabriel wanted her and perhaps, in his own way, cared about her, he'd made it perfectly clear that beyond obtaining her forgiveness for his part in Peter's death, all he'd ever wanted from her was a physical relationship. She could give him the forgiveness he so desperately needed, but he could not give her the forever-after kind of love she wanted.

When Hawk awoke, the first face he saw was Rorie's. She sat by his bedside, all fresh and golden and beautiful in the morning sunlight that filtered through the closed blinds.

"Hello," she said, her voice soft and sweet.

"Hello, yourself." He glanced around the hospital room. "Where are we?"

"In Miami. Murdock made it back to us. He and Arturo, Lazaro's guard who got Frankie to safety. Murdock had another ship waiting for us." Rorie sighed. "Frankie's here in the hospital getting a complete physical. Murdock's keeping an eye on him for me."

"Murdock's the man you need if you want to get things done." Hawk looked down at his bandaged side and then over at his bandaged shoulder. "I take it I'm going to live."

"Yes, the doctors say you'll be as good as new in no time."

"You got the bullet out, didn't you?" He had never doubted for a minute that Rorie had the strength and courage to cut the bullet out of his shoulder.

Biting down on her bottom lip, she nodded, then turned her head and wiped away the tears that had gathered in the corners of her eyes.

"How's Frankie?" Hawk asked.

"He's fine, considering what he's been through." Rorie faced him again and smiled. "I'm eager to get him home to Chattanooga and get him settled with Mama and Daddy. They've spoken to him on the phone, but I'm afraid neither of them is prolific in Spanish."

"Thanks, honey, for staying with me back there in San Miguel. You're quite a lady, you know. I'm going to miss you."

She took in and released a deep breath. "Yeah, I'm sort of going to miss you, too."

"I'm glad things turned out the way they did," Hawk said. "To be honest with you, I was never sure we'd be able to get Frankie out of San Miguel. He's a lucky kid to have an aunt willing to risk her life to save him."

"Gabriel...I..."

Every time she called him Gabriel, he went all soft inside. He couldn't bear to think about losing her, about her walking out of his life forever, about never hearing her say his name again in her sweet, sultry drawl.

"I'm sorry I couldn't save Peter and Cipriana," he said. "I'll go to my grave wishing I'd never been a part of that damn war in San Miguel, wishing I'd never— And I'm sorry I wasn't honest with you from the beginning. I had no right to make love to you." Hawk swallowed hard. Emotions he'd thought long dead resurfaced, making him feel the way he had when he'd been a scared, lonely kid.

Rorie leaned closer, lifted Hawk's hand and squeezed gently. "I think I understand how you feel. I've tried very hard to put everything in the proper perspective. While you were unconscious and I was praying for Murdock to come back and find us, I did a lot of thinking."

Hawk held his breath, hoping beyond hope that she would say what he wanted to hear.

"You aren't responsible for Peter's and Cipriana's deaths. There's no way you could have prevented what happened to them." Rorie lifted his hand and held it against her cheek. "I forgive you for being part of the madness that took my brother's life. Please, Gabriel, please, forgive yourself and free yourself from the past."

Tears misted Gabriel Hawk's eyes. He breathed deeply and tried to speak, but the words wouldn't come. He drew Rorie's hand to his lips and kissed her tenderly.

Rorie swallowed her tears. "If you're ever in Chattanooga... I know you probably don't... What I'm trying to say is thank you for Frankie's life, and I'm sure someday, when he understands everything that happened, he'll want to thank you himself."

"I was just doing my job," Hawk said. "You hired me to protect you and to get your nephew out of San Miguel. Of course, in the end, you were the one who saved both Frankie and me."

Elizabeth Landry's prophetic words echoed in Rorie's

head. *In the end it will be you who must save both Frankie and Gabriel. If you have the courage. If your love is strong enough.*

"I'll never forget you, Gabriel Hawk." She leaned over and kissed his cheek. "And I'll never regret anything that happened between us."

Rorie rushed out of the room, ignoring Gabriel when he called her name. Outside in the corridor, she leaned back against the wall and sobbed.

Murdock walked up to her. "Is he being a difficult patient?" her.

Wiping her eyes and sniffling, Rorie smiled. "No. He's... It's just me. I'm still a bit shaky."

"I've had news from San Miguel." Murdock placed his hand on her shoulder. "King Julio is dead."

"My poor little Frankie. He's lost so many people he loved." Rorie could tell by Murdock's expression that he had more to tell her. "What else?"

"Emilio Santos is dead, too." Murdock squeezed her shoulder, then released it. "Paz Santos has taken command of the renegades."

"Then there's hope for San Miguel, isn't there? With General Lazaro and Paz Santos working together to end the war and rebuild their country."

"Are you going back in to see Hawk?" Murdock asked. "I thought I'd give him an update on San Miguel."

"No, I'm not going back in." Rorie lightly touched Murdock's arm. "Will you do something for me?"

"Sure, if I can."

"Keep an eye on him." Rorie wrung her hands together. "Just until he's recovered and back on his feet."

"You're leaving?"

"Yes, Frankie and I are going home to Chattanooga today."

"You didn't tell him, did you?" Murdock asked.

"Tell him what?"

"That you still love him. That you want to be Gabriel Hawk's lady for the rest of your life."

"Well, there was no point in telling him. He'd already made it perfectly clear that he only wanted two things from me—my forgiveness and my body.'' Rorie looked directly into Murdock's sad hazel eyes. ''I've given him both. He doesn't want anything else.''

''What if you're wrong?''

''He knows where I live. If he wants me, I won't be hard to find.''

Rorie followed her mother and Frankie out of the church and down the front steps to the sidewalk. She breathed in the crisp, cool, November air. What a glorious Sunday morning! Her father's sermon had been about family. He had introduced his grandson to the congregation. Everyone had cried, including Frankie, who had clung to his grandmother's side. Rorie was so pleased that her little nephew had taken an instant liking to her mother. But then, she'd never known a child who didn't respond positively to Bettye Lou Dean's warm and gentle loving.

''I've invited the Newberrys for Sunday dinner,'' Bettye Lou told Rorie. ''They have twin boys the same age as Frankie.''

''That was a wonderful idea, Mama.''

''Are you all right, Rorie? You don't seem yourself lately.'' Bettye Lou patted her daughter's arm affectionately. ''You've been back from San Miguel for over two weeks now and—''

''I'll be all right, Mama. I just need time to…'' To what? she asked herself. To recover from being madly in love with Gabriel? To stop dreaming about him every night and fantasizing about him all day long, every day? Or to pretend that the home pregnancy test she'd taken hadn't been positive?

''What you need is a husband,'' Bettye Lou said. ''You're going on thirty years old and—''

The roar of a motorcycle engine drowned out the after-service chatter of the congregation gathered on the front lawn of the church.

''What in the world is that awful noise?'' Bettye Lou turned around and gaped at the big man riding the powerful Harley-Davidson. ''Who is that?''

Gabriel drove the Harley straight up the sidewalk, stopping

at the edge of the crowd. Rorie's mouth opened wide in a shocked gasp. Her heartbeat accelerated, the sound thundering in her ears.

"Gabriel." She whispered his name as her gaze devoured the very sight of him.

"Gabriel who?" Bettye Lou asked. "Gabriel Hawk? You mean that's the man who helped you bring Frankie out of San Miguel? Oh, my goodness. He looks like a...a—"

"Yes, I know, Mama. He looks like a big, beautiful mongrel-dog hoodlum, doesn't he?"

Ignoring her mother's continuing questions and the curious stares and murmurs from the congregation, Rorie made her way through the crowd. She stopped several feet away from Gabriel's motorcycle.

"Hey, lady, do you want to go for a ride?"

That wonderful, wicked, heart-stopping grin spread across his face. Rorie could barely suppress the joy bursting inside her.

"Where to?" she asked.

He looked at her, everything he felt showing plainly in his dark eyes. "To 'forever after,' honey. To the rest of my life, if you'll go with me."

When he held open his arms, Rorie flew into his welcoming embrace. He kissed her there, in front of her parents and her father's Sunday congregation, and before God. When he ended the kiss, she hopped on the back of his Harley and they rode off down the street.

Hawk slammed Rorie's apartment door closed and tossed the keys on the sofa. They clung to each other, their mouths mating, their hands seeking buttons and zippers. Dropping articles of clothing on their way, they hurried toward the bedroom. Hawk lifted Rorie onto the bed, then kicked off his shoes and came down on top of her. She kissed his shoulders, his chest, his belly. He stripped her naked, all the while his hands caressing and arousing, and his lips whispering erotic words of seduction.

"I love you, Rorie. I love you!"

"Oh, Gabriel, I love you, too. I love you so very much."

He lowered his head and took her mouth, possessing it with a hungry fury. She responded with equal fervor. The passion between them grew and expanded and consumed them completely.

He licked and suckled her breasts, tormenting them until Rorie begged for mercy. With swift, unerring accuracy, he checked her readiness with his fingers. She closed her thighs around his hand, trapping him.

"I want you," he said as he spread her legs apart and sought entrance to her body.

"Make love to me, Gabriel." She gave herself to him, yielding to the powerful force within her that demanded satisfaction.

He thrust into her. She arched her body, inviting his invasion, and tilted her head back into the pillow. He was hard and strong inside her as he thrust himself deeper and deeper. She moaned with pleasure.

Fast and furious, he stroked in and out, taking all that she gave. She tightened around him, then cried out as fulfillment claimed her. While she spiraled out of control, intense pleasure shooting through her body, he hammered into her, his own release coming quickly. He groaned like a wild beast in the throes of passion.

They lay in each other's arms, sated and happy beyond all reason. Gabriel caressed her hip. She snuggled against him.

The afternoon sunlight shimmered through the lace curtains in Rorie's bedroom, casting a golden glow over the bed. Gabriel lifted a strand of her hair and brought it to his lips.

"*Mia dama dorado*," he whispered against her cheek. "My golden lady."

Rorie sighed with contentment. She had never known such happiness.

Gabriel ran his hand from her shoulder to her hip. "You're getting too skinny, honey. You feel like you've lost more weight."

Lifting herself up on one elbow, she leaned over him. Her hair fell over her shoulders, covering the tips of her breasts. "I've lost twenty pounds since I met you, but if you prefer me plump, just hang around a few months and I'll put those twenty pounds back on, plus some."

"Are you trying to tell me that I'm going to have a fat wife?" he asked teasingly.

"I'm trying to tell you that you're going to have a— Wife? Did you say *wife?*"

"You are going to marry me, aren't you, Rorie?" He pulled her over and on top of him.

"Yes, of course. I just didn't...I wasn't sure you'd... Oh, Gabriel, we're going to be so happy. You and me and our baby."

His body tensed instantly. He grabbed the back of her head and forced her to face him. "Baby? What baby?"

"The baby we created the night we made love in the ancient temple."

"My God! Are you sure?"

"I'm sure. I took a home pregnancy test, and those things are very accurate these days."

He eased Rorie down on the bed and ran his hand across her stomach. "My baby." Tears welled up in his eyes. "Lady, you're incredible."

"You're pretty incredible yourself, Gabriel Hawk."

"Don't ever leave me, Rorie. Please." He held her close, burying his face in her hair. "And don't ever stop loving me."

She soothed him with her touch. "I'll never leave you, Gabriel. And I'll love you forever."

Epilogue

Gabriel glanced down at Rorie and smiled. Holding her arms open, she motioned for him to come to her. He knelt beside the chaise longue and laid his hand on her protruding belly. "He loves the music," Rorie said, nodding toward the radio on the round glass table near the pool. "Ever since I turned on the radio, he's been moving constantly."

Gabriel rubbed his palm over the fluttering movements inside Rorie. "Hey, boy, what are you doing in there? Dancing?"

A shrill, happy squeal came from the little girl cavorting in the pool with Frankie and Ronald Dean. Water splashed out onto Bettye Lou, who sat on the edge of the pool, her feet dangling off the side.

"Y'all are getting too rambunctious," Bettye Lou scolded her husband and grandchildren.

"I think our son is eager to come out and play with his big sister." Gabriel patted Rorie's tummy. "Have you noticed how he reacts every time he hears Gabi's voice?"

"Well, he'll just have to wait another couple of months." Rorie grabbed Gabriel's arm. "Help me get up, will you, honey? I think I'll go back to our room and take a nap before dinner.'' She winked at her husband. ''Don't you need a nap, too?''

Gabriel helped her to her feet, then drew her into his arms. Nuzzling her nose, he whispered, ''Do you suppose we can persuade your parents to take Gabi back to see Mickey Mouse this afternoon? Remember, we told her she could go into the park again before dinner.''

''I'll see what MaMa says.'' Rorie waddled across the hotel patio. ''MaMa?''

Hawk watched his wife—his beautiful, very pregnant wife—and his heart filled with love. Rorie had given him a life he'd never dreamed possible. She had cleansed his soul with her pure love and given him the family he had always wanted.

''No, Mommy! No!'' Four-year-old Gabriella Hawk climbed out of the shallow end of the pool and stomped her little foot. ''I want you and Daddy to take me to see Mickey, not MaMa and PaPa.''

''Gabi, your mommy and daddy spent the entire morning with you in the park,'' Bettye Lou told her granddaughter. ''Mommy's tired and needs to take a nap, so PaPa and I will take you and Frankie back to the park and afterward we'll get ice cream.''

''Hey, Gabi, I'll take your picture with Mickey Mouse,'' Frankie said.

Gabi stomped her little foot again. ''No, dammit! I want my daddy and mommy.''

Bettye Lou gasped. Ronald Dean grinned. Frankie laughed.

Rorie placed her hand on her hip, turned around and glared at Gabriel. ''When she acts like that, she's your daughter, Mr. Hawk. I've warned you about using bad language in front of her. She repeats everything she hears.''

Gabriel swooped his little girl up in his arms, tossing her over his head and then catching her. Gabi squealed with child-ish delight. Gabriel placed her on his hip, then kissed her forehead.

''You've heard me use that ugly word, haven't you, Gabi? It was wrong for me to say it and it's wrong for you to say it. Do you understand?''

Lowering her eyelids until her long black eyelashes fluttered against her cheeks, Gabi laid her dark head on her father's shoulder. "I'm sorry, Daddy. Mommy doesn't like that word, does she?"

"No, darling, Mommy doesn't like that word, so I want you to promise me that you'll never use it again."

"I promise," she said sweetly, then lifted her head and smiled. "Can we go see Mickey now?"

"MaMa and PaPa are going to take you and Frankie back to the park—" when Gabi opened her mouth to protest, Gabriel placed his index finger across her lips "—and if you go with them and let Mommy rest, I'll forget I heard you say that ugly word. Do we have a deal?"

"Okay, Daddy. We got a deal."

Gabriel handed his daughter over to her grandmother and waved goodbye, then slipped his arm around Rorie and whispered in her ear. She giggled.

"You certainly know how to handle her," Rorie told him as they walked back toward the hotel. "But then you should. You two are just alike."

"And you, Mrs. Hawk, know how to handle me." He pulled her into the waiting elevator.

Once the doors closed, he drew her into his arms and kissed her passionately. Rorie clung to him, loving the way he made her feel.

"Have I thanked you today?" he asked.

"No, but—"

"Then let me thank you."

"Gabriel, just how long are you going to keep thanking me every day for marrying you and—"

"And making me the happiest man in the world," he finished for her. "How about every day for the rest of our lives?"

"It really isn't necessary, you know. You've made me the happiest woman in the world, so I'd say we're even."

The elevator doors opened. Gabriel lifted Rorie into his arms and carried her down the hall and into their room.

"Carrying around a load like me could injure your back, you know," she said teasingly, then patted her tummy. "After all, I'm even heavier than usual, now."

"Lady, I've been carrying you around for nearly five years

and a few extra pounds don't make that much difference. Besides, I'm a big, strong man. Remember?''

He laid her on the bed and came down beside her.

"Maybe you'd better refresh my memory." She draped her arms around his neck.

"It would be my pleasure, *mi dama dorado,*" he said.

And in the quiet stillness of their vacation room, Gabriel made slow, sweet love to his wife, the mother of his daughter and unborn son, the woman who had cleansed his soul, and filled his heart with joy and his life with happiness.

* * * * *

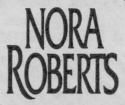

Take 4 bestselling love stories FREE

Plus get a FREE surprise gift!

Special Limited-time Offer

Mail to Silhouette Reader Service™

**3010 Walden Avenue
P.O. Box 1867
Buffalo, N.Y. 14240-1867**

YES! Please send me 4 free Silhouette Intimate Moments® novels and my free surprise gift. Then send me 6 brand-new novels every month, which I will receive months before they appear in bookstores. Bill me at the low price of $3.34 each plus 25¢ delivery and applicable sales tax, if any.* That's the complete price and a savings of over 10% off the cover prices—quite a bargain! I understand that accepting the books and gift places me under no obligation ever to buy any books. I can always return a shipment and cancel at any time. Even if I never buy another book from Silhouette, the 4 free books and the surprise gift are mine to keep forever.

245 BPA A3UW

Name	(PLEASE PRINT)	
Address	Apt. No.	
City	State	Zip

This offer is limited to one order per household and not valid to present Silhouette Intimate Moments® subscribers. *Terms and prices are subject to change without notice. Sales tax applicable in N.Y.

UMOM-696   ©1990 Harlequin Enterprises Limited

SILHOUETTE WOMEN KNOW ROMANCE WHEN THEY SEE IT.

And they'll see it on **ROMANCE CLASSICS**, the new 24-hour TV channel devoted to romantic movies and original programs like the special **Romantically Speaking—Harlequin™ Goes Prime Time.**

Romantically Speaking—Harlequin™ Goes Prime Time introduces you to many of your favorite romance authors in a program developed exclusively for Harlequin® and Silhouette® readers.

Watch for **Romantically Speaking—Harlequin™ Goes Prime Time** beginning in the summer of 1997.

If you're not receiving ROMANCE CLASSICS, call your local cable operator or satellite provider and ask for it today!

Escape to the network of your dreams.

See Ingrid Bergman and Gregory Peck in *Spellbound* on Romance Classics.

As seen on TV!
Free Gift Offer

With a Free Gift proof-of-purchase from any Silhouette® book,
you can receive a beautiful cubic zirconia pendant.

This gorgeous marquise-shaped stone is a genuine cubic
zirconia—accented by an 18" gold tone necklace.

(Approximate retail value $19.95)

Send for yours today...
compliments of ▼ *Silhouette*®

To receive your free gift, a cubic zirconia pendant, send us one original proof-of-purchase, photocopies not accepted, from the back of any Silhouette Romance™, Silhouette Desire®, Silhouette Special Edition®, Silhouette Intimate Moments® or Silhouette Yours Truly™ title available at your favorite retail outlet, together with the Free Gift Certificate, plus a check or money order for $1.65 U.S./$2.15 CAN. (do not send cash) to cover postage and handling, payable to Silhouette Free Gift Offer. We will send you the specified gift. Allow 6 to 8 weeks for delivery. Offer good until March 31, 1998, or while quantities last. Offer valid in the U.S. and Canada only.

Free Gift Certificate

Name: _____

Address: _____

City: _____ State/Province: _____ Zip/Postal Code: _____

Mail this certificate, one proof-of-purchase and a check or money order for postage and handling to: SILHOUETTE FREE GIFT OFFER 1998. In the U.S.: 3010 Walden Avenue, P.O. Box 9077, Buffalo, NY 14269-9077. In Canada: P.O. Box 613, Fort Erie, Ontario L2Z 5X3.

FREE GIFT OFFER   084-KFD
ONE PROOF-OF-PURCHASE
To collect your fabulous FREE GIFT, a cubic zirconia pendant, you must include this original proof-of-purchase for each gift with the properly completed Free Gift Certificate.

084-KFDR2

SUSAN MALLERY

Continues the twelve-book series—36 HOURS—in January 1998 with Book Seven

THE RANCHER AND THE RUNAWAY BRIDE

When Randi Howell fled the altar, she'd been running for her life! And she'd kept on running—straight into the arms of rugged rancher Brady Jones. She knew he had his suspicions, but how could she tell him the truth about her identity? Then again, if she ever wanted to approach the altar in earnest, how could she not?

For Brady and Randi and *all* the residents of Grand Springs, Colorado, the storm-induced blackout was just the beginning of 36 Hours that changed *everything!* You won't want to miss a single book.

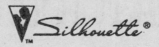

Available at your favorite retail outlet.

Look us up on-line at: http://www.romance.net

36HRS7

Available in February 1998

ANN MAJOR

CHILDREN OF DESTINY
When Passion and Fate Intertwine...

SECRET CHILD

Although everyone told Jack West that his wife,
Chantal—the woman who'd betrayed him and sent
him to prison for a crime he didn't commit—had
died, Jack knew she'd merely transformed herself
into supermodel Mischief Jones. But when he
finally captured the woman he'd been hunting,
she denied everything. Who was she really—
an angel or a cunningly brilliant counterfeit?"

"Want it all? Read Ann Major."
—Nora Roberts, *New York Times*
bestselling author

Don't miss this compelling story
available at your favorite retail outlet.
Only from Silhouette books.

▼ *Silhouette* ®